The Dibbuk Box

Jason Haxton

AFTERWORD BY HOWARD SCHWARTZ

Truman State University Press
Kirksville, Missouri

Cover design: Jamie Carroll

Library of Congress Cataloging-in-Publication Data

Haxton, Jason, 1958–
The Dibbuk box / Jason Haxton.
   p. cm.
   ISBN 978-1-61248-012-1 (pbk. : alk. paper) — ISBN 978-1-61248-060-2 (ebook)
   1. Supernatural—Miscellanea. 2. Cabinetwork—Miscellanea. 3. Haxton, Jason, 1958–
4. Dybbuk. I. Title.
BF1471.H39 2011
133.2—dc23
                                                                        2011037652

The paper in this publication meets or exceeds the minimum requirements of the
American National Standard for Information Sciences—Permanence of Paper for
Printed Library Materials, ANSI Z39.48–1992.

*To Lori, my wife, and to Ross and Laurel, my children.
In spite of my mental wanderings, my family is my greatest interest and
passion—they are my real obsession.*

"*By divine providence, a Jew believes that nothing happens by chance. The box has 'fallen' into your hands. Maybe you are the one who can unravel the mystery and bring peace to whatever is not at peace.*"

—Rabbi Yonosan Golomb, Sheffield, England, 22 March 2004

Contents

Preface

Because of my own curiosity of the item and its story, I freely chose to become connected to the Dibbuk Box. I quickly learned that in this day of instant connection through the Internet and cell phone, many thousands of people were following this artifact's journey and they all seemed to want access to the Dibbuk Box and anyone associated with it. As a result, my name has ended up on thousands of websites and blogs. Hoping to free myself from constant e-mails and phone calls, I created a detailed website to keep these people updated on my progress, but even now, almost seven years after my purchase of the Dibbuk Box, strangers still search me out to ask me about my experiences.

My privacy has already been compromised from being tied to this item, but I understand that just because someone has been involved with the Dibbuk Box doesn't mean they want to be part of an open forum to anyone and everyone. For this reason, I have been selective in using people's names. For those who have remained relatively anonymous, I use only a first name or identify the person only by relationship. For people who are already identified with the Dibbuk Box on public websites, podcasts, and forums, or who have granted permission, I have used both first and last names.

My written account of my experiences is absolutely truthful and upfront from the first pages to the final comments. I have no interest in misleading or falsifying the facts about this artifact that came into my possession through a series of coincidences. I have documented my experiences from start to finish. Here is a journey of seven years . . . watching, researching, and learning. And I have come to two conclusions, which happen to contradict each other in all details.

First, without a doubt the item known as the Dibbuk Box is a genuine artifact of amazing power and magnetism. The box clearly has some type of mystical significance, with all the required elements for ritual use. This box was created by a person or by persons with a Jewish upbringing or at least a deep understanding of Jewish culture, as is evident from the Hebrew prayer carved on the back. The manner in which the name of God is carved in the Shema hints at a deeper understanding of the Hebrew written language and of Jewish tradition. Also, the box contains a uniquely constructed piece made of multiple stones that was used ceremonially to focus one's prayer and to protect one from the direct power of God when praying. The granite stones are combined to act as a subtle energy source, much like a spiritual battery. The "tokens," or familial items inside the box are genuine and their ages span a period of one hundred years.

I have read on Internet websites that many people fear the power of the Dibbuk Box . . . and yet, in some cases, they *want* its power. People from different educational backgrounds and many cultures are drawn to it. Even insects are oddly attracted by its potency. Wherever it is stored, insects gather in colonies to be near it. Accounts of health problems, accidents, and death that follow mysteriously in its wake are numerous and are documented. Each owner of the Dibbuk Box and some of their family members swear that this item is authentic and has haunted and traumatized them.

Some members of the Portland family responsible for the creation of the Dibbuk Box believe that, once it had been released from that family, its powers were set in motion to reveal a dark story. I believe that this forgotten story is tied to the Shoah—the Holocaust—and that it centers on a single man from a small city in rural America. It was to this same city to which the Dibbuk Box was mysteriously "called," and where it now, having completed its mission and journey, permanently rests.

Second, without a doubt the Dibbuk Box is a fraud; the story was created to turn a quick profit and deceive its buyer, and its contents have no meaning beyond the obvious. It is a powerless wooden wine cabinet from the 1960s with a hodgepodge of meaningless items stuffed inside to make it appear spiritual or mystical. Other members of the same family who first owned the box have made it very clear that they know its story and that it is simply not true—it was created by a sibling with an overactive imagination.

Friends and coworkers of its creator, who have been familiar with the object from the time it was first mentioned have documented their own accounts, indicating that it was created by combining found pieces, perhaps as a hoax.

All illnesses associated with the Dibbuk Box seem likely to be psychosomatic or coincidental. The original eBay listing to sell this item identifies people who, in reality, are composites of several people with false histories. Their purported experiences with the box are untrue based on interviews. Various sources tell me that the Dibbuk Box and the written online account were conceived and created by a person who, on the other hand, continues to insist that the story was not faked and that the other sources are mistaken.

Yes, these two conclusions contradict each other, but I believe both to be true. My research over the past seven years has shown that they are indeed true. Subjectively, my personal experiences with the box and my investigations into the experiences of the others who have had contact with it lead me to believe that the box does have some unexplainable mystical or otherworldly power. Objectively, my scholarly training, years of research, and natural skepticism lead me to believe that the box is nothing more, can be nothing more, than a wooden box.

Read for yourself. Finish the book and decide which version of the truth—if any—you believe.

Acknowledgments

I have always been fearlessly curious about this world and what might exist beyond it. It is probably my Bohemian blood that stirs my interest in the unknown—passed down from my Czech immigrant grandmother, Marie Hajný, through my parents, Ronnie and Rhea Haxton, who always ensured there was a bit of untamed wilderness near our home for me to explore. My parents have been caring guides and supporters of my quests into both the known and unknown, showing a parent's pride in my smallest achievements. Now, grown and a parent myself, I have one last achievement for them to beam about—the strange tale of my experiences with the artifact that has come to be known as the Dibbuk Box.

When it became clear that I needed to organize everything I had learned and my personal records of my experiences and put them into a book, I looked around for help. Aside from keeping a personal journal and writing the occasional article on our museum for a magazine or newsletter, I never viewed myself as a "real" writer and the idea of a book seemed beyond me. Over the course of five years, I had serious discussions with four different people about writing this book with me. The first three didn't work out, so I had a good feeling when I found a writer and journalism professor to work with. We had become acquainted when we were both invited to participate in a paranormal podcast: me to talk about the Dibbuk Box and him to talk about his third and most recent paranormal book. In July 2010, he was ready to dig into my research and start writing. He stayed at my house and we created an outline and came up with a plan. I thought I had all my bases covered, but within three weeks, my cowriter had resigned from the project. To this day he is unwilling or unable to even write or speak about that time, but he did agree to let me share some of the details.

He stayed at my home and we made a plan to complete our project, then he began his trip home with a box of research material. Within hours

xiv | Acknowledgments

he called to say he had become ill and suffered a severe panic attack. A few days later, he seemed embarrassed about his reactions; he had had other paranormal experiences, but this one was different somehow. He reassured me that everything was fine and he was confident that the book would be great. Within a week or so, he was setting up interviews and going through my notes and research. Then he was injured in a home accident and immediately thought of the Dibbuk Box. Next, he began noticing strange smells near the files I had given him, he and his children became ill, and his son began to have strange tastes in his mouth. At that point, he became concerned and his wife urged him to drop the project. Concerned about his family's safety and his own health, he abruptly resigned from the project. He felt that the box wanted him gone and he would not fight it.

I understood his concerns, but hoped he would change his mind. When it became clear that he would not, I started looking again. This time, I found Giles Fowler, author of *Deaths on Pleasant Street: The Ghastly Enigma of Colonel Swope and Dr. Hyde,* and a retired journalism professor and former reporter for the *Kansas City Star.* Without Giles, I doubt this book would have been written. Giles coached me on my writing, challenging me to provide more detail (or less), suggesting word choices, and forcing me to stay on schedule. As we worked together, we became friends, and I am grateful for his friendship and for his help.

I would like to thank Truman State University Press, its director, and staff for suggesting individuals who could help my writing endeavor and for giving me the opportunity to have my manuscript published, and Barbara Smith-Mandell for her careful and skillful editing.

I am also grateful for the help of all of those who contacted me through eBay or through the Dibbuk Box website to share their experiences, their personal memories, or their expertise. And I am grateful to the former owners and to their relatives, friends, coworkers, and acquaintances who were willing to talk to me about their own experiences and their memories of events surrounding the Dibbuk Box.

Prologue

It lies just a few feet from me, entombed in a dark gray plastic, shock-proof shipping case I purchased at an army surplus store. As an added protective measure, it is further nestled within a wooden ark, a special religious container. Lined with 24-karat gold, the ark is fashioned of acacia wood from a single tree. Native to the Middle East, the acacia is known for having a sweet scent and almost indestructible hardness (from growing in one of the world's driest climates)—a perfect vessel to seal "it" away to protect me and the few others who have ventured near the thing, knowingly or not. People who seek the path of danger are plentiful these days; I hear from them weekly by e-mail pleading for access to "it." They act as if they are possessed by "it," but who am I to judge them, being likewise drawn to this risk. This thing—this "it"—goes by the name Dibbuk Box and it needs no protection from our world. Rather it is we, the curious, who have something to fear.

Chapter One

Minding My
Own Business

To be honest, it was surprisingly easy to bring the Dibbuk Box into my life. As I discovered its strange qualities, I wondered whether I really had a choice in the matter. In fact, evidence gained through my research has led me to suspect that the box found me. That was its destiny and mine too. Seven years ago I knew nothing of the Dibbuk Box. It had been in existence for almost fifty years, but I was completely unaware of it, perhaps just as it was unaware of me.

I have had the good fortune of spending most of my life working at universities, a "professional student" who was lucky enough to find a niche in academia. One perk of campus work is almost unlimited access to education and degrees at little or no cost. Beginning with undergraduate studies in art history and the commercial arts, I moved on to graduate work in counseling, the humanities, and higher education. My collection of college credits, plus my campus work experiences, finally landed me my dream job as director of a midsize museum of medical history, which is connected to an osteopathic medical school.

It might surprise you to learn that museums in general display only about 10 percent of their collections. Limitations in gallery space require a rotation schedule to show items from the collection, although prized pieces remain on permanent display. The remaining objects are stored out of sight, not unlike the contents of your attic. A big difference, however, is that the museum's objects are thoroughly documented and stored with the best long-term preservation methods available.

3

One aspect of my job and that of the museum staff is to select, study, and interpret these historic pieces, and present them in context so their relevance can be understood and appreciated. Almost daily, single items or boxes of items find their way to our office. For some artifacts, the museum is a last chance, a final home. Some of those we cannot use are offered to organizations that might be able to use them. Others are sold, or bagged and carted off to the dumpster. For my staff and me, this constant sorting of trash and treasure is a daily routine. We find ourselves almost literally wading through decades of accumulated items—a backlog of historic oddities brought to the museum by well-meaning donors who passed on anything even remotely related to medicine.

To catch up on this workload, I often turn to the nearby liberal arts university to enlist college students seeking work experience, internships, or part-time jobs in the field of museum and library collections. On rare occasions I am able to provide paid positions thanks to small museum grants. When this opportunity presents itself, I seek out punctual, autonomous, and—most importantly—low-maintenance students.

In the summer of 2003, I hired Brian, who had already performed two years of volunteer work with us, to be my part-time office manager. Brian dreamed of a museum career much like mine. His dedication to the collection and his warm disposition toward visitors and staff made him a favorite—and an ideal hire. Unfortunately, an impulsive action by Brian's roommate eventually involved the entire museum staff, to one degree or another, in a definitely high-maintenance situation, turning both the museum and my world around. I never saw it coming and, in fairness, neither did Brian.

It was on June 7, 2003, that Brian began working as a paid staff member of the museum. Not surprisingly, Brian's first week of work went smoothly. He picked up the basic skills of scheduling, transferring calls, and receiving artifacts from donors with little guidance. The dates and the details of what happened are easy for me to recall because I have kept a daily journal for well over twenty-one years. I began doing this on a whim when I learned my wife was pregnant with our first child. I thought that one day my children might want to learn about and re-experience their upbringing. That whim has grown into 140 filled journals; I can travel back to any day of my life in seconds.

These daily entries predate my knowledge of the Dibbuk Box, so I have a very accurate description of my thoughts, feelings, and actions from when I first heard about the Dibbuk Box and the evolving information I gathered after the box came into my care. It is from this trove of documented material that I am writing this factual account of what really happened.

Brian's quiet demeanor in general led me and my staff to assume he was a somewhat introverted and self-motivated person—perfect for museum work. He was fitting in quite nicely with our daily routine, which typically begins with a staff meeting, for which we take turns bringing in glazed doughnuts or the occasional coffee cake. Updates on the day's tours, incoming donations, and projects needing assistance from staff members are mixed with news on each staff member's home life. Most everyone on staff is married, with school-age children and a pet or two, living in an older home by choice. So it is not unusual for us to digress into a child's school success, the latest home renovation project, or a pet's illness, and we all freely share our life experiences with the problem at hand. Rousing discussions wrap up by eight thirty, when we part to start the day's work.

As our only college-age adult on staff, Brian had none of the life experiences of his older colleagues, and each morning I watched him sit in silence as we discussed our family lives and concerns. Was Brian bored? Definitely. But I figured our morning chats were good preparation for the day he finally left the artificial utopia of college and settled into domesticity.

So it surprised us all on the morning of Tuesday, June 17, 2003, when Brian actually spoke at the morning roundtable. Perhaps he was beginning to feel part of the museum team and wanted to be in on the domestic discussions. Or perhaps Brian had reached his limit with the ongoing saga of the arthritic dog being carried down the porch steps to do its business. Whatever the reason, Brian cleared his throat and calmly stated, "This weekend my roommate bought a haunted box."

The sudden quiet must have surprised even Brian, as all eyes turned and focused squarely on him. He could see by our puzzled expressions that he definitely had our full attention; all thoughts of kids, houses, and pets had evaporated. None of our experiences could top his statement.

Brian repeated with a little more confidence and energy, "My room-mate bought this haunted box on eBay. Really, he did, and I can show it to you." Brian got up, walked over to the front-desk computer, and started typing to pull up the eBay listing. As we crowded around the monitor, he said, "See, there it is." The image on the screen could hardly be described as scary. It was a small, worn wooden cabinet of simple design, with two doors adorned with distinct appliqué clusters of grapes. Triangle-shaped brass hinges held the doors shut and there was a small lower drawer that pulled out. This "wine cabinet" seemed a bit worn from many years of use. The image we saw only added to our initial confusion. Had we mis-understood Brian? Was this pleasant looking knickknack the "haunted box?"

We took turns reading aloud the following account by the seller, Kevin Mannis of Portland, Oregon.

> All the events that I am about to set forth in this listing are accurate and may be verified by the winning bidder with the copies of hospital records and sworn affidavits that I am including as part of the sale of the cabinet.
>
> During September of 2001, I attended an estate sale in Portland, Oregon. The items liquidated at this sale were from the estate of a woman who had passed away at the age of 103. A granddaughter of the woman told me that her grandmother had been born in Poland where she grew up, married, raised a family, and lived until she was sent to a Nazi concentration camp during World War II. She was the only member of her family who survived the camp. Her parents, broth-ers, a sister, husband, and two sons and a daughter were all killed. She survived the camp by escaping with some other prisoners and some-how making her way to Spain where she lived until the end of the war. I was told that she acquired the small wine cabinet listed here in Spain and [that] it was one of only three items that she brought with her when she immigrated to the United States. The other two items were a steamer trunk, and a sewing box.
>
> I purchased the wine cabinet, along with the sewing box and some other furniture at the estate sale. After the sale, I was approached by the woman's granddaughter who said, "I see you got the Dibbuk Box." She was referring to the wine cabinet. I asked her what a Dibbuk Box was, and she told me that when she was growing up, her grandmother

always kept the wine cabinet in her sewing room. It was always shut, locked and set in a place that was out of reach. The grandmother always called it the Dibbuk Box. When the girl asked her grandmother what was inside, her grandmother spit three times through her fingers [and] said, a Dibbuk, and *keselim*. The grandmother went on to tell the girl that the wine cabinet was never, ever, to be opened.

The granddaughter told me that her grandmother had asked that the box be buried with her. However, as such a request was contrary to the rules of an orthodox Jewish burial, the grandmother's request had not been honored. I asked the granddaughter what a Dibbuk and *keselim* were, but she did not know. I asked if she would like to [pry the lock off and] open it with me. She did not want to open it, as her grandmother had been very emphatic and serious when she instructed her not to do so, and, regardless of the reason her grandmother wanted to keep it closed, she wanted to honor her grandmother's request.

I decided to offer to let her just keep it, as it seemed to me that it must be a very sentimental keepsake. At that point, she was very insistent and said, "No, no, you bought it!"

I explained that I didn't want my money back, and that it would make me feel better to do what I thought was an act of kindness. She then became somewhat upset. Looking back now, the way she became upset with me was just plain odd. She raised her voice to me and said, "You bought it! You made a deal!"

When I tried to speak, she yelled, "We don't want it!" She began to cry, and asked that I please leave—now, and she quickly walked away from me. I wrote the whole episode off to the stress and grief that she must have been experiencing. I gathered up my items, paid the cashier, and quietly left.

At the time I bought the cabinet, I owned a small furniture refinishing business. I took the wooden cabinet to my store, and put it in my basement workshop where I intended to refinish it and give it as a gift to my mother. I didn't think anything more about it. I opened my shop for the day and went to run some errands leaving the young woman who did sales for me in charge.

After about a half hour, I got a call on my cell phone. The call was from my salesperson. She was absolutely hysterical and screaming that someone was in my [basement] workshop breaking glass and swearing. Furthermore, the intruder had locked the iron security gates and the emergency exit and she couldn't get out. As I told her to call the police, my cell phone battery went dead. I hit speeds of 100 mph getting back to the shop. When I arrived, I found the gates locked. I went inside and found my employee on the floor in a corner of my office sobbing hysterically. I ran to the basement and went downstairs. At the bottom of the stairs, I was hit by an overpowering unmistakable odor of cat urine (there had never been any animals kept or found in my shop). I flipped the light switch, but the lights didn't work. As I investigated, I found that the reason the lights didn't work also explained the sounds of glass breaking. All of the light bulbs in the basement were broken. All nine incandescent bulbs had been broken in their sockets, and I discovered that the four-foot long fluorescent tubes—all ten of them— were lying shattered on the floor. I did not find an intruder, however. I should also add that there was only one entrance to the basement. It would have been impossible for anyone to leave without meeting me head-on. I went back up to speak with my salesperson, but she had left.

At the time, I thought perhaps my worker became angry at me somehow—for her getting locked in my shop (anyone passing by might have locked the outside gate—although this had never happened before) and to get even with me [had] trashed my basement. For me, that was the only logical answer, as I knew no one else was found to be in my shop with her and [that no one had left but she].

She never returned to work (after having been with me for two years). She refuses to discuss the incident to this day. I never thought of relating the events of that day to anything having to do with the wine cabinet, instead I felt I had a disgruntled worker, nothing more.

Then, things got worse.

As I already indicated, I had decided to give the wine cabinet to my mother as a birthday gift. About two weeks after I made the purchase, I decided to get started refinishing it. First I removed a small rasp hinge and lock. I was surprised to find that the cabinet has a unique little mechanism. When you open the little drawer at the bottom, an internal mechanism causes both doors to open at the same time. It is very well made of mahogany wood.

Inside the cabinet, I found the following items: one 1928 U.S. wheat penny; one 1925 U.S. wheat penny; one small lock of reddish-blonde hair (bound with white string); one small lock of black hair (also bound with white string); one small granite statue engraved and gilded with Hebrew letters (I have been told that the letters spell out the word *SHALOM*); one dried rosebud; one wine cup; [and] one very strange, black cast-iron candlestick holder with octopus legs.

I saved all of the items in a box intending to return them to the estate. The family has refused these items, so they will be included in this sale of the cabinet.

After opening the cabinet, I decided not to refinish it. Instead I cleaned it, and rubbed in some lemon oil. It was at this time that I noticed that there was an inscription in Hebrew carved into the back of the cabinet. I have no idea what it says or if it is significant. I have included a picture of that inscription below.

On my mother's birthday, October 28, 2001, my mother called to tell me that she was going out of town with my sister for three days, and we postponed celebrating her birthday together until she returned. On October 31, 2001, my mother came to my shop. We were going to have lunch together, but before we were going to leave, I gave her the wine cabinet as her birthday gift. She seemed to like it. So, while she examined it, I went to make a quick phone call before we left for lunch. I hadn't been out of sight more than five minutes when one of my employees came running into my office saying that something was wrong with my mom.

When I went back to see what the matter was, I found my mom sitting in a chair beside the cabinet. Her face had no expression, but tears were streaming down her cheeks. No matter how I tried to get her to respond, she would not, she could not. It turns out that my mother had suffered a stroke. She was taken to the hospital by ambulance. She ended up suffering partial paralysis and losing her ability to speak and form words (she has since regained the ability to speak). She could understand things being said to her, and could respond by pointing to letters of the alphabet to spell out words she wanted to say.

When I asked her the following day how she was doing, she teared up and spelled out the words "N-O G-I-F-T." I assured her that I had given her a gift for her birthday, thinking that with all the excitement she didn't remember.

But, she became even more agitated and spelled out the words "H-A-T-E G-I-F-T." I laughed and told her not to worry. I told her I was sorry she didn't like the little cabinet and that I would get her anything she wanted if she would promise to get well soon.

Still, I didn't associate [any of this] with the cabinet itself or [with] anything paranormal. Frankly, I don't think I ever even used the term paranormal until this last month.

I'll try to make this short now. I gave the cabinet to my sister. She kept it for a week, and then gave it back. She complained that she couldn't get the doors to stay closed and that they kept coming open. There are no springs in the door mechanism and I have never found that the doors come open.

I gave it to my brother and his wife who kept it for three days and then gave it back. My brother said it smelled like Jasmine flowers, while his wife insisted that it put out an odor of cat urine.

I gave it to my girlfriend who asked me to sell it for her after only two days. I sold it the same day to a nice middle-aged couple. Three days later, when I came to open the shop for the day, I found the cabinet sitting at the front doors with a note attached to it that read, "This has a bad darkness about it." I had no idea what that meant. Anyway, I ended up taking it home.

Then things got even worse.

Since the day I brought it home, I began having a strange recurring nightmare. Every time I have the horrible dream it goes something like this: I find myself walking with a friend, usually someone I know well and trust. At some point in the dream, I find myself looking into the eyes of the person I am with. It is then that I realize that there is something different, something evil looking back at me. At that point in my dream, the person I am with then changes into what can only be described as the most gruesome, demonic-looking hag that I have ever seen. This hag proceeds then, to beat the living tar out of me. I have awakened numerous times to find bruises and red welt marks on me where I had been hit by the old woman during the previous night. Still, I never [connected] the nightmares [with] the cabinet, nor do I think that I ever would have.

About a month ago, however, my sister, and my brother and his wife came over to my house for dinner and decided to spend the night as it was very late and no one wanted to drive back home. The following morning, during breakfast, my sister complained that she had had a horrible nightmare. She said that she recalled having had it a couple of times before, and went on to describe my nightmare exactly to the last detail. My brother and his wife froze as they listened, and then chimed in that they had both had the exact same dreams of an abusive hag during the night as well. The hair was standing up on the back of my neck and still is. As we talked, it became clear that the common denominator was that each of us had had the nightmare during the times that the cabinet was in our respective homes.

I called my girlfriend and asked if she could recall having any nightmares recently. Right away she described the same nightmare, same hag, everything. When I asked her if she remembered the date when she had the nightmare, she said she could not. Then I asked if it happened to be the night before she gave me the cabinet back to sell for her. She paused for a bit and then said, "Yeah! Hey, how did you know that?"

Now then, since my family discussion, it seems like all hell is breaking loose. For a week afterward I started seeing what I can only describe as shadow things in my peripheral vision. In fact, numerous visitors to my house have claimed that they have seen these shadow things. I put the cabinet in my outside storage unit and was awakened when the smoke alarm in the unit went off in the middle of the night. I then got up and I went to see what was burning. I opened the door and didn't see any smoke. However, I did get hit with the strong odor of cat urine. I went back inside, and the smell was there in my house. I DO NOT OWN A CAT AND I NEVER HAVE. I went back outside and grabbed the cabinet.

I brought it back inside and tried to research it on the Internet. While I was surfing the net, I fell asleep and once again had the same freakin' nightmare. I woke up at around 4:30 a.m. (when it felt and smelled like someone was breathing on my neck) to find that my house now smelled like jasmine flowers, and just in time to see a HUGE shadow thing go loping down the hall away from me.

I would destroy this possessed thing in a second, except I really don't have any understanding of what I may or may not be dealing with. I am afraid (and I do mean afraid) that if I destroy the wine cabinet, whatever it is that seems to have come with the cabinet may just stay here with me.

I have been told that there are people who shop on eBay that understand these kinds of things and specifically look for these kinds of items. If you are one of these people, please, please buy this cabinet and do whatever it is that you do with a thing like this.

Help me.

You can see that I have no reserve price or minimum bid. If I can make things any easier let me know and I will do everything within my abilities.

One more note. On the same day my mom had her stroke, the lease to my store was summarily terminated without cause.

The measurements are 12.5" x 7.5" x 16.25"

ALL OF THE ITEMS THAT I ORIGINALLY FOUND INSIDE THE CABI-NET ARE INCLUDED IN THE SALE AND WILL BE DELIVERED WITH THE CABINET.

June 12 at 2:15 p.m. the following information was added:

There is no way that I can respond to all of the e-mails I've received since I put this thing online. I'll try now to update and answer the most common questions I've been receiving.

1. No, I am not religious.

2. No, I do not wish to have or participate in any sort of exorcism, or case study, or photo sessions at my home.

3. No, I will not sell any of the individual pieces which were originally found separate from the other pieces and the cabinet.

4. No, I do not speak Hebrew nor do I know what the word "keselim" means. I don't know that the word is even a Hebrew word.

5. At the end of the auction, I have decided to take an opportunity to speak with the winning bidder for two reasons: a) To make sure that the winning bidder is a serious adult who has employed some valid reasoning skills in making the decision to accept whatever this is. I will not be judgmental. Do whatever you want or need after the sale. b) To offer full details of the events that [have] transpired. After I have carried out those responsibilities, and upon payment, I will have the cabinet and its contents delivered by U.S. MAIL, FED-EX, or UPS to the winning bidder. At that point, I will have no further involvement with the matter in any way, shape, or form. Period. It is your problem.

6. To all of you who have offered to pray, I may not be religious, but I am certainly open to the possibilities—no matter what your religion might be. THANK YOU!

June 14 at 5:21 p.m. the following information was added:

> Here is another update for everyone following this listing.
>
>   NO! No, I will not circumvent, or make any deals outside of EBAY—
> EVEN FOR MORE MONEY THAN THE FINAL AUCTION PRICE!!!
>
>   If you want to win the auction and have the kind of money some
> of you are offering, there shouldn't be any reason why you cannot sim-
> ply place your bid in an open, honest fashion. I'm sure you can under-
> stand why I might be suspicious of your motives.
>
>   ALSO. . . .
>
>   For those of you wanting to know if I am still experiencing any-
> thing out of the ordinary, I thought everything was going OK until I got
> home on Friday—the 13th of June—and found that the fish in my fresh
> water aquarium—all 10—were dead.
>
>   I'm still hoping that all of this is coincidental crap.

As the last words of the "Haunted Dibbuk Box" eBay listing were read, there was complete silence. Brian had managed to do what, in my mem- ory, no one else had ever done—leave my staff speechless. This story was very strange and compelling. It didn't matter whether we wanted to think about it or not, whether we wanted to believe the story or not, the Dibbuk Box had entered our museum team's consciousness and it was scary.

As soon as the initial shock had worn off, the questions poured forth: Why do you want this thing? When is it coming? Where are you going to keep it? What are you going to do with it? Do your parents know what you're up to? Quiet, introverted, and conflict-free Brian and his story of the haunted box crept into every conversation for the rest of the day.

Before leaving work, I printed off a copy of the eBay auction story. Not being able to keep this odd tale to myself and knowing my wife had no interest in such things, I told my children about the Dibbuk Box. At the time, my son Ross was thirteen years old and my daughter Laurel was nine. I read the story to them as a spooky bedtime treat and they squealed in delight with each chilling detail about the box and its unlucky buyer. Afterward, they were filled with questions about this scary object that would soon be delivered to our town. Mostly they wanted to make sure it would be nowhere close to our home. I assured them that this box would be at an apartment miles away with a bunch of college students and that it would not—could not—hurt them.

The next day, my daughter shared the story with her girlfriends and classmates at her Catholic school. This was probably not a good idea. Several of her schoolmates had been to our home, and had seen my display cases filled with old pottery and ancient idols staring out coldly. Having seen these things that could unnerve the average adult and that nobody else had in their homes, the girls decided I must have the Dibbuk Box stashed somewhere in our house, and many decided they wouldn't come to any more sleepovers.

At work, I had more questions for Brian. I was curious about his roommate and how he had come to buy the Dibbuk Box. Brian explained that Joseph was one of two roommates from the past school year, but neither planned on returning to the apartment for the fall semester—they both had made other living arrangements. Brian had recruited several other students to replace those leaving. However, these new roommates had gone home to work for the summer and would not be back until just before classes resumed in August.

Brian planned to stay alone at the apartment over the summer in order to keep working at the museum. Since the spacious apartment would otherwise be empty and Joseph, the former occupant, had not yet moved out his belongings (his parents were professors at the university and lived close by) Brian invited Joseph to stay with him three months of summer, rent free, provided he would help pay for utilities. Joseph of course accepted, later extending the deal into the fall semester. The two didn't keep much food in their refrigerator that summer, and it was on one of their rare trips to the store to restock that Joseph first mentioned finding "The Haunted Jewish Box" while surfing for the bizarre on eBay.

Joseph quickly filled Brian in on the key points of the haunted box's story and when they returned from the store, showed Brian the listing on eBay. There were only a few days left before the auction would close. Joseph wanted the box and suggested that he and Brian split the cost of the bid. The two decided that, if they won the auction, they would examine and test the box for its haunted properties. If they discovered it truly did contain a malign spirit, they would entomb it in the apartment basement so the entity could haunt future inhabitants of their rundown building.

Brian seemed untroubled by this inconsideration. He felt that leaving the haunted box would pose no moral issue for him, mainly because it was someone else who had originally tampered with the spiritual world, so he and Joseph would be free of guilt for any strange occurrences that followed. And anyway, the seller's account on eBay suggested that the box's spirit was more a nuisance than something life-threatening. Joseph figured another option was simply to resell the mysterious cabinet when they were done testing it for ghostly attributes.

Because Brian was footing most of the apartment costs that summer, he decided not to help buy the haunted box. He told Joseph, however, that he had no problem with him keeping the haunted box on the premises should he win the auction. Sure enough, Joseph was the winning bidder for the Dibbuk Box at a cost of $140.

Over a year later, the seller, Kevin Mannis, related the following on his AOL Public Journal (dated November 25, 2004), in which he told what occurred after the eBay auction.

> After the auction, I contacted the buyer. I wanted to get some kind of an idea of what kind of person would go to the lengths he had gone to in his efforts to buy the Dibbuk Box. Surprisingly the buyer seemed to be an ordinary individual from the Midwest, a college student, who told me he bought the box because he really wanted a wine cabinet. The buyer told me that he had no interest in any "paranormal" aspect of the box, if it even had one. To be sure, I gave the buyer several chances to pull out of the purchase to the extent that it became somewhat annoying to him.
>
> Finally, certain that I was acting responsibly with a mature and responsible buyer, I accepted payment for the box and sent it out the same day. Since owning the Dibbuk Box a sort of invisible haze of negative energy had invaded my personal space—which suddenly lifted on the day I sent the box to the student who bought it from [me] on eBay. Although I had come to believe that having the Dibbuk Box was the source of many of my problems, it still seemed strange to feel the optimism return to me once the item had gone. I hoped the negative haze or whatever it was would not ever return.

Based on what Brian told me and the museum staff about why his room-mate wanted the Dibbuk Box, it was obvious that Joseph had not been completely honest with Kevin about his motives for purchasing the box. But at least Kevin was reassured enough to go through with the sale.

Joseph wasn't one to complain, but to Brian, it seemed to take unusu-ally long for the Dibbuk Box to reach its new home in Kirksville, Mis-souri. He thought it strange that the previous owner, who was so eager to get rid of the "haunted thing," had not sent it away more quickly. Kevin had owned the box for almost two years before deciding its supernatural powers were too much for him to live with. Kevin said he shipped the box the same day it was won, but he shipped the heavy, midsized package by the cheapest rate, and it traveled for a week and a half before finally arriv-ing in Kirksville. In the meantime, its new owners had all but forgotten about it.

At first, Brian didn't realize the haunted thing was already sitting in his apartment. He had come back from a class that morning and was heading for the bathroom. As he passed through the living room, he was hit by an overpowering stench of urine—a smell he had never noticed there before. He figured the bathroom needed a good scrubbing, think-ing perhaps that Joseph had missed the toilet—inconsiderate behav-ior from someone he had generously allowed to stay over the summer rent-free.

But there was no sign of an accident in the bathroom and when Brian returned to the living room he found that the stench was centered in that room. He also noticed balls of wadded paper strewn about the room. And then, for the first time, he saw the Dibbuk Box. It was sitting on the floor, closed. Apparently, Joseph had hastily torn open the pack-age before heading off somewhere.

At once, Brian remembered the eBay description, which had men-tioned a strong urine smell as one of the box's odd characteristics. The bad odor creeped him out, but to his relief, the foul smell cleared on its own a few hours later.

Chapter Two

Second Thoughts

A FEW DAYS BEFORE the Dibbuk Box reached Kirksville, I had left town to prepare a major health exhibition at the Smithsonian Institute's Arts and Industries museum. I was still in Washington on June 25, 2003, and was unaware of Brian's discovery of the mysterious cabinet on his living room floor that same day.

When I got back to my hotel around six o'clock after my day's preparations, my father-in-law, who had traveled to see the exhibit opening, was in the lobby and seemed very agitated. He told me there had been a disaster. My first thought was that something had happened to my wife or kids, who had joined me in Washington for the event. To my relief, my family was fine, but an odd windstorm had toppled a hundred-year-old silver maple tree in our front yard and it had crashed onto the porch. The incident set off the intruder alarm in my home, and neighbors called my office. Museum staff members had arrived quickly to coordinate the removal of the massive tree before it could do even more harm to the house. They also took photographs, which caught hundreds of orb-light images all over the fallen tree. Some believe the orbs that show up in photos to be spirits or ghosts.

Even before the box arrived in Kirksville, my colleagues and I had begun joking that anything that was odd or went wrong at the museum was the fault of the Dibbuk Box. Staff members groaned that we would be cursed by the haunted wine cabinet. "Oh no, the Dibbuk Box!" became our line to taunt Brian. Because it was summer, Brian was at the office all day long, giving us ample opportunities to poke fun at his weird tale. I was probably the worst teaser of the group.

While I was in Washington and speaking with the staff by phone, I had kept up the running routine: "Has it arrived yet? Has it destroyed

the museum with its Jewish wrath yet?" The jest took on deeper meaning following the windstorm that came close to wiping out my home. Now our staff's favorite line was, "Don't mock the box!"

This seemingly personal attack by the Dibbuk Box turned my previous curiosity into a more serious chain of thoughts. I explained to Brian that I was knowledgeable about both ancient artifacts and antiques of the last two hundred years, and told him I would be very interested in seeing this haunted box with all its contents. I hoped to determine whether this wooden box was a genuine spiritual artifact or just something cobbled together out of someone's yard sale junk. Brian told me he would be happy to let me view the "haunted box" once he and Joseph had checked it out themselves.

I was interested in examining the piece, but I was also cautious. Wishing to avoid any risks to my family through exposure to the Dibbuk Box, I planned to examine it either at the museum or the students' apartment a few blocks away. I had hoped to examine the box within the month, but perhaps Brian didn't believe my interest was sincere or perhaps he was too preoccupied with work and summer classes to follow up on my request.

By late fall, my patience was wearing thin and I hoped Brian would let me know soon that the box could at last be inspected. The eBay description had made a deep impression on me, but as Brian's supervisor, I hesitated to seem pushy or weird about it so I refrained from pressing the issue. I decided to wait until mid-December to bring it up, feeling that would give Brian and Joseph ample time to do whatever it was they wanted to do with this object.

Fortunately, a natural opportunity to press the issue was at hand. Each year I give a lecture for a psychology class at Truman State University about the spiritual context of ancient art pieces—small statues of idols and pieces of pottery, using examples from my private collection of ancient artifacts, some of them several thousand years old. On Wednesday, December 17, 2003, when I arrived at the classroom to deliver my lecture, I was both surprised and pleased to see that Brian was taking this winter mini-course. My presentation included examples of gravestones, types of ghosts, and the Vedic practice of palmistry that stretches back six thousand years. Students have always enjoyed handling the real artifacts I bring to class and hearing the tales of exotic civilizations. Often they interrupt the talk to share their own experiences with the paranormal.

After class, I saw Brian hanging back with several students. It seemed the perfect opportunity to broach the topic of the haunted box and its availability for inspection. Finally, I thought, I would get to see the box. I called Brian over and asked whether I could drop by later to view the Dibbuk Box. Brian apologized for not letting me know sooner, and explained that Joseph had been behaving erratically for some time and had left the apartment months ago. Then, over Thanksgiving break, he had returned to collect his belongings, including the mysterious wine cabinet. So it was gone, Brian told me. He no longer had access to it and he wasn't sure of Joseph's current whereabouts.

It is odd how I suddenly felt a great emptiness and loss just because I had missed my opportunity to see this strange artifact. I figured that was the end of the matter, but I could not entirely clear my mind of the story or the artifact. It haunted my thoughts, lurking just below the surface. A few days later, I was thinking about that damn box again, so I searched the Internet for historical insights into objects like the Dibbuk Box. That is how I located Joseph's personal blog about his and his roommates'

experiences with the curious artifact. The following account is from
Joseph's blog posting:

> I bought the box from the first seller (Kevin Mannis) in an eBay auction
> around June of 2003, out of curiosity about the "haunted" box. After
> receiving a deluge of e-mail about the box, I set up a web site to answer
> some questions, which I stopped updating in September and haven't
> updated to this day because I didn't want to talk about it with anyone.
>
> For the sake of information, I found that a dibbuk/dybbuk in Jew-
> ish folklore/mythology/teaching/whatever is a misplaced spirit that
> can neither rise to Heaven nor descend into Hell, essentially stuck in
> Limbo or purgatory. Here's another definition I found: 1. (Jewish folk-
> lore) a demon that enters the body of a living person and controls that
> body's behavior. Synonyms: dybbuk. 2. Evil Spirits, that cause mental
> illness, rage and changes of personality. The spirit or soul of a dead per-
> son that inhabits the body of a living one, with sometimes evil, some-
> times positive results.
>
> If you believe in paranormal phenomena, the box contains or is
> possessed by at least one dibbuk, possibly two, as the grandmother
> stated: a dibbuk, and keselim. Keselim is a term similar to a Turkish
> word that means "priest." This would probably correspond to the
> pair of wrapped strands of blonde and black hair. Or, it could be the
> Jewish word "Kessem" which is more a description of objects used in
> magic than a system. The hair, wine cup, coins, rose and candlestick
> are kessem.
>
> The Hebrew carving on the back, to my knowledge, is a relatively
> common Jewish prayer: "Hear O Israel, the Lord is our God, the Lord is
> one. Blessed is the name of his honored kingdom forever."

Joseph also had an online public log of events:

> I was doubtful of the "haunted" box, and I still don't believe in the para-
> normal. What happened in August and September [was] likely coinci-
> dental, so I will relate it as I originally wrote it down in a log.
>
> Sunday, 31 August 2003: Over the last week some interesting,
> though possibly coincidental, items of note have come up. Firstly, I
> share a house with six other people; we have been taking turns sleep-
> ing with the box in each of our rooms.
>
> Two people are now complaining of burning eyes, one is listless
> and depleted of energy, and another became spontaneously sick. A

few days after these ongoing annoyances started, the air outside our house was filled with small bugs for several hours....

Last night (Saturday) we discovered that the box, now located in the back corner of the house, had come mostly open, though it had been shut and it seems unlikely that anyone could or would have touched it. Asking around, nobody had been near it.

Wednesday, 10 September 2003: Though it seems impossible to prove that the box is a direct cause of misfortune, we have definitely seen a tidal wave of "bad luck."

Strange odors now permeate the house, the dumpster out back overflows with trash and decay, one roommate suddenly got bronchitis, and I broke a finger.

Several mice have died in the engine of one car, and more electronic devices seem to be dying every day: x-box, toaster, TV, and watches.

The online log of events ended by mid-September when the fun began yielding to real concern, then fear.

Brian told me that their previously boring apartment had suddenly become a bit of a hangout for many students they had met early that semester. Usually the new guests were given tours of the place, which included an introduction to a pet piranha called Chew Bacca. Two refrigerators also were on display, one of them containing a steak wrapped in its original store package dated three years earlier. And of course the "Haunted Jewish Box" would be shown. Often women guests were not informed about the box or its haunted history until after they had touched it or were forced to handle it. Then they'd be told that they had been cursed. It freaked out most of them.

I knew this was true because I met one of their female prey quite by accident. I was giving my lecture on ritual artifacts to a psychology class a year later. During the wrap-up discussion, a student by the name of Sarah mentioned that she had been cursed by a "Jewish box thing." Acquaintances at the apartment had talked her into putting her hand inside the cabinet with the hair, coins, and other strange items. It upset her, and she had not forgiven the guys for betraying her trust. For several weeks after the incident, she'd been bothered by an unnerving feeling that something—a leechlike "darkness"—was physically "attached" to her, so she had gone online to see what could be done to shake the feeling, or the curse.

In hopes of locating some authority that could offer aid, Sarah found help from the website titled Learn How To Remove (learnhowtoremove. com). Along with information on removing tough stains, it provided advice on eradicating curses. The first sentence was a paraphrase of a quote from Eleanor Roosevelt:

> "No one can make you a victim without your consent." Thus, if you
> believe in your own power, removing a curse becomes a moot point. If
> you have a negative outlook, you will no doubt become vulnerable to
> the words of those who seek to cause you undue harm.

Sarah prayed to be freed from the "attached" thing and to be granted awareness of the good in her life not the evil. She told me that, in time, the dark presence seemed to leave her. Her story confirmed Brian's account of using the box to scare female guests.

My feelings of regret and loss at failing to get access to the Dibbuk Box lasted only another month and a half. I guess Brian had recognized my sincere interest and had seen my disappointment when he'd told me the box was gone, so when he learned that the box would soon be sold by auction on eBay, he immediately sought me out. I could have a chance at owning it, if I was still interested.

Brian also told me a few other incidents that had caused him to suspect something deeper was at play. Aside from the erratic behavior of the Dibbuk Box's distressed owner, who moved from apartment to apartment as if stalked, Brian described in greater detail his roommates' odd physical ailments that would appear and then vanish overnight. Then, the constant replacement of light bulbs and all things electrical had become a financial drain on everyone in the house. When the residents returned to school after Thanksgiving break, they were not displeased to find that the Dibbuk Box and its owner were gone. Soon life at the apartment became upbeat again and free of the constant problems that had disrupted the daily routine while the box was there.

Despite Brian's creepy stories, I was still cautiously curious about this mysterious Jewish wine cabinet, but I probably would not have been brazen enough to bid on the Dibbuk Box when it came up for auction again had it not been for my friendship with Michael Callahan, a medical school acquaintance who became my confidante. Michael worked as an admissions counselor for the medical school, where his wife, Erin, was a second-year student. Because Erin was studying much of the time, Michael had a lot of time on his own. One of his hobbies was performing a magic act; his interest in performance magic drew Michael's attention to the box.

Michael stood out in any crowd, partly because of his shaved head, which was carefully wrapped during the cold winter months. He had an athletic and compact build, and was just enough bigger than average to make people cautious about approaching him, although he really was a kid at heart. But the most interesting thing about Michael was his eyes. His large pupils reminded me of dark caves; his eyes were like windows into far-off places and the deepest recesses of his soul. If you believe in the existence of "old souls," that was Michael—wise beyond his years and with a yearning to learn. Then there was Michael's personality, which can best be summed up as clever, inquisitive, and energetic, a useful combination of traits for someone who, once set on a course of action, cannot be deterred from his goal. But Michael got his way not through force, but because he overflowed with charm and could summon a childlike wonder from even the most humorless person.

One evening, as a special treat for my son, Michael visited our home to perform an elaborate magical illusion. He produced what seemed a perfectly ordinary navel orange and allowed my son to examine it thoroughly. It was just an orange, except when it was peeled, it revealed a whole lemon, and when the lemon was peeled, it revealed an entire chicken egg. Michael then broke the egg over my son's head, releasing a glittering cloud of confetti. Those few moments of entertainment had required an intricate, highly skilled, and careful setup.

As a rule, illusionists do not share the secrets of their craft, but Michael made an exception this time, showing my son the effort required to create the illusion. Michael and I became friends and found out that we shared many interests. But I didn't tell him about the Dibbuk Box or its history until one day in January 2004 when he came to me with an idea he was having trouble working out.

Michael wanted to create a show that could use his illusionist skills and provide a small income outside his regular salary. Inspired by a ghost tour he had taken in New Orleans, he wanted to develop a walking tour of Kirksville that would focus on sites of ghostly encounters and strange deaths. He and I already walked the streets of Kirksville while I pointed out locations and told him the weird lore and macabre tales I had collected over the past twenty-three years. Michael wanted to end his tour by inviting the participants into his home, where he would have an illusion set up to culminate the experience with a "paranormal" climax. His quandary was how to come up with a plausible reason for this sudden "haunting" within his own house.

The Dibbuk Box offered what seemed like the perfect solution. By incorporating the story of the Dibbuk Box into his walking tour, he could have a haunting anywhere he chose. After all, the box was in Kirksville and it contained a captive spirit. Knowing the lengths to which Michael might go, I wasn't sure I wanted to tell Michael about the Dibbuk Box, or whether I wanted to be any more deeply involved with the actual artifact. So I decided to avoid the issue of having the actual box physically present for Michael's tour by offering to help him create a replica spirit box, reasoning that Michael was providing entertainment, so his story didn't need to be the absolute truth.

As I pondered whether to share my idea, an opportunity to discuss this with Michael came up. Having lived in Colorado most of his life, Michael was an expert snowboarder. Ross had become pretty good on our snow-covered backyard hills, so he was thrilled when Michael offered to provide some pointers. Among other things, Michael would show him how to scoop and pack snow to create sturdy snow ramps for going airborne and making tricky jump-spins. When we arrived at Michael's home on the morning of Ross's lesson, I was determined to tell Michael about the Dibbuk Box and explain how a homemade knockoff of the actual artifact could be used to pull off the spontaneous "haunting" he hoped to stage for his walking tour.

We loaded my truck with snow shovels and a thirty-gallon plastic garbage can and drove to a local park's sledding spot, known as Suicide Hill for its steep incline that ends at an active street. As we drove, I turned the subject to the Dibbuk Box. I told Michael that, with the right artifact, he could apparently cause a spirit to appear at his command anywhere he liked. Michael was clearly baffled, but I let the words "Dibbuk Box" play in his mind.

Michael was clearly growing impatient with my silence as we pulled up to the hill. Finally, while unloading the truck, I began to tell him the story from memory. Ross, by my side, chimed in at key points of the tale, which added credibility to the telling. Sometimes we stopped talking briefly to work on our ramp project, then I would continue from where I had left off. By the time we put the final touches on the snow ramp, we had told Michael everything we knew of the Dibbuk Box. He mostly stayed silent as we talked, but now he wanted to know how he could get his hands on this Dibbuk Box.

I let Michael know that the "haunted box" was available on an eBay auction, and the auction would continue for several more days. But he didn't need to buy the actual artifact; he could simply use the eBay image of the box and the description of its contents to build a replica for his own use. Michael made it clear that he'd consider this option only if the real thing could not be won. I asked him why and he said that when we shared the story with him, the intensity and the emotion of the telling had the same effect on him as a campfire tale told to a circle of awed listeners. Michael wanted to tap into that same kind of emotional excitement for his performance, so nothing would do but to display the real object. Besides, why go to the trouble of recreating something that was already perfect and had a truly eerie history? And if the Dibbuk Box came with a haunting spirit, so much the better, right?

Right! His was not a question but a pronouncement of assumed agreement. Michael was making sense; I should have known to use more caution. Maybe my own deep-seated desire to get my hands on this artifact saw Michael's statement as the justification for taking the leap I'd been psychologically avoiding. When I got home, I pulled up the auction announcement on eBay and stared at the box's taunting image. I hesitated to make that first opening bid for 99 cents, finding myself unable to click the "Place Bid" button. Although the counter showed that hundreds had looked at the listing, no one else had bid so far. Perhaps they thought it just a prank and didn't wish to be made fools of, maybe they assumed that genuine curiosities like the haunted Dibbuk Box never showed up on eBay, or maybe after reading the description they were too scared to bid. I knew the truth about this item, and Brian, who had lived with the malevolent object, was absolutely sincere about its powers. I sensed the honesty in his eyes and the caution in his voice whenever he spoke about the Dibbuk Box, so I had a convincing testimonial that wasn't available to other casual lookers.

On February 3, 2004, with Michael's vow to come to my aid should I have any second thoughts or disturbing experiences, I made up my mind. Michael had promised that if I ran into serious trouble, he'd intervene and house the cursed box himself. His commitment was all it took for me to break through my mental conflict and place a low bid to test what would happen. We decided I would place the bids because Michael had never used eBay, so he had no user account set up and he did not understand the tricks bidders use to boost their chances of winning. I had been using eBay for over eight years and was pretty good at scoring nice buys at low prices. As I was the one doing the bidding, if I won the Dibbuk Box, it would become metaphysically tied to me, becoming my problem and responsibility. Later, at a time of personal fear and need, Michael would fail me. But on this snowy February day, such a turn in the plot was unimaginable. My friend had spoken sincerely and I trusted him. I went online and pulled up the listing. The Dibbuk Box loomed on the screen, daring anyone to make a bid.

For the auction, current owner Joseph had reposted the original description from when he bid and won the Dibbuk Box, including his own testimonial and warning at the bottom. Here is that addition:

> I don't really want to talk about anything [that happened] between September and January, so I'll just say that I'm selling the box now for a couple reasons:
>
> 1. Around October 6th, I started feeling bad, with trouble sleeping. This problem has persisted through today. I live alone now, and as of late I have noticed replacing a lot of burnt-out light bulbs and getting many unusual car repairs. . . .
>
> 2. I've started seeing things, sort of like large vertical dark blurs in my peripheral vision.

3. I smell something like juniper bushes or stingy ammonia in my garage often, and I have no idea what from.

4. Most disturbingly, last Tuesday (Jan. 27, 2004), my hair began to fall out. Today (Friday) it's about half gone. I'm in my early twenties and I just got a clean blood test back from the doctor's. Maybe it's stress related, I don't know.

5. Anyhow, for personal reasons I very strongly do not want this box anymore. I hope there's someone on eBay that will take this thing off of my hands. (I would just throw it away in the woods or something, but I know there has been some interest in it in the past.)

I reread the entire story and my eyes caught the lines from the first eBay listing in which the granddaughter had shouted at that first buyer, Kevin Mannis: "You bought it! You made a deal! . . . We don't want it!" Was I ready to take the risk? Not just to buy this thing, but to make some *deal*? A deal with whom, or better yet, with what? I was eased by the thought that I was not alone in this matter; Michael would be here to help me.

I entered the first bid, ninety-nine cents with a proxy amount in the sum of eighty-one dollars, to see what would happen. Nobody challenged my bid to own this haunted box until the auction's final hours several days later.

Chapter Three

Taking Possession

BIDDERS ARE ALWAYS trying to pay the lowest price in online auctions, and I have learned to hold my top bid until the last few seconds so that bidding does not become a personal battle of wills. Judging by the fact that nobody had challenged my initial small bid, I guessed that the serious bidders would come in with their higher bids towards the very end. I was correct.

The last time the Dibbuk Box was up for auction, Joseph's winning bid was $140. Auctions have their own psychology, and over the years I have seen that when an item's value is known from an earlier sale, bidders will refuse to pay double that amount. I felt confident that the online bidding for this item would be similar, so in the final moments, I planned to "proxy bid" double the previous winning amount of $140 and add a few more dollars just as a precaution. If my guess was correct, I would win the Dibbuk Box; if I guessed wrong, another bidder could outmaneuver me and take the prize. If I did not put in the highest bid, there would be no time for me to counter another's bid. Time would run out, the auction would close, and I would lose. I didn't even want to think of that possibility. I needed to guess right.

I truly expected the ending bid to be closer to the original winning price, maybe a little over $140. I was very wrong—this item was different. As I waited on Monday, February 9, 2004, the final morning of the auction, the hours edged closer to closing bid time and I was disturbed to see that the number of hits (viewers or lookers) on this eBay listing doubled in mere hours to 5,500. There was a lot of interest in this item, which was not a good sign for a bidder. This was a crazy number of hits for an item that could only be known by word of mouth or by e-mail. The word was out, and I was no longer confident of winning the box. There were too many odd variables involved with this item. As the seconds ticked in that last minute, I had to move to the eBay bidding page where I would enter my final bid in one lump sum and be cut off from seeing what others were bidding.

It seemed like my whole body was pulsing from the pounding of my heart. I can't remember ever being as on edge as I was in this bidding. My thoughts were going over and over my plan and I was poised to strike. I kept telling myself to be steady; keep focused on the important final seconds; don't bid too early and give someone else time to counter with a higher bid, or too late and not be able to register the bid. In the back of my mind I was also worried that a sudden computer glitch would block me from bidding. My mind raced with all the possibilities. Then, among all those other thoughts came a truly bizarre qualm: Could all this agitation and nervousness be caused *by the Dibbuk Box itself?* Was there more going on then typical bidder's stress? Focus on the seconds . . . Stay present . . . Ready . . . Now click! I sent my proxy bid of $286 with a mere fourteen seconds left to go—neither too early nor too late.

It was over one way or the other. I took deep breaths as I navigated to see the auction's ending results. At the top of the auction site for the Dibbuk Box I read:

Bidding has ended for this item (agetron is the winner) Winning bid: US $280 History 51 bids

I was the winner! After worrying about the auction most of the week, I was glad it was finally over, but I had yet to take possession of the box (an interesting word, "possession"). I would learn soon enough, as previous owners had, that this moment would be only the beginning of the Dibbuk Box's impact on my life.

I hadn't known that Michael was in his office upstairs monitoring the final bidding war. Moments after it was all over I heard someone leaping down the stairs to my office and Michael lunged through my door. Out of breath, he gasped, "Tell me your eBay identity is *agetron*." Michael's wide eyes implored me for the answer. He had been counting on me to use my skill to win so he could learn the haunted wine cabinet's secrets: Did it have a trapped resident spirit after all? Was it ours?

I smiled and told him, "Yes! I am *agetron*. We've won the Dibbuk Box." At this, my friend whooped and danced a bit, releasing his pent-up anxiety from the bidding war. I empathized with his joyous antics—I felt much the same, but I'm not really the whooping and dancing type. Waiting and not knowing how it would turn out had put a good bit of stress on me. Now it was over. I just needed to pay up and claim my prize.

The auction required me to pay $25 for shipping and costs in addition to the bid. However, as Joseph and I actually lived in the same city, there was no reason he couldn't simply hand deliver the artifact to the museum and receive my check for $280. I figured he'd be happy to, for two good reasons: he'd have his profit, and he'd be rid of that damned box. Soon the mysterious cabinet would be available for my inspection and for Michael's use in his spooky paranormal show.

Not long after the auction ended, I was surprised to be contacted by my fiercest competitor for the Dibbuk Box, Jennifer R. of Portland, Oregon. Jen had found my e-mail through eBay and was writing to explain how the Dibbuk Box auction had caught her interest. A friend had e-mailed her the eBay listing for the Dibbuk Box, so she had checked it out and was immediately hooked by its story, as the paranormal had always fascinated her and the Dibbuk Box offered her a chance to experience the alleged spirit and to research its story. Jen continued: "I am a scientist by training [in geology] so I started asking the 'whys, hows, whens, whos, and mostly what-ifs.' I have lived in Portland my whole life, and felt connected because my location is also the box's origin. I came very close to winning the Dibbuk Box."

This was her first-ever eBay auction, and she had become confused by the bidding process. In a live auction bidders take turns back and forth raising their bids, but eBay works differently. Every time Jen bid on the box, the higher bid amount indicated that I was still the top bidder, showing only that the price had increased and that she had not advanced. This was due to my proxy bid, which countered hers each time she upped her price. After trying several times to gain the upper position—and seeing only that it cost her more each time—Jen became frustrated. Thinking that somehow she must be bidding against herself, she stopped making new bids for just a few seconds trying to understand what she might be doing wrong. During her pause, the auction ended.

Initially, Jen had mixed feelings about bidding on the artifact. A part of her had welcomed the chance of something strange occurring, but another part was fearful of unexpected consequences, in particular about the effects the box might have on her young son. She decided that maybe fate had played a part in the outcome and that the box was not meant for her. Still, she told me, her fascination hadn't ended when her bids failed. She had felt attached to this item and when the auction ended she'd had a deep sense of loss that had taken a long time to dispel. She worried that the new owner would hide the Dibbuk Box and the strange story would be buried forever. Meanwhile, she had searched eBay for days, hoping the box would return. She said, "I wanted to reach out to you, the owner." While searching, she had come across my e-mail address and now she wanted me to keep her up to date.

After hearing her story—and about her obsession with the box—I pondered on the power the box had over people. I also realized just how close I had come to losing the bid and the box. If Jen had not stopped when she did, she would have passed my money limit and the Dibbuk Box would have been hers. Maybe it was my destiny to win the box, along with the responsibility for figuring out this enigma.

Within minutes of winning the Dibbuk Box auction, I had e-mailed Joseph hoping to hear from him quickly. After several hours had passed and I had received no response, I also left messages on his answering machine. I was now invested in owning the Dibbuk Box, and I feared that Joseph might have changed his mind about the sale. Did he want to keep the box in spite of the problems it had brought him? Joseph had once commented to Brian that when he had won the Dibbuk Box, its previous owner had seemed reluctant to let go of it.

Frustrated by Joseph's failure to respond the first day, I remembered that both of his parents were on the faculty at the university. It would be simple to get their names and home phone number, so I decided to call them to see if they knew their son's whereabouts. Even Brian, who had seen Joseph earlier during the week, wasn't sure whether he was living at home or at another student's apartment.

His mother answered my call and said Joseph was usually at home in the evening. When I explained that I was trying to reach her son to pay for the Dibbuk Box, she didn't know what I was talking about. During the nine months Joseph owned the box, he had never once mentioned the item to his mother. She put her husband on the phone, thinking maybe he knew something about it and could help me. His father informed me that while he knew Joseph had been keeping a wooden box in their garage the past month, his son had not told them about its odd history or the problems it had brought him. Joseph's dad found the whole situation somewhat alarming and thought it was good that I take the box off his son's hands. He was certain Joseph would be at home that evening, and promised to tell him that the check was ready and that I would appreciate Joseph delivering the box to the museum the following day.

Joseph never called, and I began to worry that something was wrong. Was he planning to keep the box after all? I was frustrated, to say the least, that the Dibbuk Box seemed to be toying with me—staying just beyond my reach. Then I received a call from Brian, who told me that Joseph had asked him to pick up the check and handle the delivery himself. Joseph wanted nothing to do with the new owner. By turning the dealings over to Brian, he would never have to meet with me or spend another moment with the sinister box.

In fact, I learned from Brian that Joseph had turned the box over to him even before the eBay auction ended. This was how Brian found out the box was up for sale again. Brian had been the only apartment resident during those early months with the Dibbuk Box who hadn't had a chance to sleep in the same room with it, so Joseph had given it to Brian once it was up for sale. Once it was ensconced in Brian's bedroom, he wished the thing were somewhere else. During the seven days of the auction, Brian had suffered high stress, energy drain, and restless sleep. Brian too was more than ready to be rid of it.

He finally delivered it at one in the afternoon on Tuesday, February 11, 2004. He showed up at the museum carrying a rather large cardboard shipping box and wearing a concerned look. When Brian tilted the shipping box, I could see the Dibbuk Box inside, encased in bubble wrap. My pulse quickened. It had been almost nine months since I first learned of this mysterious artifact and now it was finally mine. The first thing I wanted to do was figure out exactly what this thing I now possessed was.

I took the cardboard box from Brian and found it was a lot heavier than I had anticipated, perhaps about twenty-five pounds. A glint of warm, reddish wood peaked out from a tear in the plastic, and its weight in my hands brought the reality of the situation to me: It was finally here . . . I owned it . . . I was the new master of it . . . or was I?

His delivery completed, Brian didn't stay to see what I would do next. He had made it clear the past few days that he didn't trust this item and the trouble that seemed to come with it. He turned and walked out of the museum, not pausing or looking back, and I was pretty sure he would not approve of my intention to store it at the museum, even just for the night. Excited as I was to get my first full look at the new purchase, I felt it only fair to wait until Michael could be present. I hauled the cardboard box into a room just off the museum's largest gallery, where it hardly stood out among the clutter of teaching supplies and cardboard boxes of other items waiting to be sorted.

Filled with excitement, I called Michael. He couldn't be free until seven thirty that evening, and would need me to give him a ride to the museum where we would conduct our inspection together. The anticipation made it hard to keep focused on my work, but I tried not to think about what was ahead and keep myself busy for a few more hours.

That evening I drove over to Michael's home to pick him up. As we drove back to the museum, I told him I had already received a few e-mails from media reporters interested in learning about the Dibbuk Box and writing articles about it. Michael asked me if I realized what was happening. I asked what he meant, and he said based on the ever-growing interest of journalists and the growing number of eBay users who viewed the site, the Dibbuk Box was on the brink of becoming a symbol, an icon, an entity unique unto itself. More than twenty-five thousand different eBay users had checked out the box on the auction site even *after* it had been sold. Given the curiosity it had already generated, its audience of online watchers might just keep growing to millions. This box was something odd and wonderful. Michael kept repeating that he could hardly believe he was present at the beginning of it all. It was, he said, the most amazing experience in the past three months of his life. Maybe Michael was right, this was going to be a lot of fun!

We arrived at the dark and empty museum. Staff, faculty, and students had long since headed home and the rooms and hallways were running on limited lighting to cut down on utility costs. I unlocked the exterior door, then the museum's inside entrance. The sounds of gears rotating and bolts being pulled back seemed louder in the empty place, which is always creepier at night when echoing noises pierce the darkness and hints of skulls and other human parts are partially visible in the dim safety lights.

I left Michael in the workroom and headed to the storeroom to retrieve the cardboard box. Our first act was to unwrap and examine the Dibbuk Box and check out the various tokens inside of it. Once we had scrutinized the box and its contents, we planned to store the artifact in the museum. I could see that Michael was really enjoying the slow, careful process of freeing the Dibbuk Box from its shipping container and bubble wrap, and I was taking my time enjoying the physical discovery of this artifact. I had waited nine months to see it, and there was no need to rush now. Brian never mentioned anything about Joseph receiving the promised documentation from the seller when the Dibbuk Box arrived, so those materials were not in the shipping box.

The worn cabinet showed spots of missing veneer, a few scratches, and some gouges. This kind of wear could be expected of an item several decades old. In spite of the damage, it was still a choice piece. The mahogany wood glowed warmly. I pointed out to Michael small nail holes on the top edge of the box and on the top of one door. I held the door where I found the holes and imagined a small hinge with a rasp lock to hold the door shut. When I tried to open the doors using the "trick" lower drawer, the doors would not budge. So it was indeed possible for a small hinge with a tiny lock to keep the whole unit shut—drawer and doors. I released the door with my hand and pulled the drawer to open the doors. When the doors opened, a scent not unpleasant was released—it was neither jasmine nor cat urine, but was woody, clean smelling, and a bit intoxicating. I liked the smell and found it to be addictive.

Attached on each side of the two doors were wooden holders with holes; could these be to hold something like a scroll? More likely, they were meant to hold bottles of wine, resting on the bottom holder with the top of the bottle going through the hole in the top holder. But they could also be used to hold wine glasses. Within the cabinet were all the pieces that had been described in the auction listing. I was ready to explore more.

Anticipating the need for a backdrop while taking pictures of the box, Michael had brought a large length of blue velvet material that he often used in his illusionist performances. I removed the interior items, the tokens, including the two bound locks of hair, and gently placed them on the soft velvet. With these objects on the table, I next brought out a black light we use to show kids the amount of germs and dirt left after they wash their hands. I knew that if there were any kind of biological residue, such as blood or skin particles or traces of cat urine, the ultraviolet rays would expose it instantly.

The light immediately showed a glowing spot on the front of the box. On close examination I found it was merely candle wax that had somehow dripped on the outside door, perhaps from the odd, octopus-legged candlestick we had found inside. Otherwise, the box seemed to be clean, down to the wood, of any organic substances. As we pored over the outside of the strange object, Michael suddenly shouted with excitement. He had found something—a mark. When I looked where he was pointing, I saw what seemed to be a capital letter *N* written in black permanent marker, or some other ink, on the lower edge of the box's side. Thinking aloud, I suggested that it could have been written there to help the owner align the box to the north, in which case its doors would face to the east. I had read that directional aligning with the sunrise to the east was a common feature of ritual items dating back to the time of ancient civilizations. If the box had been used by a Jewish family for some religious purpose, a mark aligning the box in this manner would make perfect sense because in a synagogue, the ark is aligned so that people

facing it are facing Jerusalem, which in the continental United States would always be to the east.

Using museum-standard white gloves, we checked the items that had been inside the cabinet. First there was a gleaming metal cup. It had been plated in silver, long worn off, exposing a golden glow of brass beneath. This item also bore a capital *N* on its lip, which was cracked and distressed from years of use. It made us wonder whether there was a relationship between these matching *N*s. If this box had served as an altar of sorts, might these marks have aided the user in some way, perhaps for some spiritual ritual unknown to us? Neither Michael nor I had an answer.

Picking up the first lock of hair, I felt a bit uneasy. From whose head, in what time period, had this reddish-blonde lock come? The somewhat curly and tangled mass of long strands was tied in the middle with a white thread to hold it more or less together. Next, I selected the ebony-black lock of hair. It was so dark that a tint of blue shone off the surface. It too was tied with a white string, but the hair was stick-straight, there was more of it, and it was cut to less than an inch. As a result, even the binding thread had not prevented bits of the hair from shedding away onto the velvet.

The largest item within the wooden container and what caused the box to weigh so much was a sculpture of four different colors of granite stones, assembled in an odd design that seemed to defy gravity. The largest section of stone was brilliant white, peppered throughout with gleaming ruby dots and flecks of black. The whiteness made these random spots visually leap from the surface. This stone had four Hebrew letters carved deeply and filled with copper. No doubt it took great skill and time to do this kind of work without breaking the stone. Later, I learned that the letters spelled out the Hebrew word *shalom*, which means "peace."

The remaining objects were a dried rose, a thing from nature now dead, and two pennies whose dates of 1925 and 1928 linked the objects to years long ago. I wondered what was important about those dates: perhaps a birth or a death? Based on the familial tokens and the Hebrew lettering on two of the pieces, I reasoned that the box, itself an unusual but not unique item, had belonged to someone Jewish who must have added the carved lettering. It had been described as a wine cabinet. Could it have been used as part of the Shabbat ritual of lighting candles and reciting blessing over candle and wine?

Based on the design and hardware, I placed the box circa late 1950s or early 1960s. The simple, modern design and its accents, the hinges and drawer pull, pretty much gave away its creation date for me. The mechanism that caused the doors to open when a small lower drawer was pulled out seemed unique and ingenious in its simplicity. I was told that this item had been created after World War II. My dating of the box put it in approximately the right time period, and the contents were of a similar age or older, as I would expect.

It had passed my visual test and physical inspection. I believed it was a genuine, serious artifact, but its original function was still a mystery. Could it have been created to hold some spiritual entity like a Dibbuk? When it came to that spiritual question, I wasn't sure. Looking at the wooden box with its contents spread before me, I could see nothing that reminded me of any other occult artifacts I had studied or read about, and no obvious reason for these objects being together.

Next, I decided to explore it with my hands without looking at it. I pulled off my gloves, closed my eyes, and rested my palms on the top of the Dibbuk Box. To my surprise, it was warm to the touch. I opened my eyes briefly, then closed them again and continued. I pressed down firmly on the box to get a sense of its hardness, and was startled when the wood itself seemed to shift, almost as if it had a pulse. I had the distinct impression that I was pressing on the surface of water that rippled under my hands. Startled, I opened my eyes. The wooden object was as solid and unyielding as ever. Once more, with my eyes closed, I tried to *sense* the box by touch. This time the wood seemed to melt under the pressure of my fingers, and suddenly I felt a sharp pain in my side that migrated up into my stomach. The pain was so intense I could hardly breathe. It would torment me for many hours. I washed my hands thoroughly and put the gloves back on.

Despite the pain throbbing in my belly, Michael and I took a few photos before calling it a night. We arranged the contents in front of the box with the doors slightly ajar for effect. Then I rearranged the items inside, just where I'd found them when I first opened it. The pieces were a tight fit and had to be arranged in a specific order so the drawer could be closed firmly and the outer doors could be shut. The candlestick goes in first, then the large granite stone piece, and then the cup, each article fitting tight against the other. The fit seemed too perfect to be coincidental.

Once the box was closed, I lifted it from the velvet cloth that Michael had brought and pushed the soft material toward Michael to pack up. It was the first time I noticed the concerned look in his eyes. He asked if I had some sticky tape he could use. I placed the Dibbuk Box on the table and fetched some clear packing tape used for shipping museum gift shop orders. Still wearing the white museum gloves, he pulled off a strip of tape, wrapped it back on itself so his hand could fit inside, then started patting the fabric with the sticky side. I realized he was attempting to retrieve any loose bits of hair that had fallen from the black lock. After patting the whole thing over, he threw the tape into the trash and repeated the procedure two more times. All I could do was watch in disbelief.

Caught in this act of compulsive behavior, Michael told me he wanted to avoid bringing home even the tiniest particles of "Dibbuk Box hair" that might possess spiritual properties. I had to chuckle. It was the first time Michael showed any suspicion that there might be more to this thing than the eye could see. I half hoped he would dream of the hag and receive a good beating, but the growing pain in my stomach made me suspect I was the box's chosen victim.

Michael's behavior and my abdominal pain put me on guard, so I decided the best course of action was to keep the box in a storage area at the museum. For the time being at least, it would rest among the museum's collection of human bones once used as teaching aids and cruel-looking instruments used by long-ago physicians—far enough from my home that my family and I would be safe, just in case. Michael wasn't the only one who felt a bit nervous after handling the piece. He wasn't volunteering to keep it at his house and I certainly didn't want the box in my home, at least not until after we had examined it further. Another reason for waiting before moving this item was to see if any mysterious problems might manifest themselves within me. I took the Dibbuk Box into the back storage area, placing the box so the side with the black-inked N was facing north and shoving it tight against the wall so its doors or drawer could not open on their own. Then I turned off the lights and let it be for the night. I could not have guessed that my plan for housing it at the museum would fall apart before the week was over.

During the twenty-minute commute home, I was comforted by knowing the Dibbuk Box was safely tucked away to view and ponder at my leisure without involving my family. So far so good. Only Michael and my staff knew of my purchase and the box's arrival that day. Lori was firmly planted in the physical world. In twenty-one years of marriage, I had never known her to give any credence to matters of the occult. But I still felt it was best not to mention any of this to her—this was to be my investigative project alone. When I arrived home, my thoughts of the Dibbuk Box were replaced by my son's talk about sparring in tae kwon do and my daughter's exasperation with a girl who had made rude comments about items she had brought for show and tell.

By the time I went to bed that evening, I was exhausted. But my sleep, if you could call it that, was anything but restful. I kept seeing images of an old woman with dark, sunken eyes and flyaway white hair that crackled with blue static electricity. Visions of old faces would morph into other faces horribly disfigured by cuts and wounds. I saw face after face, and then the image of the white-haired hag with hollow eyes watching me would return. I would wake up, only to fall asleep and dream of a huge store full of household items for sale—like an old five-and-dime store. Three times in a row I dreamed of this store. A pleasant, small-framed old woman with white hair stood in the middle of the store, trying to help me. I looked around, not really sure what I had come to buy. Then she wanted to show me something important. She pointed to a glowing white, two-foot-square box as if that was what I needed. It seemed to be just an empty box about the size of the Dibbuk Box. I was not sure what she wanted from me, if anything, but a few months later I would encounter that very woman in the least expected setting.

When I awoke in the morning, my stomach was still churning in pain. Coincidence or not, it had begun while I was handling the Dibbuk Box. I got up to shave and shower. I splashed warm water on my beard stubble and looked into the mirror for the first time that morning. I was startled by the bloody, red eyes staring back at me. These were not the bloodshot eyes of an exhausted person—it looked like I had been poked in the eyes with a stick. I was puzzled by their freakish appearance—and they hurt. I flushed my eyes with my wife's contact solution, trying to get the red toned down a bit. Then my wife stepped into the bathroom; she took one look and asked what happened. I honestly told her that I didn't know. She suggested I get them looked at by a doctor soon.

I had done nothing before bedtime to injure my eyes. I knew it wasn't from allergies—not with six inches of snow outside—and I hadn't been near any animals. The wood of the box was a varnished mahogany veneer, nothing that should have caused an allergic reaction. The only thing different in my daily routine was that I had touched the box last evening for several minutes. My hands were exposed to its wood, but I had washed them thoroughly afterwards.

When I got to work, I was bombarded with inquiries about my eyes. I said I didn't know what had happened, but I was pretty confident it wasn't an infection. It had come on too suddenly and was too severe. Though my eyes looked horrible and continued to hurt badly, they didn't itch or seep any goo. Maybe I had rubbed them during my restless sleep. I figured they would heal in a few days, so I tried to ignore the pain and go about my business. Lori had planned for us to meet up with Michael and give him some photos I had taken of him doing snowboard stunts and working with Ross on the snow ramps at the sledding hill. My wife wanted to thank him in person for being such a good role model for our son, and providing him such entertaining activities. When we caught up with Michael, he was taken aback by the change in my appearance. He motioned at my eyes and I waved him off.

It soon became obvious that he had told Erin about his fascination with the Dibbuk Box and our experiences with it the previous night. Erin turned to my wife and remarked on the strangeness of this "wooden box thing" the guys had acquired. My wife's ears perked up. She said she hadn't a clue of what we were talking about. There was an awkward silence as spouses looked at each other. Finally, I explained it was just a project Michael and I were working on, something for one of his magic performances. I insisted it was really nothing. Ignoring my hint to drop the subject, Erin offered to show my wife the Dibbuk Box's listing on eBay. My stomach ached, but I was pretty sure it wasn't the box's fault this time. Lori and Erin headed off to Lori's office to see this project I was involved with. Alone with Michael, I asked, "How was your night?" He said he hadn't slept well, probably due to all the excitement. He asked about my night, and I told him how awful it was. He asked, "And your eyes?" I said it was nothing, and that I'd woken up this way. He shook his head and went upstairs to start his workday.

A few hours later, I ran into my wife on the way to a campus awards ceremony to recognize staff. I had been nominated to receive the "Above and Beyond Duty Award" by some medical students I had assisted with research on the history of medicine. After the ceremony, my wife was a changed woman. As we walked back toward our offices, she told me bluntly that she disliked the idea of me owning "that box." It was "a stupid waste of money," she said. I was to get rid of it right away and sell it back. I've never seen her that mad. She gave me the silent treatment for two days. I decided it best not to let the topic of the Dibbuk Box come up again.

And I had decided I would definitely keep the box . . . at the museum.

Chapter Four

Questions
from All Sides

Checking my personal e-mail account for the first time in several days, I found hundreds of messages from people who were aware of the eBay auction and wanted to know whether I, as the newest owner, had experienced any paranormal episodes. It gave me a strange sense of importance to find I had such a range of followers—writers, professors, sports stars, paranormal specialists, religious leaders, and average people on the street—all writing to ask how I was getting along with the box and telling me about their own encounters with the supernatural. Inquiries came from every state in the country and even from other countries, including England, Australia, Norway, and Germany. This new experience only made me more determined to solve the mystery of the Dibbuk Box. I felt like these people trusted me to get to the bottom of this puzzle, even though it was completely beyond my life experiences to date.

One of the first to contact me was Max Gross, a writer for the *Jewish Daily Forward*. Founded in 1897 as a Yiddish newspaper, the *Forward* is now a weekly news magazine that appears online as well as in print form. It surprised me that such a serious-minded paper was interested in this "Dybbuk Box" topic. When researching the word "dibbuk," I had learned, among other things, that Hebrew and Yiddish use a non-Latin alphabet, so when they are transliterated into the Latin alphabet, there may be more than one spelling for a word. The short *i* sound, for example, may be transliterated either as *i* or as *y*, and the more common spelling of the word is "dybbuk." I decided to stick with "dibbuk," however, because that is how the word was spelled in the original eBay posting. Using this alternate spelling makes the online searches more likely to come up with discussions of the actual item.

I had little to add on the topic beyond what was in the eBay listing, but Max said he was under a tight deadline—the very next day—and wanted any help I could offer as he wrote the story. Being wary of his motives, I checked out his previous articles in the *Forward* and found they were lighthearted fare, such as a story about the curative powers of chicken soup. He seemed to be whom and what he said, so I promised to do what I could to help. Max was only able to contact me through eBay and with my permission, so I felt that I would be able to keep some personal distance and keep my identity confidential.

First and most importantly, I told Max, I did not want my name or geographic location to appear in his story. There are too many crazy people stalking the Internet. I did not want them showing up at my door—or in my life. Also, the college student who had sold me the box wished to remain anonymous. Max assured me that would be no problem and that I could be identified generically without using my name. After he had interviewed me over the phone, he requested an image to go with his story, which he planned to call "A Box Full of Bad Luck." I provided two different digital images from the photos that Michael and I had taken just the night before. All seemed well and it felt good to help, but when I saw the article online the next day, I was angry, to put it mildly, to find that Max had disregarded our verbal agreement and published my full name, my profession, and where I lived. The only things he left out were my phone number and street address, both of which were easily available. I also found that the article had reached a huge audience, well beyond the *Forward's* usual readership, and that it could be accessed online by simply typing "Dibbuk Box" on any Internet search engine. Suddenly my name and story were on numerous websites on the paranormal and blogs of the curious. I never wanted—and I never expected—to suddenly have this level of exposure to an unknown audience with unknown intentions.

All kinds of people were soon phoning or e-mailing me at the museum or at my home. Several people demanded that I turn the Dibbuk Box over to them, adding that they would arrive for it in a few days. Others wanted me to join their demonology groups or Wiccan cults, or to tell me how this item had infiltrated their already plagued lives. Pagans, Christians, and Jews alike found me and wrote. There was no way I could keep up with the communications even if I wanted to, and in many cases I didn't. Because of that one article, I suddenly had no privacy. And Joseph wrote me a bitter letter telling me how upset he was that his name had appeared in print, and the incident undoubtedly drove a wedge between us.

To halt the constant barrage of phone calls and e-mail letters, I had to make my home phone number unlisted and change my e-mail address. This stopped many would-be contacts, but truly interested people could follow the clues to my location and place of employment. This was a wake-up call for me. From here on, I would not trust any journalist to respect my anonymity. My solution was to set up a website without my contact information that would allow people to access information on the Dibbuk Box, but not my personal identity. For the merely curious, that information seemed to be enough.

Still angry from my last interview fiasco, I wondered how to deal with another writer who had contacted me just days after I'd won the box and before my trust in reporters was shattered. Leslie Gornstein, a freelance writer for the *Los Angeles Times*, had pleaded for my help in preparing her own story about the Dibbuk Box. She had been given the potential story lead from a close friend in the newspaper business, and, once again, word of mouth had passed along the bizarre tale of the box. Leslie made it clear that she thought the story might give her a much-needed break, enabling her to get more work assignments with the *Times*. I called her and said I was having second thoughts about working with her or any writer. I explained my current problems, brought about by my "paranormal outing" by the *Forward* writer. She agreed that what had happened to me was wrong, but assured me that she would never share confidential information without permission. She then promised that before submitting her final draft for publication, she would clear every word of it with me. Leslie wanted the story, but she also wanted me to be comfortable with the way it was told. She realized that my family and job came first for me, and that this new development in my life was just a passing interest, a short-term hobby.

In the end, I believe I made the right decision in trusting her. Leslie was a professional and true to her word. Over the next five months, she and I exchanged e-mails, and chatted regularly on the phone as she assembled her article. The article took so many months to write because just as she'd come close to submitting the story, I discovered some new information that caused her to start over from a new perspective. At last, she could delay no longer and turned her story in to the *Los Angeles Times* Entertainment editor, and it was published under the title "Jinx In a Box."

Leslie promised to call me when the story was in print. Good to her word, she did so and even sent me two copies of the newspaper. When I received the papers and flipped to the Entertainment Section, I was impressed to see that her story was given an entire page and included a good size color image too. It shared space with updates on Hollywood films, actors, live performances, and shows in town. The Dibbuk Box story, featured as it was, stood out as something very different and odd from the normal news fare, even by Hollywood's standards. As she'd hoped, the article brought Leslie a good bit of recognition and success with the paper. With my promise to help her completed, I never thought I would have any reason to hear from or have any further contact with Leslie Gornstein again. It was nice to have such a positive outcome with her, so I could move on.

In those first few days, I had also received an e-mail from Steve Maass, president of the Long Island Paranormal Research Group (LIPRG). Steve contacted me just before his move from Long Island in 2004. Within a few years of his move from Long Island to Asheville, North Carolina, LIPRG disbanded and the website closed. Steve has since created the Asheville Paranormal Phenomena Observation & Research Team (APPORT). Steve describes this new group as having originally formed in 1995 under the name Long Island Paranormal Research Group, and states that APPORT continues to document phenomena that are not unnatural, but simply uncommon.

Steve had been tracking the Dibbuk Box since it first appeared in an eBay auction. He had done considerable research on the box and was willing to offer me both historic data and advice about the object's alleged paranormal powers. Steve was the first paranormal researcher to contact me, but before long dozens of paranormal groups were asking if they could visit and do an investigation. Steve directed me to his organization's website, http.liprg.com (now replaced with APPORT on facebook.com). I went to the site and learned that the organization had been around for several years and provided a section that listed, with images, its paranormal investigations to date. The Dibbuk Box had its own separate information tab and was identified as a subject of ongoing research. The comments seemed professional and there was a good following making appropriate inquiries and offering comments. I asked Brian if he knew anything about Steve Maass, and he told me that Joseph had received several e-mail inquiries from LIPRG, usually warning them not to open or take lightly the powers of the Dibbuk Box. I decided to reply to Steve, but I would be cautious until I learned more about his motivation concerning the haunted box. The last thing I needed right then was to be stalked by some nut job seeking to gain power through this purportedly haunted object.

I checked into Steve and confirmed that he was a public school music teacher, which made me feel a little more comfortable about him. Coming from a family of teachers, I know how much time and dedication teaching requires, especially teaching music, which often requires after-school hours as well, so it seemed unlikely that Steve would have the time and energy to be a fanatic. From talking to Steve, it became obvious that his passion for teaching carried over into his interest for paranormal work, as seen through his LIPRG website, which was well organized and thorough. Over his years of working with paranormal investigations, Steve had built a solid network of people in the paranormal field. And knowing that Maass is a common Jewish surname, I thought perhaps he had a special interest in paranormal things related to Judaic folklore.

With my current concern over the eye problems and the odd dreams I was having, the most useful information he could provide at the moment would be how to protect myself from dangerous supernatural forces. Within our first few e-mails, Steve sent me a page detailing experiences and his research in spiritual oppression, and an article he had written with the Dibbuk Box in mind. It was entitled "Sacrifices to Spirits, and How They are Made," and provided a historical perspective on how people have dealt with spiritual energies over the centuries, including processes of succumbing to and appeasing demons. At the time, those rituals seemed like a guaranteed way to bring even more trouble into my life and I wasn't sure I would ever be desperate enough to try them. Still, I tucked the article away in one of my files, just in case I changed my mind.

Steve also informed me that in June 2003, while monitoring the auction for the Dibbuk Box, he had learned of Joseph's winning bid and immediately sent him an e-mail. In fact, Steve had e-mailed Joseph a number of times, but Joseph had said little. Even when Steve sent him specific information on the box, Joseph merely wrote back that the material was "interesting." Steve felt that Joseph had pretty much ignored his offers to help and his warning that messing around with this artifact was a serious matter. Communication between them ended, but Steve kept watching the Internet for information about the Dibbuk Box and was excited, but not too surprised, to see it reappear on eBay. When Steve wrote to me, as the box's new owner, he hoped I would want help from an expert in the paranormal, perhaps from one of his contacts or even himself.

Still, I found it odd that Steve's e-mails seemed somewhat wistful when discussing the Dibbuk Box. Considering how much effort he put into tracking the artifact, doing research, and warning the owners not to trifle with it, I could not understand why he didn't just bid on it himself. Then he could have had complete control over this thing that seemed to occupy so much of his time. The eBay records indicated that he had never once bid on the Dibbuk Box. I asked him why he had not bid for it, and Steve said he had wanted to more than anything from the moment it first appeared on eBay, but when his wife read the description of the box and his preliminary research on it, she put her foot down. Steve told me that weeks before he learned of the Dibbuk Box, he had purchased four reputedly haunted dolls, one of which had caused a series of unnerving incidents in their home. After that experience, the idea of living with this haunted box was too terrifying for his wife to consider. She was no novice to the spirit world, having joined Steve on countless research trips to haunted homes, mental asylums, and scenes of horrific violence, but did not want to take the risk of having the Dibbuk Box in her home. Considering how my wife had reacted, I could understand Steve's dilemma. Steve had seen the Dibbuk Box as a potential subject for one of his greatest investigations, but his regard for his wife's concerns was more important to him than actually possessing the artifact, so instead he chose to keep up with the box's manifestations from a safe distance, and offer information and advice whenever possible.

I, on the other hand, was not at a safe distance from the Dibbuk Box, and I began to experience a variety of unpleasant physical symptoms with no cause I could pinpoint. I have been blessed with healthy genetics. All of my known ancestors, my parents, and my siblings have enjoyed excellent health and long lives, and my family and I rarely see a doctor except for annual checkups. Good health is easy to take for granted when you have it, so imagine my concern when my normal well-being seemed to vanish overnight. The only explanation I could think of for these sudden health problems, rational or not, was this new addition to my life—the haunted box.

The troubles began within days of buying the Dibbuk Box. Besides my blood-streaked eyes, related vision problems, and the sharp pain in my abdomen, I began having ailments that were completely new and frightening. By merely swallowing accumulated saliva, as we all do, I began to choke. Even the smallest sip of water would "go down the wrong way," or into the windpipe rather than down the esophagus. The feeling of something in my windpipe would take weeks to go away, then it would start again. It felt as if I was drowning, and these choking attacks continued for years until the box was spiritually sealed. I also started having a very nasty, bitter, metallic taste in my mouth and nothing I did could rid me of it. I tried gargling with mouthwash, constant toothbrushing, and popping breath mints, but I could still taste the bitterness. My physician told me I had dysgeusia, an altered sense of taste that induced foul, metallic flavors. It can come on suddenly for no apparent reason and vanish just as suddenly. Not surprisingly, I felt stressed by these physical problems and began to have trouble sleeping, no matter how tired I was.

Although I had used cotton gloves when I handled the Dibbuk Box, I did touch it with my bare hands for a few moments. I had thoroughly scrubbed my hands afterwards, but I began to wonder if I had somehow gotten contaminated, an idea also raised by several people who were following my experiences through e-mails. Could previous owners and their family members have passed on their illnesses and mental disturbances to me? They had suffered such varied symptoms as strokes, hair loss, violent dreams, and fears they were going mad. Could this wooden box somehow have been coated by accident, or maybe on purpose, with substances that would harm anyone who handled it? It would have been relatively easy to do, but what kind of person would do such a thing? Now that the idea had entered my mind, I knew I'd have to check it out.

I was familiar with the possibility of poisonous artifacts from working at the museum, where we had dealt with preserved tissue specimens and turn-of-the-century medicines likely containing cyanide or mercury, which were commonly found in medical laboratories and doctors' bags. Using information collected from Brian Spatola, collection manager at the National Museum of Health & Medicine, and several online sources (National Library of Medicine, National Institute of Health, and Medline Plus), I learned that many of the symptoms described by previous owners were the same for those who'd been exposed to and inhaled ammonia. These included hallucinations and the sense of smelling cat urine. I wondered if the finish on the surface of the box might be producing toxic fumes of some kind, or if indeed a cat had previously urinated on the box. Ammonia is a major component of cat urine, which could work towards explaining these odd coincidences. However, the black light I had used when Michael and I first examined the box would have shown cat urine as a biological substance on the box's surface (or inside), but there was none. Also, Kevin's surface cleaning with lemon oil would have eliminated urine residue, had it existed.

Other symptoms of mild exposure to ammonia include temporary blindness, eye irritation, conjunctivitis, coughing, throat pain, wheezing, and upper respiratory irritation. Kevin, the first to sell the Dibbuk Box on eBay, had described violent dreams and a smoke alarm going off for no apparent reason. The presence of ammonia in the air could increase the likelihood of a fire, but the fumes alone could not set off an alarm. I learned from the Centers for Disease Control (CDC) website that mild cyanide exposure could produce these immediate effects: rapid breathing, restlessness, dizziness, weakness, headache, choking, nausea and vomiting, and rapid heart rate. Many of these symptoms seemed similar to symptoms I was suddenly experiencing. I felt a cold emptiness inside—had I been poisoned? I was trying not to panic, but I felt a powerful need for logical answers. I was not ready to dismiss the possibility of spiritual attacks, but first I would concentrate on a non-supernatural explanation. At the moment, my physical ailments were pointing to a different culprit—physical contamination. Using a chemical test kit from the museum, I began examining the box's wooden surface, interior, and contents. The tests require that you swipe the object with chemically treated cloths or cotton swabs, and watch for changes and reactions. Using this method, we can test for ammonia, mercury, cyanide, and other harmful residues. My tests on the Dibbuk Box showed no unusual or harmful chemical residues. It was a relief to find that the only coating on the Dibbuk Box was a simple varnish, similar to sugar water. Many early varnishes were made largely of sugar for a cheap but hard finish. With my fear of chemical contamination now relieved, I was left to ponder other causes of my sudden and growing list of health issues. Was it mere coincidence?

Why would my ears become feverish and scarlet-colored in just minutes and remain that way for days? Why had my body broken out in head-to-toe welts and hives that would vanish suddenly leaving no signs of having been there, only to reappear in a matter of seconds? My skin would itch all over, as if from the inside, and scratching provided no relief. One morning, I discovered that I had scratched patches of skin until they were raw and bleeding. Was my research into spiritual oppression causing psychosomatic symptoms to appear throughout my body? Whatever the cause, it didn't seem to matter, because the physical evidence and discomfort was real.

Often I would lie awake all night, hoping that exhaustion would finally put me to sleep, but no such luck. Members of my family were the first to notice the deterioration of my health. Knowing there was no chemical contamination, I began to wonder if I had contracted some microscopic germ from that hair within the box. Perhaps some horrible disease had caused the violent coughing and choking. Fearing the worst, I arranged for a thorough checkup with our family doctor, who performed every possible test, but found me disease-free and in excellent health (but noted that losing ten or fifteen pounds would make it even better). I had no explanation for the symptoms that were growing more severe each day. To make things worse, I began receiving e-mails from people who felt that they and their families were fighting similar problems just from having read about the Dibbuk Box on eBay or my website.

Was it all simply a case of mass hysteria, or was I indeed dealing with a different, supernatural threat?

A woman named Blair wrote to tell me that ever since reading the Dibbuk Box story in her office with her boss, she had lost her sense of taste, gotten pinkeye, and smelled the stink of cat urine. She had also watched as her boss jerked back and forth uncontrollably. Her family and her boss had all come down with strep throat in less than eight hours. Her warning: "Whoever controls the picture of the Dibbuk Box online needs to take it down immediately!" She believed that images of the box were somehow releasing small portal openings of evil all over the Internet. Every viewer was receiving "negative spiritual-energy ghosts" in their offices and homes. It seemed odd, but Blair had gone to the trouble to write me about her situation and her symptoms mirrored mine.

A father named Mike wrote to say he had sought me out as the box's owner so he could warn me against opening it. The spirit contained within wished only to deceive and destroy, he said. While reading of the box's history, Mike had smelled several disgusting odors mentioned in various accounts. He had two small children and wished to protect them from danger. Both had become seriously ill just recently, he said, so this would be his last e-mail to me. He closed with the warning, "No one on this earth has the power to destroy what's in that box."

Dan, another e-mail correspondent, wanted to share "something strange" that had happened to his wife. He wrote:

> . . . she is very spiritual and into energy, and chakras and whatever. . . . About a week after [she] read the story of the Dibbuk Box, she started to develop rash-like spots on her chest and neck—a few at first and then a full breakout of this strange awfulness. Two days after the spots started we ended up at the hospital where they told us it was Pityriasis Rosea. Never heard of it! The doctor says nobody really knows what it is or how to fix it. . . . My wife immediately blamed the Dibbuk Box story. I don't know, but she insists she knows that is what caused [her problem]. It took three months for these spots to go away.

Again, having some of the same symptoms I could only empathize with her problems. Were all these problems related to the Dibbuk Box?

One letter was especially interesting, and it shed some light on the idea of a box as a container for some kind of spirit. A soldier named William wrote to me:

> First off I want to start by saying I am not a religious "kook" or a paranormal researcher or anything like that. I have been around the paranormal though throughout my life. I am currently a US Army soldier with the 182nd Airborne Division based in Fort Bragg, NC.
>
> Before I was at Bragg I was stationed in Italy, and I've actually heard something similar to this story while I was there, but this was about a year or two before the Dibbuk Box made its debut on eBay.
>
> Because I was in Italy I was a bit of a party animal and made a lot of acquaintances overseas. Also, when I was a young boy I grew up in a real haunted house and had a lot of VERY real experiences there. Ever since that time in my life I've been drawn to the paranormal. So while I was in Italy, I inquired with a lot of the locals to find haunt[ed places] where me and my soldier buddies would go to check them out. I've been to some crazy places. . . .
>
> Anyways, while I was inquiring about things of a ghostly nature I actually met a kid who told me about a ritual (Jewish guy by the way) that his grandmother used to do to trap spirits.
>
> Now I never heard about this Dibbuk box before last night. I just happened across a site that was talking about eBay auctions and your site was linked. I found the story intriguing to say the least, but then it struck a nerve with me when I read about the contents of the box. It was very similar to what this guy told me about in Europe.
>
> The hair had something to do with it, almost like a yin and yang sort of thing. The contrasting black and light hair brought like a positive and negative energy that was supposedly like a vortex of sorts to trap spirits. He did say something about coins with the dates on them but I forget the purpose.
>
> BUT, in his stories all of these (or similar) items were brought together for a different purpose. They were intended to trap a spirit for the express purpose of becoming possessed. They would trap the spirit and then use a cup or chalice to "drink in" the spirit.
>
> I seriously apologize for all these sketchy details, but I never really paid that much attention. I mean I found it interesting but at the same time a lot of stuff he was saying was going in one ear and coming out

the other. He kind of rambled on a lot when he spoke, on top of that he spoke broken English.

    If I remember more I will definitely stay in touch with you. I know this box isn't for sale, but I REALLY wish I could buy it. . . .

Meanwhile, members of my museum staff started having concerns. Brian was the first to suggest that the artifact was harmful to those in its proximity. He was not pleased that it was stored less than twenty-five feet away from his workstation. At a Monday morning staff meeting, he mentioned that he'd had an unusually bad weekend. He had gone to the nearby city to meet up with some friends, but the weekend had quickly started to go bad. Little things that didn't matter had led to harsh words and a threat of a fist fight. Everything the group did—whether it was eating out or trying to get tickets for a show—seemed to take on a dark cast. In the end, all of them left angry. Once they were home, however, none of their troubles made sense to them. The rage had been contagious and seemed to have come out of nowhere. The biggest source of Brian's distress was that his father had suffered a serious fall, breaking five bones in his wrist and knocking him out of work indefinitely. What Brian clearly wanted, if only as a precaution, was to have the Dibbuk Box moved away from his work area.

Another staff person who shared office space with Brian was not present at the meeting to voice any concerns because she was away. Soon after the box had arrived, her sick grandmother had taken a sudden turn for the worse and had died, so my coworker had gone home to be with her family. I did not want to believe that the box could have been involved in any of this, but all at once my normally upbeat staff was in disarray, burdened with each others' problems and feeling drained of energy. I was concerned. All were well aware of the box's haunted past. I told them that, as a precaution, I would take the box away from the museum when the workday ended.

I did not care whether the phenomena were physical, mental, or spiritual. My intention was to take up Michael on his pledge to store the box at his home if it was giving me more trouble than I could handle. Well, it was! It seemed unlikely that Michael would be distressed by the kind of incidents that were truly starting to scare me. Tales of grim occurrences attributed to the Dibbuk Box had only energized him to find out more about it, so why not let him take charge of the box for a while? One thing was certain: some of the museum staff no longer welcomed this artifact at their workplace.

I tried phoning Michael at his home but got no answer. That evening, I set about wrapping up and repacking the Dibbuk Box, wondering whether I should move it into my own house until I could drop it off with Michael. I never figured that storing it with other museum artifacts would be a problem, but the box's history was too strong and I felt obligated to keep it at a distance from my employees. I called again, but there was no answer, so I left another message. In the end, I wrapped the box snugly with bubble wrap, put it into a shipping box, and locked it in the covered bed of my pickup, where it could remain secure until I was able to deliver it to my magician friend.

The next morning, I was up early and called Michael's home phone number again. No answer. My wife and daughter had left hours earlier to go shopping in another town. My son, Ross, and I were the only ones at home, and he wanted me to drop him off at a friend's house to work on a miniature working catapult for a class project. As he was filling his backpack with the materials needed for his project, I decided that I would drop him off first at the friend's house, then head for Michael's place to deliver the Dibbuk Box. I was growing frustrated that Michael had not returned my calls. I needed to leave the artifact with him until I could come up with a long-term storage solution, but still, no answer. My frustration was now turning to panic. Where the hell was he? He and his wife rarely went out for more than a few hours on any given day. I listened to the ringing on the other end of the line, waiting (ring), hoping (ring), on and on. My stomach, now just a dull pain that had never gotten any better, was aching. Several days had passed since I'd handled that infernal box. What had I been thinking when I decided to obtain this artifact and probe its inner power? Ring! Ring! Nobody there. Come on Michael, or Erin, pick up the phone! Nobody was home and I reluctantly gave up trying.

After putting down the phone I was suddenly struck by a sickly sweet smell, like jasmine, yes, jasmine flowers. The odor was potent—almost intoxicating in its strength. It seemed to surround me. I was familiar with musty damp smells from my home's basement, and the smell of Murphy's Oil Soap from scrubbing the 100-year old pine wood floors, but this was not an odor that I had ever picked up anywhere in our venerable Victorian home. Where had it come from? The house was pretty tightly sealed from the cold of winter, so it couldn't have entered from the outside.

I knew that previous owners of the Dibbuk Box had mentioned the same kind of aroma that had come and gone for no apparent reason. It certainly was not my wife's perfume, which was light and hardly noticeable. My nine-year-old daughter used no scent except for her bubble bath. This scent belonged to neither. Besides, they had both been gone for hours, and this was a recent, lingering smell. I walked around the room sniffing, trying to track the source of this strange heavy odor. It seemed to begin and end in the spot where I had stood when trying to call Michael. Just then, my son came into the room and wanted to know if I was ready to go. I asked him to walk over to me. His typical child response was to stay where he was and ask me what I wanted. "Just come over here for a second to where I am," I repeated. "You'll see." He strolled over, and at once I knew he had caught the mysterious odor. His expression was incredulous and a look of fear came into his eyes. But I certainly didn't expect him to come out with what he said next: "Dad? You've got the Dibbuk Box!"

Surprised by Ross's words, I asked him to sniff out where the smell was coming from. I stepped away from the area of the scent and asked him if this odor was somehow emanating from me. He sniffed over my shirt and arms, the front of me, my back, and said "No," it wasn't on me at all. Next, he walked around the room's perimeter, sniffing high and low. He left the room and came back in. Finally, he said, "Dad, it is only right here where the desk and phone are." I asked, "Just in that small patch of space and nowhere else?" Ross said, "This is freaky." I assured him everything was okay, it was nothing, just a smell, but he didn't seem convinced. Why that odd scent had caused him to accuse me of having the Dibbuk Box seemed like a fairly big leap. Sure, I had told them the story of the box and its scents, but that was eight months earlier. I told him that I did have the Dibbuk Box, but it was not inside our home. Changing the topic, I reminded him that it was time to get him to his friend's house to work on that class project. I was glad to have a reason to leave both the room and the house.

We went out into the fresh and pure February air, crisp from the cold and the snow. I opened the garage and told Ross to hop into our nice new pickup. It was only two months old and still had that new-car scent. As Ross climbed in, a concerned look came upon his face. I knew what he was going to say because I could smell it, too. The truck reeked of cat urine like a used litter box—inside my new truck! We did not own a cat and never had, but we had friends who did, so we recognized the stench. Ross exclaimed, "Dad this is bad. Get rid of that box." We had brought fresh air in with us, so the odor cleared a bit and the new-car smell returned, but knowing the Dibbuk Box was in the back of the truck left me uneasy and apprehensive. I thought it best not to let Ross know the box was traveling around with us. The trip to his friend's house would be brief, then the box was headed to Michael's house. I mumbled that maybe a cat snuck into our garage and used it as a litter box, and maybe we had picked up some soiled dirt on our shoes and brought it in the truck. That was a plausible explanation. Ross seemed to accept it, but I wasn't so sure. That smell was in the truck before we even entered into it.

I also had to acknowledge something else: that same odor had come to me the previous night in our newly added great room. At the time I'd convinced myself it was just my weary mind playing tricks on me, but this morning my son confirmed that these scents were real. I had to admit that I'd been trying to dodge the truth. And what about the awful metallic taste that came and went in my mouth? Perhaps the smells had somehow distorted my sense of taste.

I dropped off my son and then went straight over to Michael's house. Maybe something was wrong with their phone. When I arrived, there was no sign that he and his wife had been there that night or this morning. The house was dark and the car was gone; they had obviously gone somewhere and I was stuck with the Dibbuk Box.

It was not until the next day that Michael returned my call. He wanted to know if I was all right because he had gotten multiple messages on his answering machine. I said, "No! I am not all right." I told him I needed a break from the Dibbuk Box—and I wanted to be rid of it right then. Michael laughed as I told him about the odors, sickly sweet and foul. He said no problem, bring it over in a couple hours. He would put it in his basement, which already smelled because of his cat's litter box and even had a jasmine scent from a plug-in air freshener. Relieved that I would be free of the box, I apologized for being such a jerk about it and thanked him, saying I would be over in about two hours. I finished up a few household chores, thinking it would not be long until I was rid of the Dibbuk Box. I was about to leave to drop off the box and pick up my son when the phone rang. It was Michael. I told him I was just leaving and asked, "What's up?" He said I could not come over. I was incredulous. Michael continued, "Really, don't come over with the box today." I asked him why, and he said he had suddenly become very ill. He said that he would call when he was feeling better, but for now he was too ill. He apologized and hung up.

I stood there staring at the receiver. A few hours ago he had been laughing about my problems with the Dibbuk Box. Suddenly everything had changed—this spontaneous sickness was very strange. Several of the college students had become ill when they first encountered the box. Maybe the Dibbuk Box didn't want to leave my home just yet, and somehow it caused the sudden sickness in my friend. It was not a comforting thought, but the thought was there. The box would not leave me, or it would not let me leave it. First the unusual health problems, and now these strange signature scents had infiltrated my home. I felt unhappy and responsible for my predicament. Having the Dibbuk Box in the truck rather than in my house didn't seem to matter. I moved the box upstairs to a closet in an unused room. I wondered what would come next. It was time to see a second doctor to look for some much-needed answers.

The following day, I went to see an optometrist about my bloodshot eyes. They were not healing and my vision was becoming blurred. Maybe there was some physical reason. First I went to the local optometrist at the department store. I have never worn glasses, so the only time I have my eyes checked is when I renew my driver's license. The optometrist said he saw no problem other than a bloodshot condition, probably caused by spontaneous drying. I thanked him, but wondered if another opinion might be needed.

I made an appointment with another optometrist who also happened to be a friend because his son went to my kids' school. The eye doctor did a very thorough check. First, he checked for any physical damage, scratched areas, or other injury using a variety of high-powered magnifying lenses. He also looked for any signs of disease. After examining my eyes for half an hour, he made his diagnosis: I had a "spontaneous eye event." My eyes had developed dry spots that caused them to become bloodshot. He recommended prescription lubricating eye drops, noting that I would need to use them for a long time, possibly for the rest of my life. This was not the news I wanted to hear. He added that I shouldn't be surprised if my vision had gotten a little worse because of this condition.

I used the lubricating drops generously, and after a few days, the redness cleared completely, but not my vision. And the drops were not a permanent solution—if I missed a day, the redness would return immediately. Still, for the most part I'd begun looking normal again. But my relief was short-lived because new issues erupted around me. Within two weeks of taking possession of the Dibbuk Box, my home seemed to take on a distinct chill. Even as the outside temperature warmed up, the temperature inside the house dropped. Normally, setting the thermostat at seventy degrees was fine; now, even at seventy-eight degrees, we couldn't seem to keep warm. We started layering clothes and checking the thermostat regularly. The higher thermostat setting did no good—a cold presence had settled into our home.

Another odd development was my sense that something was touching my hair as I wrote in my journal each evening, but no one else was present. I decided to have my hair cut much shorter, thinking perhaps the length was making my hair heavy or causing a pull. Even with a cropped cut, the feeling of something brushing across my hair continued. It was unnerving. Equally so were the popping noises heard throughout the house. They seemed to come from within the walls and ceiling. We were all accustomed to the settling noises of an older house, especially when temperature changes caused expansion or contraction in the wood, but this was different. I knew it wasn't my imagination, because my kids were also disturbed by overly loud pops.

More and more often, I began catching glimpses of shadows and shifting reflections in the windows at night, but there was nothing in the room to make a shadow or a reflection. One evening, while working on my computer in a brightly lit room, I watched a shadow move across the floor. It seemed to expand and drift, gliding under my chair like a dark cloud. Then it passed and moved on through the wall. It made no sense because the room had a fixed central light, not free-standing lamps whose small movements might allow shadows to roam. Streaks of light, apparently without a source, were becoming a frequent sight at night. It was as if fireflies were streaking around the area where I sat, leaving three to four inch trails before vanishing. My son would sit and watch them. One evening he pointed out an uncharacteristically long tail of light that streaked along the wooden baseboard and out of sight. At first, the speed and suddenness made him think it was a mouse, but following its direction proved that it was indeed pure light. It seemed the more I paused to watch these light specters, the more I seemed to notice.

The experience of seeing these lights reminded me of the Magic Eye Inc. 3-D illusions popular in the 1990s. To the casual observer, these images seemed to be nothing more than random repeating designs of tiny intertwined images, colors, and patterns. However, if the observer stared at the tiny images and then slightly unfocused their eyes by looking through the image and focusing at a distance, an entirely, new 3-D image would suddenly loom forward at them. So, you see, it is possible to create an image that appears to be different from the objects that compose the image, like photomosaic images, or to create a cognitive illusion, such as an image that could be either of two things depending on the assumptions of the viewer. But there are also physiological illusions, like afterimages, that result from excessive stimulation of the eyes and brain by things like brightness, color, or movement. I began to wonder whether our assumptions about what we were seeing, and our brains' ability to interpret what our eyes perceived meant that we might be missing seeing things that were all around us because we don't know how to properly look for something right in front of our eyes. Maybe this has something to do with seeing shadows, flashes, and unexplainable light movement. I really don't know how else to explain what we were seeing, but it seemed real.

At that point, I was not sure if these seemingly paranormal phenomena in my home were caused by the Dibbuk Box, or if they had some other psychic origin. Over the hundred years of our home's history, it had been the site of four deaths, including that of a nineteen-year-old man who died

Magic Eye® 3-D Viewing Instructions: Hold the center of the top image right up to your nose. The image should be blurry. Very slowly move the book away from your face, try not to blink, and a 3-D hidden image will magically appear!

in the very room we were using as the computer room—the room where I had seen the drifting shadows. That room had been my son's bedroom years earlier, but he asked to be moved to another bedroom in the house because he could not seem to get restful sleep. This was one of the locations where the bizarre occurrences seemed most concentrated. Could the eerie events have been triggered not only by the Dibbuk Box, but also by the very house in which they took place? Maybe these things had been going on for years, but we hadn't stopped and watched long enough to see them. This newfound awareness of the possibility that other entities existed in my home was strange to me. Whatever the cause of these phenomena I was experiencing, I could not make them stop. I wanted to return to a time before these phenomena began, but I could not.

Chapter Five

Searching for the Truth

AFTER STEVE MAASS and I had exchanged e-mails for a while, we finally spoke by phone. In a lengthy conversation, we spoke about the Dibbuk Box and my recent unsettling experiences. I told Steve I would appreciate his help, and right away he sent by e-mail a variety of lengthy passages on Jewish spiritualism. The first item he sent suggested that I could slow, reduce, or maybe even completely stop the health problems and paranormal activities I had experienced since acquiring the Dibbuk Box by performing an appeasement ritual. By now, Michael should have been well enough to take over the care of the Dibbuk Box. I called him and he sounded fine, but when I let him know I wanted to drop off the box that afternoon, he asked me to hold on for a minute. After a lengthy pause, during which he talked to his wife while covering the receiver with his hand, Michael told me he was sorry, but he couldn't care for the box until at least next week. He explained that a close friend of Erin's would be visiting for the week, and she didn't want the Dibbuk Box at their home because it might bother her friend. Michael had promised he would take care of the box when I needed him to, but this was the third time he had not been available. First he was gone the entire weekend when I needed him to take over its care, and second when he agreed, then backed out after he suddenly became ill. Now due to his wife's guest, I was again thwarted in my efforts to drop off the box with him. So much for his promise to be there for me if I needed him. He felt that the situations that prevented him from watching the box were beyond his control, and maybe they were. But maybe the Dibbuk Box had some hand in the events. It seemed as if the box didn't want to leave me, or for me to leave it. If that was the case, I needed to take action on my own.

In the almost four weeks since I had bought the Dibbuk Box, my life had become driven by health problems and possible paranormal activities. I had to regain some semblance of control over my life. If I could not suspend these things completely, perhaps I could at least get a break. One of the passages Steve had found was from *The Key of Solomon the King*, a fourteenth- or fifteenth-century book of magic incorrectly attributed to King Solomon. The passage gave instructions on how to appease a spirit. I decided to try it, or something like it.

CONCERNING SACRIFICES TO THE SPIRITS, AND HOW THEY SHOULD BE MADE

In many operations it is necessary to make some sort of sacrifice unto the Demons, and in various ways. Sometimes white animals are sacrificed to the good Spirits and black to the evil. Such sacrifices consist of the blood and sometimes of the flesh.

Then perfume and sprinkle it according to the rules of Art.

When it is necessary, with all the proper Ceremonies, to make Sacrifices of fire, they should be made of wood which hath some quality referring especially unto the Spirits invoked; as juniper, or pine, unto the Spirits of Saturn; box, or oak, unto those of Jupiter; cornel, or cedar, unto those of Mars; laurel unto those of the Sun; myrtle unto those of Venus; hazel unto those of Mercury; and willow unto those of the Moon.

Then say: "May this Sacrifice which we find it proper to offer unto ye, noble and lofty Beings, be agreeable and pleasing unto your desires; be ye ready to obey us, and ye shall receive greater ones."

Performing a spirit appeasement ritual with a burned offering was completely alien to my Methodist upbringing and my training in counseling. This very idea completely challenged my notions of normal behavior, but at the time, nothing in my life seemed to be normal. Of course I would never harm an animal to placate a spirit, dark or light, but I had an idea of something that might work—I would use the items from inside the Dibbuk Box. Maybe using those items would get the attention of whatever spirit was involved and show it that I was growing tired of it, and I was getting bolder too.

For the sacrificial pieces, I settled on two long strands of the reddish-blonde hair and a few strands of the shorter black hair from the box's drawer. I hoped that any spirit, whether light or dark, would accept these as a sincere offering. I wrapped the pieces of hair and a scented pinewood twig with pine needles still attached (left over from a batch of holiday potpourri) in a piece of plain typing paper on which I wrote, "Better gifts shall come to you from me." I signed it and gave the paper a good dousing with my men's cologne (the requisite "perfume"), then I folded the paper into a tight small square around the hair and pine twig. I took my small sacrifice to the privacy of my detached garage and shut the door.

Striking a household match, I lit the edges and dropped the burning square to the earthen floor of the garage. It burned slowly, but completely. The whole time the flames leaped, I chanted "better gifts shall come, better gifts shall come from me." I had no idea what those "better gifts" would be, but I promised them anyway. As I watched, the glowing embers crackled and faded, and the rich, smoky pine scent rose up in warm wisps. In the chant, I made some kind of a long-term commitment with whatever might be causing me problems, and that commitment bothered me. It was a promise that, in my heart, I did not want to make, but at the time, I felt I had no choice but to try this ritual. I was ready to try almost anything to regain my health and stop the malicious attentions of whatever lurked inside the Dibbuk Box—if anything at all was there.

In the pitch black of my garage, I could smell the scent of the offering amid the moist and earthy smells of the garage. I thought about the unexplained cat-piss smell from a few days earlier, but that smell was gone. With the ritual complete and the offering consumed by fire, I buried what few ashes remained, along with the burnt matches, in the garage's gravel and dirt floor. I stepped out of the garage convinced that I had, in a sense, cleared the air, and could make a fresh start in dealing with this artifact. I told myself that the Dibbuk Box was just a jumble of harmless things, and the ritual had just been a precaution of sorts. I had certainly handled worse items at the museum, like human remains. This was nothing. Breathing in the cold night air, I felt that a weight had been lifted from me.

Feeling cleansed and hopeful, I strolled back to the house. The night sky was clear with sparkling stars—so much space out there, so much unknown. I felt like anything was possible. I was sure that if the ritual succeeded, I would notice immediate changes for the better in my daily life. And for the next week, all paranormal mischief did seem to quiet down. Who could say whether it was the ceremony that had brought me physical relief, but at least I felt better. And although I found it strange that I had resorted to this ancient ritual act of appeasement, at that time I had no idea what else I could do.

Now that I had a respite from my troubles, I could return to my original reason for buying the Dibbuk Box—to research its history and its meaning. I had received a lot of information about paranormal aspects of the box and paranormal phenomena in general from Steve and the other paranormal researchers who had contacted me since I had acquired the box, but I wanted to look at aspects of Jewish practice and folklore. When he first sold the Dibbuk Box on eBay, Kevin reported that the original owner was a Jewish woman from eastern Europe. It did not seem unusual that a Jewish household might have a wine cabinet to hold the wine, cup, and candlesticks used on Shabbat, but the idea of the box itself being a religious item was unusual. I talked to several rabbis and to a docent at a Jewish museum and it was an enigma to all of them. The box had been described in the original eBay auction as being a very secret and personal piece to the grandmother. I wondered whether the original owner might have been influenced by a Catholic tradition of home altars, or by Jewish folklore or superstition, or even by an interest in spiritualism or the paranormal to create some kind of a personal altar or devotional object. Thinking of other cultures and traditions, I wondered whether the stone statue had been used as a focus for personal prayer and even as some kind of buffer between the person praying and the power that is God. Such an item might not be typically used by those of the Jewish faith, but such an item is not unheard of either and is even common in some other cultures and religions.

One rabbi I communicated with, Hasidic Rabbi Golomb of Sheffield, England, suggested that the stone statue might have been used as a devotional object, perhaps being made with broken pieces of a headstone, although they seemed too thin to be from a headstone. Guided by Rabbi

Golomb, I theorized that it could have been some kind of a devotional object, but this theory was not so much based on scholarly research or a deep knowledge of the history of Jewish practices. Rather it was more of an opinion based on my broad knowledge of practices in various traditions and cultures, and the fact that the original owner of the box had apparently been involved in various nontraditional practices. Although personal altars and devotional objects are not common in Jewish homes, I did find a store called Devotional Furnishing that sold an item resembling an open box on a stand and identified it as a *mizbeach me'at* (miniature altar), stating that "This altar can be used to house a significant icon to help focus energy for prayer or meditation."

The types of items located within the wooden cabinet seemed reasonable for devotion and family keepsakes. Saving items like a lock of a child's hair is not just a Jewish tradition, nor is drying a flower from some special occasion, but candlesticks and a Kiddush cup for Shabbat are clearly Jewish items. Many Jewish homes display items like a shofar (ram's horn) and Hanukkah candlesticks, and decorative mezuzah holders (containers holding parchment on which the Shema is written) are placed on doorposts. Sculptures or wall hangings with a Jewish text or the word "shalom" are also popular decorative items. So it is not uncommon that a person might have a special decorative cabinet in which they store small items related to their spiritual life. But why the original owner put these particular items together in this cabinet and what the cabinet meant to her was a mystery.

Hoping to learn more about the artifact's background, I tried to locate Kevin Mannis, who had first sold the box on eBay after acquiring it at an estate auction. The eBay account described him as an Oregon antiques refinisher. Joseph had given me the telephone number he had called when he spoke to Kevin about the purchase, as well as an e-mail address. I called, but the phone number was no longer in service, and my e-mail messages were returned noting that the address was no longer valid. I wondered if Kevin had changed his phone number and e-mail as I did after having so many people contact me about the box. I would have to try some other way to find Kevin. All I knew was that he lived (or had lived) in or near Portland, and that he had a mother and some siblings in the area.

By happy coincidence (or maybe not), on the very day I had won the Dibbuk Box I was offered the chance to take a museum exhibit to a conference for physicians in Portland, Oregon. Under any conditions this would be a fantastic opportunity, but visiting Portland, where the box had originally been bought at an estate auction and where antique-shop owner Kevin lived, would provide an ideal opportunity to research the history and the secrets of the mysterious box. The event in Portland would take place in June. I was to give a historic overview of medical treatments for head trauma and display various museum artifacts to the conference attendees. The conference would run three days, leaving me a solid day and a half to dig up any information I could about the Dibbuk Box's creation and its previous owners. I had three months before the conference; I would use that time to make thorough preparations.

The first order of business was to locate Kevin and ask whether he would guide me to the sites described in the eBay listing: his antique shop, the Jewish cemetery where the old woman was interred, and her home where he had attended the estate auction and bought the Dibbuk Box. Following up on clues from his eBay ad, I found a listing in Portland for a woman with the last name of Mannis; perhaps she was a relative. I took a chance and called the number. There was no answer, so I left a message saying I needed to reach a Kevin Mannis concerning a business transaction. Within hours I received a call back. The woman was suspicious and demanded to know how I'd found her phone number, and what business transaction required reaching her brother. I explained that when the number I had for her brother didn't work, I checked the Internet White Pages website for the name Mannis and had found just a few listings for that particular name. I was hoping if I called them all, one might have a connection to Kevin. The woman was clearly distressed that a stranger could so easily find her phone number. I told her I was calling about "a small antique wooden box, like a wine box," that her brother had sold. She said she didn't appreciate having me call her and insisted that she knew nothing of a wooden box. I apologized, but said it was really important that I reach Kevin as soon as possible.

Her tone softened briefly as she acknowledged that her brother had collected antiques for some time—things he sold at his shop in downtown Portland, but heated up again as she made it quite clear that she and her brother's wife were not on speaking terms with Kevin, and they wanted no contact with him at all. She didn't even have a phone number for him. With that, she demanded I not bother her again and hung up.

I was confused. In his eBay listing, Kevin indicated that he, his sister, his brother, and his sister-in-law were all on friendly terms, often having dinner together and even spending nights at his home. This didn't square with his sister's remarks at all and I began to wonder if Kevin's version of the Dibbuk Box story was less than true. But then again, she had confirmed that Kevin Mannis did indeed own an antique shop in downtown Portland, and I had verified that at least one member of the family was a current resident of Portland. It was possible that Kevin and his siblings had become estranged after he sold the box. In light of my recent troubles, I felt it was important to verify all of Kevin's claims that he'd gotten the Dibbuk Box from the estate and family of a 103-year-old Holocaust survivor, plus the information about his shop, and the events concerning his family's experiences.

I now had several names of the Kevin Mannis family, but I decided to try something else to locate more of the family. Using an investigative website, I ran a search on the family name Mannis in Oregon. I learned that apparently only two families of that name lived in the entire state: one family was in Portland, and the other was near the coast. Looking over the names and ages, and the information on family relationships, I concluded that Kevin's father was named Richard and that he was deceased. The site indicated that Kevin lived with his mother. To learn more about the family, I decided to turn to a genealogy website. A friend on the museum staff had an account with a genealogy website loaded with family resources from immigration records, census addresses, birth and death records, family trees, and more. She agreed to do a search for me, and we found a comment posted by a Mannis relative, who explained that the surname Mannis was an unusual name based on the original Russian-Jewish surname Mnfesky. No wonder it was changed to Mannis. The surname seemed oddly close to the biblical word "manna," for the edible, nourishing mold provided by God to sustain the Hebrews during their desert wanderings.

The writer explained: "supposedly my grandfather actually made up the name, or changed it from Mnfesky. I am supposed to be related to every Mannis since there are so few. My father's name was Richard Mannis, and my grandfather and grandmother were Irving and Ethel Mannis." Actually, the surname Mannis is also from Scotland and is more common in the eastern United States, but the name seemed to be quite rare in Oregon. If the person who posted this comment was a relative of Kevin's, I now had the names of his grandparents as well.

Unfortunately, only the sister I had called had a listed phone number—and who knows, after my call maybe she too had her number unlisted. She had made it clear I was never to call her, and I respected her request for privacy. I checked the grandparents' names against immigration records and death certificates on that same genealogy website, and discovered that Ethel was a Russian-Jewish immigrant who had arrived on the East Coast in the early 1900s and she was already married with a listed occupation as a portrait artist in the 1929 census. She had died at the unusually advanced age of 102 or 103 (records listed two different dates of birth for her). It struck me as pretty odd that Kevin had identified the original owner of the Dibbuk Box as a Jewish woman who had lived to be 103. The similarity hardly seemed to be a coincidence. If the Dibbuk Box was an item from the woman's estate, what was its link, if any, to the writer of the genealogy note and his grandmother Ethel Mannis?

I now had several leads to follow once I got to Portland, but I had even more questions. Was Kevin related to Ethel Mannis? And was it Ethel Mannis who had originally owned the box and whose descendants sold it in an estate auction? Because Ethel had emigrated from Russia, she had probably adopted that name when she arrived in America and her original and/or Hebrew name could have been different. But if Ethel Mannis and Kevin were not related, why did he not mention the coincidence of them having the same last name? Or did he even know the name of the original owner? If he was a relative, why would he not want that to be known? In Kevin's eBay account, he claimed not to know Hebrew, but if he was descended from Ethel and Irving Mannis, might he not have picked up some Hebrew from his grandparents? Of course, if he did know a few Hebrew words, that wouldn't mean he could read the Hebrew alphabet. The Dibbuk Box story from the eBay listing appeared to be perhaps a mixture of truth and untruth, all entwined. But for what end? I decided I would sort it all out.

I started considering my options. The search would be difficult, given the distance between me and Portland. I needed to have someone in Portland to look through any documents that were accessible only in person. Knowing that college students are always looking to make a few extra bucks, I called the job-placement office at the University of Portland, and advertised for a short-term research assistant to search through back issues of the *Oregonian* newspaper for information on the Mannis family and the alleged estate sale. The pay was minimum wage and the hours were completely flexible.

Within a few days, I had an inquiry and hired Alyssa, a sharp student who would spend a few hours each day looking for two things: obituaries and estate auction announcements. She was to look through microfilm of the *Oregonian* from January 2001 through January 2002, dates selected based on Kevin's statement that he had bought the Dibbuk Box at a September 2001 estate auction held by the family of the original owner after her death. Just to be on the safe side, I had Alyssa search the entire year of 2001, and also search for obituaries of women who had lived to be over one hundred years old and for auctions held in the months before and after the date Kevin mentioned.

Several weeks later, Alyssa told me that she had checked all the newspapers and had found nothing resembling an obituary of a centenarian, or an estate auction or estate sale of a century-old Holocaust survivor. I was starting to doubt whether the Dibbuk Box had come from an estate auction at all, and beginning to suspect that the box had originated somewhere else, possibly within Kevin's own family. If this was so, what was the family story behind the piece?

I next asked Alyssa to check obituaries once again, this time for a Richard Mannis, who might be Kevin's father, along with his parents, Ethel and Irving. In just a few days, she had a solid piece of information. It seemed that Richard Mannis had died of a heart attack in 1990. The obituary listed his children among surviving family members, including his son Kevin, his mother, Ethel, and a family member living in Las Vegas, Nevada. If I could track down this other family member, she might shed further light on Kevin's grandmother, Ethel, his family's Jewish background, and the mystery of the Dibbuk Box. The obituary listed a Jewish cemetery and a rabbi officiating at the service, so it was clear that Richard Mannis was Jewish. An Internet search turned up the Mannis relative who had been living for some time with Ethel Mannis in Las Vegas.

I had learned several facts: (1) most likely there had never been an estate auction in Portland in 2001 or it would have been advertised in the local paper to draw bidders; (2) no Jewish woman of a hundred years or more was listed as having died in that time period in the Portland area; and (3) the Mannis family was Jewish.

The Dibbuk Box had put me in contact with an interesting array of professionals involved in spiritual investigations including teachers, scientists, religious leaders, members of pagan cults (which truly opened my eyes to a whole new belief system), and many curious people who wrote friendly notes with offers to help in any way possible—all I needed do was ask. However, I continued to suffer from a number of recurring and unexplained health issues, particularly vision problems, choking, hives, fevered ears, and a constant metallic taste in my mouth. I was excited as my trip to Portland drew closer because I hoped to find answers that would help remedy my problems. In the meantime, I e-mailed a relative of Ethel Mannis whose name had turned up during my Internet searches for Kevin.

In my e-mail message, I introduced myself, explained how I had found her address and what details I was looking for, and included a link to the Dibbuk Box website. When she responded, she said it was strange to receive the link to the Dibbuk Box when she was home alone in the midst of lighting a *yahrzeit* (memorial) candle and saying the Mourners' Kaddish (prayer for the dead) for family members and for all Jews who had died, particularly those who died in the Shoah (the Holocaust). She had darkened the room and had just lit the candle and begun her meditation as she gazed out at a full moon hanging low and bright in the night sky. Her peace was disturbed when she heard the computer jingle, alerting her to an incoming e-mail. She wasn't expecting to hear from friends or family that night, but she checked and found an e-mail from a stranger asking about Ethel Mannis, the very person who had been most on her mind as she prayed. It seemed to be some kind of sign from beyond. Was Ethel reaching out to her on this night? This relative believed it might be a good time to use the spiritual energy of that evening to try to remove

the bad luck that had come to Kevin and all others involved with the artifact, but she made it very clear that while she was interested in spirituality and even spiritualism, she would have nothing to do with anything
dark.

The relative interrupted her meditation to respond, commenting
with a touch of humor on the odd timing of my message and asking
whether I was aware that it was Yom HaShoah (Holocaust Remembrance Day) and that around the world Jews were lighting a candle and
saying the prayer for the dead. I wrote back saying no, I had no idea,
but I had felt compelled to write to her just then despite the late hour.
Over the next half hour, I sent off a quick volley of questions and she
answered. Did your grandmother practice *kishuf,* Jewish magic? Did she
own a small wooden cabinet with grapes on its doors? What did she do
with her life? Did Kevin spend time with her? How did she die? Where is
she buried? Do you have a photograph of her? She confirmed that Ethel
Mannis did own a lot of antiques and had for a time lived with Kevin in
Portland, Oregon. According to the family, Ethel was born with spiritual
powers and was superstitious. Ethel received premonitions that helped
her financially in life; she wore what she considered her lucky clothes,
and believed in the power of symbolic writing, which she could (and did)
create. She never discussed the old country where she was born, instead
telling people she was from Boston. She may have felt guilty for not being
as traditionally religious as other family members, although it is likely
that she had been more observant while living with Kevin, as her son
Richard would have expected. The relative said she believed that Ethel,
and for that matter anyone, can diffuse power out of any object con-
necting soul to nature. That is an aspect of mysticism. The relative also
wrote that without a doubt, Ethel had attempted to communicate with
spirits and was a true believer in spiritualism. According to the relative,
the spirits are always trying to communicate with us, and Ethel truly did
conduct séances with family members. She told me that, in her opinion,
the box is merely a box, and that Kevin had placed the items in it. She also
told me that although Ethel was interested in mysticism, she would not
have had anything haunted (such as a haunted box), but rather her possessions were blessed with positive energy.

In a later e-mail, she sent a photograph of Ethel, plus the information that Ethel and her husband, Irving, had made a small fortune as owners of a sundries store (a small department store selling all kinds of household items) in Las Vegas that had opened just when that city was starting to grow. When I opened the attached photograph, I saw a very familiar-looking, white-haired, petite old woman. It was the same old lady I had dreamed of over and over the night after the box arrived. In my dreams, the woman was standing at the center of a large store pointing to a glowing white box. Thinking back to my memory of the dream, I realized it had taken place in the type of store the relative had described. And when I told her about the old woman in my dreams and her resemblance to the photo of Ethel, the relative was surprised but took it all in stride. Perhaps Ethel had owned the mystical Dibbuk Box at one time, though the relative said she had never seen such an item in Ethel's apartment.

Was Ethel Mannis the creator of the Dibbuk Box? How many 103-year-old Jewish women could there be in the Portland area who practiced *kishuf*? Maybe it was Ethel Mannis who was reaching out to anyone close to the box. In the e-mail message with the photo, the relative also mentioned that in her last few years, Ethel had stopped dying her hair reddish blonde, its natural color for most of her life. I thought about the reddish-blonde lock of hair bound in white thread that was tucked inside the drawer of the Dibbuk Box, and the lock of black hair too. Okay, no more e-mail messages. I asked if I could call so we could speak personally. She sent her phone number and I immediately called. While we talked, I jotted down the information she gave me. Among other things, she was able to provide insights into this Jewish immigrant named Ethel—her daily activities, her dalliance with mysticism and magic, and what Ethel had taught her about these occult subjects.

The relative and Ethel had shared an apartment in Las Vegas for several years. Afterwards, Ethel had moved to Portland and lived with Kevin for a time, before moving into a nursing home. Kevin and his grandmother had been very close. Ethel had lived an exceptionally long life, and was active and able to care for herself to the end when the flu brought on congestive heart failure (there are those heart issues again). Ethel must have been quite an independent woman. When she and her husband sold their store after many years, Ethel had managed to clear a small fortune and had been able to live independently until the final years of her long life.

I was able to locate the nursing home where Ethel had spent her last six years and spoke to a nurse who had known her well. The nurse described Ethel as quite "spunky," with the ability to take care of herself, and said she was forceful, talkative, matter-of-fact, and direct. The nurse said that Ethel charmed everyone and is dearly remembered. The nurse did not recall her ever having a wooden box of any type. She died on September 24, 1999, of pneumonia and old age, and was laid to rest at the Home of Peace Jewish Cemetery in Sacramento, California.

I asked the relative if she had recently communicated with Kevin, and she said she had not. She described Kevin as smart, gifted, and talented, and probably a little spoiled. When I asked if she had his telephone number, she hedged. Perhaps, it might be better for me to obtain it from someone else in the family. She suggested Kevin's younger brother.

Chapter Six

Finding Kevin

On Wednesday, June 24, 2004, at six thirty in the morning, I boarded the plane for Portland, carrying a practically indestructible suitcase containing my medical exhibit. This trip would be my best chance to find and meet Kevin Mannis, whose eBay listing had triggered my quest to solve the mystery of the Dibbuk Box. The plane trip was uneventful, and when I arrived at the hotel where the medical conference would take place, I checked in and put my luggage in my room before setting up my display of the personal effects of the founder of osteopathic medicine next to the conference registration booth. While I worked, I thought about how I might try to get my own unlisted phone number or address if I were in my hometown. Then it hit me—the courthouse records in Hillsboro, the seat of the county including Beaverton, where Kevin now supposedly lived.

After the lunchtime rush ended and the next session had begun, I put away my materials, grabbed a sandwich, and headed to Hillsboro. Traffic was tied up coming from Hillsboro, but my drive to the town was a breeze. Staff members at the courthouse were helpful in checking public records for me, and within minutes a search of the county tax rolls yielded both an address and a recent telephone number for Kevin Mannis. The information I had searched months to locate was there for the price of a single photocopy. I noticed that the phone number on the courthouse copy was different from the one Joseph had provided me, which was no longer in service.

As I drove back to the hotel, I was surprised to find that the earlier traffic jam had evaporated, so thanks to this bit of luck, my absence had been brief and the attendees were still in the lecture room. I hoped my luck would hold when I called Kevin later. That evening, I tried to collect my thoughts for this important phone call. I took a deep breath and dialed, my pulse quickening with each ring.

The phone was picked up and an elderly woman said, "Hello, who is this? What do you need?" Her speech was hesitant and slow. I replied, "Oh, sorry to bother you. I just need to talk to Kevin." The elderly voice returned, "Hmmm . . . just a minute." There was a long pause. When she returned to the phone, I was surprised to hear her say that no Kevin lived there. Then she added, "How did you get this number?" I thought fast and replied, "Look, I have an opportunity for Kevin to get paid to write the rest of a story that he started about a wooden box he sold on eBay." I said I had $150 for him if he would just call me at the hotel and speak with me for a few minutes. "But he must call tonight because I'm only in town for one more day." The woman said she would see what she could do, but added that no Kevin lived there. Knowing this was his phone number, I asked if she would take a message just in case he showed. It took her awhile to find paper, and as I spoke she repeated each part of my message several times. I gave her my name, the name of my hotel, my phone number, and my room number. The woman sounded tired, or maybe angry at being disturbed, but somehow I knew Kevin would call. Later I learned she was Kevin's mother, who Kevin had written about having suffered a stroke and having lost her ability to speak after touching her son's gift, the Dibbuk Box.

Sure enough, Kevin called close to midnight. When my phone rang, I knew it was him. When I answered, he gave his name and then said nothing more. The ball was in my court. I asked pleasantly if he'd gotten my message. Kevin replied, "Message? No not really." He said that when he'd returned home a short while ago, his mother told him he'd had a call from a man named "James" about "a wooden something." She said the caller wanted to write something and pay him for it. She didn't have a phone number or any other information. Kevin said he checked caller ID, which gave the number of a Portland hotel, so he called it, mostly out of curiosity. When the desk clerk answered, Kevin made a guess and asked to be connected to Jason Haxton. He had known for months that I'd been trying to track him down. First he'd heard my name from his sister, then he saw it on a registered letter I had sent to his mother at their shared address saying I would be in Portland soon and wished to speak with him.

Kevin asked me what my problem was and what I wanted. I answered that I was sorry, but I had been driven to find him because of that infernal Dibbuk Box he had sold on eBay a year ago. "You see," I said, "I now have it." He paused for a moment, then said, "You now have it?" I replied, "Yes, and it is acting up." Kevin said he knew it—the box had come back into his life and it would continue to haunt him. Then he asked, "Can I trust you?" I assured him he could. He said he was thirty-nine years old, and for most of those years he'd been in the public eye for various positive achievements; he mentioned his theater work, told me he was a gold-medal skater, and claimed he had written the musical score for NASA's *World View* CD. He said his father had been a prominent lawyer and his uncle had been a sheriff. Kevin blamed the Dibbuk Box for all his problems during the last two years. "After it came into his life," he said, "I lost all my businesses, my health, my friends, and I still suffer." He told me his story was all true and began retelling the events I already knew from his eBay postings: his dreams of being beaten and the events at his small antique shop in the Wax Building on West Burnside Street. At that point, he said, his life had been destroyed; maybe I could help him pick it back up. Maybe we could trust each other. If there was any good to the Dibbuk Box, perhaps he and I might be able to find it together.

He explained that before the Dibbuk Box came into his life, he would go to auctions daily to buy art pieces, furniture, antiques, and decorative kitsch. He said that the box, forgotten, unwanted, could have been left anywhere a thousand times, but somehow it had survived to come to him. I wished he would show me everything: his former shop, the place where the auction was held, and anything that might shed light on the family to whom the box first belonged. He gave me his cell phone number so I could reach him immediately, and suggested we meet the following day. Before hanging up, he commented that it was strange; if anyone had asked him six hours ago if he would be talking to me, he would have answered, "No way, never!" Everything was so different now. We were working as a team to solve a paranormal mystery.

As I hung up, I was still feeling amazed. In one call, I had gone from having no contact with Kevin to complete access. My work with the exhibit was done, so I'd have a full day to ask questions, explore sites associated with the Dibbuk Box, and take photographs of everything. I packed my clothes and stowed the exhibit materials I'd brought to Portland. Nothing but the Dibbuk Box all day tomorrow! I could hardly sleep thinking of everything that had occurred. I would share them all with Kevin and hopefully he would be able to give me some answers.

I called Kevin first thing in the morning. He had a few errands to run and suggested we meet at around three in the afternoon at the Beaverton Starbucks. Having Kevin's address, I knew that the Starbucks was only a few blocks from Kevin's apartment. He said we could talk for a while, then if I wanted, I could drive and he would direct me to his old shop and other locations mentioned in his eBay listing.

The next evening, I recorded the events of the day in my journal. My first impression of him was surprising; he was a towering man, big and solid, not someone you'd want to mess with. But he seemed a gentle giant—gregarious, intelligent, friendly, and easy to laugh with. He said he had not really been trying to avoid me, it was just that family members and others had never followed through on getting us together. Other people I had been in contact with had mentioned my interest in meeting him, advised him to be cautious, and left it at that. As we drank our giant coffees (we refilled twice before we were done), I caught him up on everything that had happened since he had sold the Dibbuk Box to Joseph. As he had said in his eBay listing, Kevin had never contacted Joseph again or checked on what had happened with the Dibbuk Box once he was free from it. Once it was mailed, he wanted to forget the two years of hell it had caused him and his family, but, he said, he had never become truly free of its curse. I told him about the 141,000 eBay visits to view the haunted object, the *Los Angeles Times* story by Leslie Gornstein, Joseph's bad fortunes with the box, and my troubles. Kevin was dumbfounded. We took a break so he could go home and visit the website I had created and read some of the material that I told him could be found on the Internet. In two hours we would reconvene at the same Starbucks, then drive to his former shop and other key sites, and finally finish the day with a nice dinner. Looking back to my meeting in Portland, I felt that Kevin was trying to make sense of the Dibbuk Box enigma too, and that he wanted to inform others about our discussions.

The following are entries from Kevin's AOL Public Journal of November 25, 2004, five months after our first meeting. He had already recounted his experiences after he shipped the Dibbuk Box to Joseph.

There seemed to be a noticeable change in the atmosphere around my home. I have never been one who was even the slightest bit prone to having any kind of a feel for something like I am trying to describe now. The emotional atmosphere of my living environment became palpably less tense. It is just a matter of fact.

I started thinking about all the things that had started working again, happening again, since I finally had gotten rid of it. Had I somehow become a modern scapegoat by bringing this item into my life? Back in biblical times, when things seemed worse than normal, the whole town would gather together and a goat would be brought forth. Each person was offered the opportunity to lay a hand on the goat and transfer from himself to the goat any sin, bad deed, perceived wrong, or whatever else was bothering the person or community. Once all the bad and evil was placed upon the goat, it would be sent off into the desert taking all the "evil whatever" with it. Perhaps this item was nothing more than a psychological version of the scapegoat—only to touch it was to transfer the bad and evil into whoever handled it. It was a scapegoat or scape-box that behaved in the reverse. The power of negative thinking with this item seemed to run rampant throughout the Internet cosmos. There was something about that box that was real. I had really experienced it. My family had really experienced it.

At the very end of my auction listing for the Dibbuk Box on eBay, I had written that after the sale I didn't want to have anything more to do with the box. All things being equal, I would have had to stand by that statement. But things weren't all equal now. Things were pretty insane. The current owner—Jason, the curator—had gone to a great deal of expense and effort to make contact with me. And, it wasn't like I was going to be taking the box back, or giving a refund on it . . . G-d forbid! All Jason was asking, and a couple of hundred thousand others, was for me to try and find the people I had purchased the box from, then see if they would kindly explain the nature of the diabolical enigmatic entity they somehow managed to [pass as] a cheap yard sale find.

That was all he asked. I could do that and still maintain a safe distance from the possessed item. Roughly seven months had passed since selling the Dibbuk Box when I started getting strange phone calls. Calls were coming in with odd static that completely prevented me from hearing the callers. I also started receiving mail from a trickle of people who said they had watched the eBay auction for my wine cabinet and only wanted to get some sort of update as to how I was getting along. Some said that they wanted to make sure I was still alive. That was a little odd.

One day when the mail came, there was a registered letter that required my signature to receive it. This document came from a man who began by writing that he was not a "wacko." He described himself as an academician who worked as a [museum] curator. . . . He said that he was trying to find me to make sure that I was all right and not in any danger. He went on to explain that he was contacting me on behalf of the museum he worked for to inform me that the museum had purchased the box from the young man who had purchased it from me on eBay. He thought it would please me to know the box was being kept under lock and key and under the 24-hour supervision of museum staff. It was his intent at this point to search me out and offer a sizeable amount of money for my agreement to be interviewed about the box and its origin. I was exasperated at this point (I tossed the letter into a pile of unanswered correspondence next to the phone). I was set upon ignoring the obvious "wacko" who had sent it.

I did not try to hide my attitude when the guy called me two weeks later. I acted noticeably put out [and] with a great deal of contempt upon finding that he had flown here to Portland, Oregon, and was calling me. I was actually in a state of disbelief when I demanded what in the hell he thought he was doing, and why in the hell he was attempting to do it to me.

It caught me by surprise when he immediately shot back without missing a beat that he was trying to solve one of the biggest mysteries he had ever heard of. We both held our tongues in shock for what seemed like a day until the curator broke the silence with a simple question. He asked me if I had seen any of the information about the box [and whether] I was on the Internet? I quietly told him that I had not. He then told me he understood why I had been responding to him the way that I had. He told me to go to the eBay site where I had originally sold the box and, once there, to look at the visitor counter at the bottom of the page. Afterward, he asked that I go to the Google search engine and type in the words "Dibbuk Box" and watch what came up. He said he would call back in one hour.

I went to the eBay auction site and did what he requested. My jaw must have hit the keyboard of my computer when I first saw the computer tally of people who had read the listing. I blinked like they do in movies to make sure I was really seeing what I was really seeing. The counter tally was at 141,651. In other words, 141,651 individuals had gone to that site for the first time. I knew from the count that I had taken at the end of my auction that they would have had to have done so after my auction ended. I didn't have a clue as to what was going on. I saved the page and went on Google. I typed in the words "Dibbuk Box" as the curator had instructed. I blinked. I got up and walked around. I got a glass of water. I returned, closed my eyes, then I slowly opened them.

What I saw was astounding. Hundreds upon hundreds of websites had come up. Professional sports teams, automobile owners associations, political party propaganda news sites, and every sort of site of the wildest variety of interests had articles, discussions, reprints of my eBay listing for the Dibbuk Box, and chats devoted to this object like there was no tomorrow. I sat there stunned with amazement trying to make sense of it all. A half hour must have gone by in the interim period and the phone rang. I didn't even say hello. I cautiously asked the curator what was going on? The curator was a bit amused by the whole thing and said he had empathy for the state of shock I must be experiencing. Then he started to explain.

He told me that it was unclear at this point whether the college student who had originally purchased the Dibbuk Box from me really did so for the utility of the wine box himself. As the curator continued, he described a series of mishaps that my eBay buyer had suffered, which began precisely on the day he had taken delivery of the box. Many with him suffered too—no good deed goes unpunished. The curator told me that many of the people involved in getting rid of the Dibbuk Box had come to suffer a strange malady that affected their eyes. The symptoms involved extreme drying and swelling of their eyes and other physical ailments. Many of them consulted physicians, but were told there was really no medical explanation for their sufferings in terms of viral infections, irritants, etc.

> I asked the curator how they got rid of the box? He said that the friends and family of my dazed buyer had reposted my original accounts, added a brief narrative that described what had happened to him and his roommates, and resold the Dibbuk Box on eBay.

That was how Kevin perceived our meeting in Portland, and for the most part it was the same as I recalled it, although he got a couple of details mixed up, including his impression that it was the museum and not me personally that had bought the box and was taking care of it. The evening after our meeting, I wrote about our talk in my journal. Sitting at the coffee shop, I had brought Kevin up to speed on Joseph's and my own experiences over the past year living with the Dibbuk Box. Now I asked if he would fill me in on his life with the box. Much of what he said repeated material from his original eBay listing. However, he gave me a fuller account of the key incident that occurred when he gave the box to his mother, and he told of several other strange occurrences during the time he still had the Dibbuk Box in his shop. Some of these stories he had not discussed on the original eBay listing, believing they would add unnecessary length to the story, but I was able to get the information in more detail later.

As luck would have it, a few months later some colleagues who did multimedia work for the university had some work to do in Portland, Oregon. They said that if Kevin would come by their hotel in downtown Portland, they could do a video-recorded interview for me. Kevin agreed, so I sent him contact information for my colleagues—the date, time, and address—along with a few questions for the interview. Following are the stories that Kevin shared with me at the coffee shop and during that interview, transcribed verbatim from the videotape with some bracketed clarifications based on our conversations.

> My mom was actually the first person I gave it to, and my idea [after buying it at the estate auction] had been [to clean it up a little bit]. I was actually going to strip and refinish it completely. However, I looked it over and decided it was in pretty good shape. Sure, it had a couple of blemishes, but they're the kind that added character to it. So I just put some lemon oil on it and gave it to [my mother] pretty much as I had received it. My mom's birthday is on October 28, and we were not able

to get together that year on the 28th. We postponed seeing each other until a couple of days later, the 31st, which was Halloween.

Mom had come down to my shop that day and spent the morning with me just talking. I remember we were having just good quality time together. I was just getting ready to open up the shop [when] she suggested that maybe she could go upstairs and open up the shop for me. When I [agreed], we were down in the basement where my workshop was located. It was a great idea. So she went up, and I went up also, and that is when I gave her the wooden wine box . . . I said, "Happy birthday, mom." I then left her there and went downstairs to make a few phone calls before taking my mom out for a meal.

I had three other people that were working for me at the time. They were all downstairs with me except one young male worker who was up with my mom. Shortly after I'd given her the box and she was upstairs [opening up and preparing for customers] I was surprised when [my worker] came running down the steps and told me, "You've got to come and talk to your mother. There's something wrong." Confused, I said okay. I hurried upstairs and immediately realized there was something very wrong.

Mom was sitting in a wing-backed chair that was for sale in the shop. I said, "Mom, is everything all right?" She didn't respond to me. I could tell that she could hear me, but she was not able [to speak to me]. Then she just started crying. And when I say crying, tears just welled up and started rolling down her face. [She had] no expression. No movement. Again, I asked, "Mom, is everything OK?" The first thing [I thought] was that she was having a stroke. And I was correct about that. So I grabbed the phone and called 911 to have an ambulance come.

At that point, two customers—a couple—came in the door of the shop. I told my shop foreman to explain to them that we were having a medical emergency and that they would have to excuse us and please come back at another time. . . .

I was on the phone with the ambulance and I heard him tell them this, and they said, "No, we're not coming back at another time." At that point, the man reached into the breast pocket of his coat, the woman reached into her purse, and [they] produced FBI badges and guns, which they proceeded to level at us. Shocked, what could I say? I was on the phone with the ambulance at the time. I just kind of watched in amazement as they put my two employees into handcuffs [and in came] literally 50 or 60 different FBI agents, Secret Service agents, immigration and naturalization agents, DEA enforcement agents, ATF agents, Portland policemen, county sheriffs, and probably a few I'm leaving out. Not because I want to; I just can't remember all of them. But they were all there and they came streaming through the front door of my little shop. While all the time, my mother sat like a crying statue in the chair.

This place was maybe 15 to 20 feet wide by about 30 feet deep. . . . They came pouring through the door and right down into the basement, all of them with guns drawn, all of them with very serious attitude. It was very clear that this was not anything to poo-poo, so to speak.

They were kind enough to allow me to keep telling 911 what was wrong with my mom [and to ask them to send an ambulance]. They were also kind enough to allow me to go downstairs after the ambulance did arrive and to get medications that my mother had with her at the time. They said they were going to search the premises and take anything that had an electronic memory chip in it. And I said, "Why?" I didn't get an answer. I never did get an answer. What I did get, almost a year to the day later, was a soft apology from them. No explanation as to why anything was taken or confiscated. I got everything back that they had taken, and there were volumes of things.

Essentially that event put me out of business. They took cash registers, a laptop computer, a regular computer . . . my desktop, calculators, cameras, anything that had an electronic chip in it. They took all the discs that I used to compose music on, all disks with my records. My landlord contacted me a few weeks later and told me, "I heard about the police being here—I don't know what you are up to, but here is your notice. Your lease is ended—pack up and move out." Huh? I had always been on good terms, paid my rent on time and actually had discussed with him the possibility of expansion into the adjoining space. What had happened?

During the next year, I guess the police went through each one of those discs and each memory chip bit by bit, looking for something that, again, I have no idea what it is. But they've all been returned to me, along with an apology for any inconvenience. A real mystery and shitty timing. Anyway, at that point I was more concerned about my mom.

The odd thing, too, was they didn't arrest anybody, they didn't charge anybody with anything. Obviously there was nothing to be charged with, but they did come in and make this search and seizure, and I guess they didn't want me to be in the way because they suggested that I go and check on my mom at the hospital after the ambulance left. Befuddled by both events, I went to the hospital. Mom was my first concern.

[At the hospital] I went to my mom's room in the . . . intensive care unit where she was being kept. She had a pad of paper and a pencil [and] was able to write. [She had written:] "NO GIFT!" In all the excitement and in view of her obvious health problem I thought somehow she [had forgotten] about the present, and I gently said, "Mom, I gave you the nice wooden box." To which she furiously scribbled a new note. "HATE GIFT!"

This was bizarre to me. Out of all the things in the world, [and with] everything that was going on—the raid, all of these government agencies, [her stroke]—the only thing, the paramount thing on her mind, was to tell me that she hated her birthday gift. At which point, I said, "Forget the gift. I'll get you something else, don't worry about it." It was really kind of overwhelming. Anyway, she said she hated the gift and that was that. We're not going to push the subject. She doesn't really talk too much about it now [and] I don't really know anything else about it.

Kevin told me of another incident he recalled when he put the Dibbuk Box up for sale after his mom had refused it.

It occurred at the shop [where] I had a guy working for me . . . who went by the nickname of Shorty. Well, my staff, Shorty, was downstairs in the workshop, and I was upstairs.

Along comes a punky looking kid, kind of a street bruiser. He walked into the shop and wanted to know if Shorty was around. And I said, in a joking manner, "No he's not 'a round,' he's 'a skinny,' and I'm the one who is 'a round.'" The guy didn't really like that and called me an A.S.S. I replied [that] I was a smart ass. He looked around, and not seeing Shorty upstairs [he] proceeded to go down the stairs. I said, "No, you can't go down there," and at that point my foreman was coming up the stairs and backed [the intruder] back up into the main floor. This made this punk real upset.

I didn't care who he was. Bottom line was, he was not going down into my restricted area. And I said, "I'll go get Shorty, but you can't go down there, okay?" He started swearing, and I said, "Okay, look, you're going to have to leave the shop NOW." And the foreman and I started to eject him. Not forcibly but gently, moving toward him and continuing, "You have to leave." That didn't go over too well with this guy. He grabbed an antique straight-edged razor that happened to be set in a display area on the showroom floor. He then lunged at me, and he did a pretty sloppy job of it.

I backed out of the way, and he crashed forward—and ended up hitting the counter on which the Dibbuk Box was sitting. When he hit, he knocked the box off the counter and it fell to [the] floor, doors sprawled open.

At that point the foreman and I physically grabbed Shorty's punk brother under the arms and escorted him out the door. When we got him out the door, he started goose-stepping and giving the Nazi Sieg Heil [salute] and referring to me in some pretty derogatory manner the whole time. It was a pretty odd spectacle. I looked up from his strange behavior to see a police cruiser was coming down the street. The police cruiser pulled up on the sidewalk. [The officer] and his partner didn't say anything. Didn't ask me anything. They just arrested [the intruder], put him in the car, and drove off.

[I] came to find out that the punk was Shorty's brother. Hearing all the commotion upstairs, Shorty came up and said. "I'm really sorry about that. I should have told you my brother just got out of prison. And he doesn't mean anything by his actions. He's actually pretty harmless, but he's kind of a ruffian and you must have rubbed him the wrong way.". . .

They let Shorty's brother out of jail that night after they'd taken him down there and rebooked him [or] whatever they did with him at the station. However, the brother died the following morning, about two blocks from my shop. He had his belt wrapped around his neck and a hooded sweatshirt that was pulled up over the head, and they labeled it as suicide. There in the middle of the street. It was very, very bizarre. To my knowledge that was the first time that anything had ever happened that was actually hostile towards the box, and perhaps the first possible victim I guess—in short order [now I suspect that the Dib-buk Box actually took vengeance on the person that toppled it to the floor—it may have felt threatened]. At the time I didn't associate [the incident with the box].

Not long after Shorty's brother's death a police officer came into the shop. [I was] not sure why he had appeared. He had been involved in the arrest and the hauling off of Shorty's brother and wanted to check in to see that everything was all right. He said he didn't know there was such a shop and wanted to look around. It was nice to have a new customer, regardless of the situation that brought him to me. He took a perfunctory glance about the store and watching him I saw his eyes land on the box across the room on the same counter that it had been knocked from earlier.

He briskly strode up to it [and reached out] to touch it. Then he stopped [and his hand recoiled]. He slowly backed away. His [earlier cheerful face] looked white and concerned. He immediately left the shop without saying another word. It had looked like a guaranteed sale. I am used to watching customers [become] smitten—something strikes their fancy or revives some distant memory and they must have the item. He had that look, too, until he almost touched the box. Maybe his training caused him to be alert to [subtle signals]. He left so quickly, and because he never returned, I never found out what caused him to change [his mind] so quickly.

My friends then recorded Kevin's response to this question: "Beside the odors and broken lights, did anything else ever happen in your down-stairs workshop? You said there is only one way down and the only natural light comes in through tiny, barred, street-level windows." Kevin said,

Well, I learned of an incident that took place while I had been away at the beach for a couple of days. My family has owned for years a beach cottage several hours south of Portland. When I returned and was opening the gate to my shop, I was [approached] on the sidewalk by one of the locals, one of the transients that are there on the street every day. . . . He came up to me and said, real accusingly, "You're going to end up killing somebody down there," pointing to one of the small windows. And I said, "What are you talking about?"

[The drifter] said, "Listen, I know what you do down there. I saw it. We all know what you do down there." Again, I asked, "What are you talking about?" He actually brought me over and pointed down. He said, "You see that? You can see right through there. You should watch what you're doing and not let other people see if you're going to be involved**."** I said, "Involved in what?" And what he described to me was eight or ten guys in dark black coats and black hats, in the basement, dancing around, having some sort of a party. He actually described dancing in a circle—around and around, faster and faster. Which . . . is impossible because I was the only one who had access to my shop. I was the only one who had a key, and I hadn't been there for three days. Nobody else had had access. This guy was real adamant about the fact that he had seen what he had seen. And I was real adamant about the fact that what he was saying was impossible. I certainly wanted to know if somebody had broken into the shop, so I listened."

He just kept saying, "You just got to be careful what you're doing down there because somebody's going to get killed." And that was it.

We were then joined by yet another gentleman, and, oddly, he confirmed [the story of] what they had seen the previous morning at about 4 o'clock in the morning. They got real upset with all the noise and commotion, and walked up the street, and that was that. This is, of course, at a time when the box was being kept in the basement.

Aside from that event, here is something less visible but that affected me more psychologically. The reason I picked this shop for my business is because it had a very pleasant feeling about it. It's an old building. Very, very pleasant feeling, and customers, friends and family would make comments about the fact that when they walked in [they noticed] a very warm atmosphere. The windows were floor to ceiling, and it was very bright. . . .

That changed after the box was purchased. At the time, I didn't relate [the atmospheric change] to the box. But after it arrived, people had a claustrophobic feeling. People felt . . . an oppressive feeling. And [it was not just happenstance that] they would actually go out of their way to tell me this. Or to tell one of the people that worked for me, "You know, there's just a real bad feeling about the place." That was about the time that I [as well as my sales manager, my employees and friends] started seeing, out of [our] peripheral vision, dark kinds of shadow figures that had a definite movement to them. How do I put this? Things that move like they're human, things that move like a person moves, but [they're] a shadow.

These are things I didn't really talk too much about until the night that I decided, I'm coming out with everything that I've experienced and I'm putting it on eBay. I am telling it all....

I had made the connection. Whether . . . it's a correct assumption or not, my [sense was that] there was something to this box. And [I've] got to admit, rationally thinking about it now, and with the luxury of time and distance, [that this idea] may have been the wrong thing to think at the time. But to me, there was something that was coming from the box. And I didn't want to give that something to somebody else. When you give something to somebody, it's usually somebody [you know and like]. And [I've] got to tell you . . . , I wouldn't want to give this to anybody that I really liked, [I have only told you some of the problems that I have had—a lot more occurred that is very personal]. But [it has been so bad] I wouldn't want to give any of that to anybody I didn't like, either. So giving [the box] away was not really an option.

What I wanted to do was . . . to get some help [with this thing]. And, I wanted to put [the box out to the public] where maybe there was somebody who knew what it was or knew how to deal with it, and would want to. Not only that, but [somebody who wanted the box] enough that [he or she was] willing to commit to it. You know, I put it up for .99 cents. I could have put it up for anything. I could have had a big reserve price. I could have really talked it up, I guess, which was not really my intent.

All I wanted to do was to say, "This is what's happened. I have no idea why or if I'm even right. But if there's somebody out there who can help me, if there's somebody out there who knows a little more than I, please step in and do what you can." And that's basically why I put [the story] on eBay. And decided to sell [the Dibbuk Box]. Money was obviously not the motivating factor. I put it on there for less than a buck. And it didn't make a lot of money. And that's fine with me also, because it would have been tainted money as far as I'm concerned....

So I don't know if there's anything to [the story] or not. I was telling people, "You know [this is] my take on it, but I want you to be well aware of what it is I'm sending to you." [The buyer would have] read the story, and [thought] who knows? Maybe there's something [spiritual to this box], maybe not. [Regardless] I'm buying a wine cabinet.

This ends the transcribed interview account, which matched what he had already told me over several cups of coffee.

Hearing Kevin's account, I could empathize. Some of the same things were happening at my home: the unaccountable coldness, the shadows that moved like humans and would slip behind me, or under my chair, or to other places where no light was shining to create real shadows. Kevin also described shimmering, metallic, almost orb-like figures that accompanied the shadows. I could relate to these phenomena too. Both the shadows and the metallic entities continued to play around my house in the evening hours.

After he had related his story to me, Kevin was ready to show me the physical sites. I drove and he directed me. Our first stop was his former antiques and used-furniture shop on Burnside Street. Kevin noted that the area was more cleaned-up now than when he'd worked there. Addicts and drunks drinking from brown paper bags had been the norm then. Today the neighborhood had trendy little shops that reminded me of the small businesses in a college town. Through windows I could see that his former shop at 221 West Burnside was empty. It had been absorbed into a chiropractic college and clinic that stretched from the former shop to additional space around the corner, taking up at least half the block.

I stared in wonder at the lockable iron-gated fence that stuck out from the front door. I could see how someone might easily get locked into the building if a passerby wanted to play a joke and seal him inside. I could also look into the basement from two small windows with vertical iron bars testifying to the area's former roughness. Kevin told me that an iron rod jutting from the shop had once held the sign for Addy's Market. Before he rented the space, it had been an elderly couple's mom-and-pop grocery store, selling booze, cigarettes, candy, and other small items needed by neighborhood residents. Like many small businesses, Addy's Market had closed.

Kevin said it was mainly the police raid that had led to the loss and disarray of all his business records and music material. Because of the vast number of police, it appeared that something was very wrong with both Kevin and his little shop. Not wanting any problems with the law, the landlord then asked Kevin to pack up and move out immediately. Kevin looked at me wide-eyed and said, "I honestly don't know why the police came and in such great numbers from so many agencies. I was never told what it was about."

To his face, I told Kevin, "Wow, that is so strange." However, in the back of my mind I was thinking there was no way in hell that the number of police he described would descend upon his little business and he have no clue as to why they were there. Kevin must be hiding a significant piece of this story, and the intrusion by police had something to do with this mystery. What he described just doesn't happen in America, in downtown Portland, Oregon—not the America I know. I would get to the bottom of this police story yet (if it even happened), once I was back home and could access the Internet.

It was obvious, as we looked into the former shop, that nobody else had moved in. All the other adjoining spaces had nice little businesses. Kevin's former shop appeared to be used for basement storage for the adjoining Chiropractic School and Clinic.

Kevin said he had liked the name "Addy's Market," and as the sign was already up, he decided to keep the name for his antique and furniture store. That choice for a name, though it sounded cute, in the end might have played a role in the police bust and loss of his business.

Satisfied that the shop was exactly as Kevin had described it in his eBay listing, I took a few photographs. I then asked about the location of the original auction where he had purchased the box. Kevin indicated it was in an older housing development a short distance from his former business.

We hopped into my rental car and headed down streets leading south. Then we drove back to the north. By this time it was late afternoon. En route, we stopped to see the most amazing Jewish cemetery, with a huge stone entrance, massive open gates, and old, closely grown trees. The canopies of leaves darkened this place of the dead. The heavy gravestones were marked with Hebrew text. This cemetery not ten blocks from Kevin's shop was frightening, even in the midday sun that brightened the surroundings but seemed to have no effect within the graveyard. I had no desire to go in—I could view all I wished to see from the outside in the parked rental car. But I did wonder whether or not the 103-year-old original owner might just be buried somewhere in there. I had learned that Kevin's grandmother was buried in Sacramento, but I wasn't sure about the box's creator. Maybe the age of the original owner and Ethel was nothing more than a strange coincidence. So indeed the original owner could be buried in this cemetery. Then we passed two more cemeteries only a few blocks from the first. None seemed warm and inviting. And for each of them there seemed to be a nearby synagogue, massive and exotically designed, with words in Hebrew carved on vertical columns top to bottom.

About half a mile from the last synagogue, Kevin had me pull into a labyrinth of mid-sixties homes. He told me that this was the area where he attended the estate auction at which he had bought the Dibbuk Box. Kevin was looking for a driveway that dropped steeply down to a ranch-style brick house. Kevin explained that he would know the house when he saw it because of its steep driveway. Many of the houses we passed nearly fit that description but lacked the required steep driveway. Kevin recalled it because of the extra burden it took to cart his auction purchases up the incline to his parked car.

Not finding the home on our first pass through the neighborhood, Kevin told me that there are some things you remember about each auction. He remembered the Dibbuk Box auction for the steep driveway and the upset granddaughter from the family estate who told him they didn't want the box; he bought it—now take it and LEAVE!

Kevin said that these memories of the auction were permanently burned into his memory. Kevin knew the house was somewhere near Sunset Street and had a steep driveway, it had to be close by, but he couldn't zero in on it for some reason. We circled the neighborhood several more times but failed to find the brick home at the bottom of a steep hill. Finally, Kevin apologized to me, saying he'd thought the home would be easy to locate—he was wrong. He volunteered to find the auctioneers who had worked there and ask them for the address from their records. This is where my journal entry covering my travels with Kevin had ended.

I had now pretty much confirmed the physical evidence of what Kevin claimed and had written on eBay. I had also taken photos of Kevin, his former shop, the cemeteries and synagogues, and the home neighborhood of the family who had purportedly sold the box to Kevin. During our chat the night before and our day of talking and tracking down sites, Kevin and I had seemed to hit it off pretty well. He had a sharp, somewhat sarcastic sense of humor and was obviously intelligent. He was a great talker with a keen sense for details and a vivid use of words. We ended our day at a nice downtown restaurant decorated in art nouveau style. Dinner, wine, and dessert—all were well earned. I now felt that I understood Kevin, as well as the little Jewish community that had once been home to the Dibbuk Box.

As we prepared to part ways, I gave Kevin an assignment to see if he could retrace his steps back to the auction house or maybe call the auctioneers and see if they could provide the address. I wanted him to find that family. I suggested that he might call around to several auction houses and see if they could provide the name of the auctioneers or an address.

Chapter Seven

Sophie's Story

KEVIN THOUGHT the best way to find the house where the estate auction had been held and he had bought the Dibbuk Box was to contact the auctioneers. He communicated with me about what happened through e-mails, phone calls, and his public AOL journal dated December 5, 2004. Because the auction was handled by a two-woman team, something fairly unusual in this male-dominated profession, Kevin did not have much trouble locating the auctioneers. He called them and, using the pretext that he may have dropped his watch during an auction at the house, asked for the address so he could check and see whether the family still had it. Kevin said that the auctioneers apparently hoped there might be a bit of extra cash in it for them, but when they realized there was no reward, they simply gave him the address of the house and hung up.

Kevin didn't waste any time; address in hand he immediately drove out to the house. He was excited about the possibility of figuring the "whole thing" out—whatever the "whole thing" meant. Sure enough, the auctioneers had provided the right address because right away he recognized that odd steep driveway leading down to the ranch-style house. The driveway was so narrow and steep that Kevin didn't want to drive down, but on the other hand, he didn't want them to see him walking down their drive and think he was just wandering around and might be a threat. Thinking he should have dressed better for his visit, Kevin decided to park at the top of the driveway with his car visible but not blocking the entrance. He approached the door and could hear voices coming from inside. He thought they sounded pretty normal, not the type to spend the day conjuring up demons and the like. Then again, this was the place where he had gotten the box. He knocked politely on the front door and waited.

The door opened wide and Kevin saw a familiar face. She smiled warmly, "Kevin?" It was "Deborah" (not her real name), a high school classmate. Kevin greeted her, trying to keep his tone sounding as though he was expecting to find her there, and wondered how to introduce the topic of his visit—the mystical cabinet that might have belonged to her grandmother.

After a few seconds of silence, Deborah's smile started to look less like surprised interest and more like forced politeness. Realizing he would have to say something, Kevin commented that he thought she lived over on Hamilton Court, and she reminded him that she had—twenty years ago when they were in high school—but some things just seem to change. There wasn't any easy way to bring up the subject, so Kevin asked if she remembered an estate sale at this house. Her face went blank for a minute, then she asked if he was referring to her grandmother's estate sale about three or four years ago. It was the only estate sale her family had ever had, and she had not been there, but her younger sister had been. Kevin now realized that the woman he had chatted with, the granddaughter who had become so upset, had seemed familiar because they had probably known each other in high school. Deborah continued, "I heard you bought the Dibbuk Box and some other things." Her sister had told her about the whole incident of him purchasing the box and then trying to give it back to the family. Deborah said her sister had always feared and hated the box while growing up. Then she laughed and said it was probably the box that hated her sister more than anything. Kevin didn't think that it was that funny—it must have shown on his face, because she stopped laughing. Kevin described what happened next.

> I asked what she meant about the box hating her sister and she said she was just kidding: "Kevin, it was always a big joke [in our family] that anything unpleasant that occurred was because of a dibbuk." Again my look must have been a little odd. Deborah stepped out of the house, closed the door behind her, and said, "All right Kev, it's been twenty years and we weren't even that close in school. You didn't just drop by to shoot the wind and talk about my grandma's stuff, did you? 'Cause if you did, it's a little strange. It's already a little too strange. So tell me what's up?" She went from high school pal to paranoid parapsychology cop in about two seconds.

"Okay, listen. I bought the box back at your grandmother's estate sale. It was plain crazy that your sister didn't want it, and how she said so. It got really weird that day . . ."

Deborah asked me, "Weird how?"

The look on her face, which I had been reading as bewildered and curious, seemed to become more fretful and concerned. I began to tell her some of the things that had happened to me, then I moved to the things I had been told by the current owner at the museum.

"Look, I feel stupid trying to convince you of this. I can't believe I'm even saying these things, let alone saying them out loud to you," I said.

I paused for a moment. I couldn't read her face now. Her eyes were fixed on mine, but her face was essentially expressionless. "You weren't even here during the sale. I shouldn't have bothered you. Look, tell your sister I'm really sorry about what happened that day . . . and, I understand a lot better now." I turned and began to walk away.

"It chose you," she said. That wasn't Deborah's voice.

"Yes, Kalman [my Hebrew name], they can choose." A very old lady, introduced as Sophie, had appeared in the doorway. She said, "You have been chosen by the *ru'ah tezazit* [an unclean spirit]." I stood there frozen. She added, "It has chosen you!"

"*What* can choose?" I stammered.

"*Dibbukim min ha-hizonim*, Kalman," she said. "The dibbuks from the demonic side."

Sophie seemed to be at least eighty, maybe even eighty-five years old, and looked small and frail, but her upwelling of emotion seemed to instantly drain my spirit to the core and I [suddenly] understood the meaning of the phrase "having your guts ripped out." Confused, I apologized for bothering the family and got ready to leave, but Sophie's next words stopped me: "No! It is I who stand before you begging for forgiveness." I asked her to explain and she continued, "The time has finally come. At last! The price has finally been paid; the toll has been taken. You were chosen. In his generous mercy, *baruch HaShem* has delivered me to this day, that I may see the end of the wrath that fell upon the world [as] retribution for the acts that foolishly tempted the Lord." Then more calmly, she said, "You came about Havela's Dibbuk Box, yes?"

Deborah walked over to Sophie and gently took her arm, but Sophie pulled it free and said, "Come, Kalman. We will talk, you and me. Come."

I followed Deborah and Sophie inside the house and to a patio just beyond the living room, where Sophie sat down at an ornate white cast-iron table. I sat down too and Deborah excused herself to get some tea. Sophie and I were alone, and I was afraid. Not afraid of Sophie, but of what might happen next. Sophie was staring off into nothingness. Staring back at her, I realized that I had met her on several occasions when she had attended school functions for Deborah. She and her sister had always called her Aunt Sophie, but I learned that Sophie was actually Deborah's grandmother's first cousin. It was a relief when Deborah finally returned with the tea, but then she left us alone to talk.

Sophie began to speak again. She asked me to keep one thing in mind throughout our conversation—she was sorry. She then began to apologize profusely. She was sorry for World War II, for the Korean conflict, for the killing fields of the Khmer Rouge, for Bosnia. She said she was sorry for some accident that had taken place in India involving the Dow Chemical Company back in the 1980s. She brought up more obscure names, places, and dates and I just sat there, taking it all in. Then she said, "It wasn't Havela's fault alone, if that's what you're thinking. We were all to blame, every last foolish one of us. We were so young. What were we to do?" She began to cry, and to pray in Hebrew.

I tried to comfort her. I told her that I wasn't really concerned with the box and such. I was there to see if maybe someone had found a watch I had lost during the estate sale a few years ago. And the wine box was just a wine box.

She gazed deeply into my eyes and asked, "Do you think that you get to be my age by being *furmisched*?"

"*Furmisched*?" I asked. "What do you mean?"

"I mean to ask you if you think you'll get to be my age by being stupid?' she snapped.

"No, no I probably won't." I said.

"Then stop acting that way. Don't play games with me. I know exactly why you are here and I know exactly what the box is. It is what we intended it to be. It is a Dibbuk Box."

I told her I had never heard of anything called a Dibbuk Box until I bought the one that belonged to her cousin Havela.

"Nor should you have. There had never been a Dibbuk Box until the first one we made: Havela, the others, and me. But a dibbuk is not the devil. A dibbuk does not take a human shape so much as it cleaves onto a human soul. It is a devouring parasite. A dibbuk takes possession of the very essence of a being and then plays master to the helpless puppet of a soul as it fulfills its evil premeditated purpose. I'll tell you how it came to be." She seemed to be warning me.

This was why I had come to see her. If I played my cards right, she'd tell me the story and I could be on my way. I didn't know what kind of head-trip I had gone through when I first saw her, but I wanted to hear her story.

Sophie told Kevin that she had been a girl in Poland in the 1930s in the days leading up to the Holocaust. They watched evil grow around them, but most Jews felt helpless to do anything. Sophie was a child and her cousin Havela was a grown woman, married with three children, and Havela and Sophie's mother were very close. In those days, it was fashionable to hold séances. This was of course forbidden in Jewish culture, but, Sophie said, "Things that were taboo were as alluring to the young back then as they are to young people today." Havela liked to be very modern; she was the most fashionable woman in their community. Sophie told Kevin that Havela used to have tea parties for a group of women, including her mother, and Sophie went along too. After Havela's husband and children were murdered in a pogrom and life was becoming difficult for the Jews, Havela continued to have the women gather for tea and they would pretend they were far away from the rumors of trouble to come.

Sophie told Kevin that in those times, there was little they could do about the racial laws and rising violence against the Jews, but Havela was a fighter. She couldn't fight in the normal sense of the word, so she decided to fight the war in a most unorthodox way. She decided to summon a spirit, a dibbuk to help them fight for the Jews. At first it was a game. Havela made a beautiful table cover, embroidered with the words *yes* and *no*, the letters of the alphabet and numbers, and various symbols. While the men were at prayers, the women would gather, spread out the table cover, and play at holding a séance. Havela would pretend to be a medium, and the women would ask who would marry whom, who would have children, and other silly questions.

Then one night, Havela was different. There was a rumor that conditions were going to get even worse; everyone was scared. Havela was scared too, but she was also angry. She said they had been just playing at summoning spirits, but now she insisted that the women work together to summon a real spirit. Sophie's mother said it was a sin to practice witchcraft, but Havela said it wasn't witchcraft, it was kabbalah. Sophie told Kevin what happened next.

> "Kabbalah!" my mother whispered. "What do you know of kabbalah?"
>
> Havela held up two small books. One was the story of the Golem of Rabbi Loew [a sixteenth-century rabbi in Prague] and the other was *Sepher Yitzerah* [a third- or fourth-century book of Jewish mysticism]. "I know you've heard the story of Rabbi Loew," Havela said.
>
> "That's just a fairy tale," my mother insisted.
>
> "I know the story," said Shosnana, one of the older girls. "Rabbi Loew made a golem out of clay to protect the Jewish people from the pogroms."
>
> "Its body was formed out of pure clay, but it didn't have a soul," Havela explained. "It was a living being whose mind was made from pure energy by Rabbi Loew. It was as powerful as an army and it defended the Jews against their enemies."
>
> "It is just a fairy tale," my mother exclaimed. "How can you do this? How can you give these girls such ideas?"
>
> Havela ignored her and continued. "I'm not the one who started this. This is a manual of kabbalah meditation. Not just prayer, but the means by which a man can harness the same power used by the Almighty, *baruch HaShem*, to form the very material of the universe." She paused and looked at each woman, one by one. "We can use what is in this book to fill our eyes and ears and thoughts with something other than death. We can use it to fight."
>
> She turned to my mother. "Chana, I need you. Help me keep hope. Please?" My mother began to cry. "Please? Will you help me?" My mother put her arms around Havela. "Yes," she said quietly.

Sophie stopped talking. In the silence, Kevin saw Deborah appear in the doorway. "Is everything all right?" Kevin wondered if Deborah had been trying to listen, and began to wonder whether Sophie had ever told this story to Deborah.

Sophie didn't answer. She picked up her teacup and took a sip. "So, David decided to take the train home from the airport?" she asked Deborah.

"What? Oh, wow! What time is it?"

"Why it's almost half past," Sophie began. Deborah glanced at her wristwatch and ran out of the room, calling back, "I had no idea it was so late! We'll be right back! Sorry to have to rush like this. Aunt Sophie, if David calls, tell him I'm on my way. Goodbye!"

As I heard the door slam, I turned back to Sophie and saw a most interesting sort of smile, almost mischievous. She calmly poured more tea into my cup and offered me the plate of crème-filled pirouette cookies.

"Have as many as you like," she said.

I thanked her and took a sip of tea. "Couldn't everything that goes on around the Dibbuk Box be a coincidence?" I asked.

"There is no such thing as chance throughout all of G-d's creation, Kalman," Sophie said.

Kevin told me that he learned from Sophie that the Dibbuk Box story goes back to the late 1930s. Havela and her friends thought they had discovered some sort of spiritual guide—the Dibbuk—and as time went on they found it easier and easier to communicate with this Dibbuk. Before long they were having fairly regular meetings and the spirits were becoming more and more involved in their daily lives. Then the spirits wanted the group to perform a ritual that would bring them into the natural world permanently. The group was troubled, but decided the best way to end the spirits' influence on them was to lure these spirits into this world and then trap them. They met on the evening of November 8 and called to the spiritual world into the morning hours on November 9, 1938, trying to capture one or more spirits, but things went very wrong. The entrapment failed and the otherworldly entities were instead released. What followed was a time of sorrow and tragedy for all Jews in Europe, and the group became scattered. The original Dibbuk Box was most likely destroyed during the war, and according to Sophie, the Dibbuk Box I now care for was created in Portland, Oregon, to regather and hold the same spirit or spirits that had been released on that fateful night in November seventy-three years ago and to provide answers about the reason for the Holocaust. Havela, with a few surviving family members, sought to recapture these dangerous, harmful spirits and return them to wherever they'd come from. Sophie made it clear to Kevin that she regretted she had ever become involved in the dibbuk drama—that it had ruined their lives and she hoped the world would someday be able to forgive her and Havela. Once she had told her story, Sophie told Kevin that she wanted nothing more to do with the box and asked him to keep her identity private. Kevin agreed and stood to leave, but something didn't feel right. He looked down at his feet and was shocked to find that his ankles had swollen to the size of large grapefruits. He had felt no pain and there was no discernible injury. Kevin was a champion skater; he had very strong ankles and had never experienced anything like this. Sophie thought Kevin's problem was related to the box's malign spirit, but Kevin headed to the hospital. Kevin described his problem to a nurse and after a few hours plus a few IVs, Kevin was allowed to go home. The cause of the swelling turned out to be . . . what? The ER doctor couldn't give Kevin any clear diagnosis.

Not long after meeting Sophie and his emergency room visit, Kevin found himself faced with other problems. A spiritual oppression began exerting its presence on Kevin's mother. Kevin told me about the strange phenomenon in an e-mail:

> Today my mom called me into the living room to fix the TV. I asked her what was wrong, and she started to tell me, but [the trouble] became pretty obvious pretty quickly.
>
> The volume started turning up without the remote or TV being touched. I asked my mom where the remote was and she pointed it out on the coffee table. I asked her if she had been sitting on the other universal remote that was sometimes used.
>
> She shook her head. I realized she was holding something back, so I asked her what was up.
>
> She started to tell me, but the TV volume shot up [to] full volume. I turned it down. I waited. Nothing happened. I asked her when the TV started doing this. She held up both her hands to indicate ten, then pointed to her watch and drew a circle in the air to indicate minutes.
>
> I became a little frustrated and told her to just speak out loud. She stood there looking at me for a couple of seconds. Then she raised her eyebrows, the way she raises them right before she says, "I told you

so . . ." and [began to say] "ten minutes," but as soon as she said "te–" the volume shot up again.

    She walked over and turned off the TV. Then she just shook her head and walked down the hallway toward her room. I got upset and said, "Come on, Mom. I can fix the TV." She kept walking. She went into her room and shut the door.

    I followed her down the hall and kept asking her to please come back and let me fix [the TV] for her. When I got to her door, I started knocking and asking her to come back out, but she wouldn't answer. I kept it up for a minute until she finally yelled at me, "It doesn't want me to talk right now."

    At the same time, music started blasting from inside her room and the alarm on her clock radio went off. She turned it off and slid a note under the door that read, "See?"

I spoke briefly with Kevin's mother several times when I was trying to call Kevin by phone and he wasn't home. My first attempts to get her perspective were cut short; she made it clear she wanted nothing to do with "that box." I told her that I hoped the box helped Kevin and brought no more harm; her only response was that we should stop talking about it. I explained that, to me, the scariest story concerned her reaction when Kevin gave her the box as a birthday gift, but she didn't wish to discuss it. She said that she had been in the Marines during World War II, so she was tough and not easily intimidated, but the subject of the malicious artifact was closed.

It didn't stay closed for long. Another evening, I called Kevin and his mother again answered the phone. She said she was home alone and was still hurting from an incident a few days earlier. She told me she had been troubled by a negative energy in the house for weeks, then a few days back, she felt a hard push from behind, and was flung to the floor on both knees. Now one leg was swollen from the foot to her groin. Her leg was hurting her terribly. She was pretty sure it was broken but declined to go to the hospital because it was a weekend and she believed hospital care was better on weekdays. But the pain was so great, she said, that she'd probably go tomorrow.

She told me that she had no idea when Kevin would be back, but she stayed on the phone and didn't make any attempt to end the conversation.

I realized she wanted to talk to someone. I asked if she thought she needed some form of immediate medical care for her injury. Was there anything I could do to help? She told me she wasn't sure. She seemed to sense my concern, and began to open up. I had my journal out and began jotting down details as she spoke of her misfortunes.

Even worse than the pain was the loss of her eyesight, she told me. Her glasses were no help. If only she could see again! I told her about my own vision problems, which had struck immediately after I'd handled the Dibbuk Box. At once, I realized that my mention of the box had turned her off again. She did not want to talk about it any more.

It turned out that Kevin was visiting Sophie's family again, but his request for more information was getting him nowhere. Sophie had nothing more to add. In talking to Kevin via e-mail and phone, he kept putting me off whenever I asked for Havela's surname. I wanted her name so I could confirm her death and possibly read her obituary to get more information on the family. From there I could follow backwards to check census records and even immigration records. Finally, Kevin relented and provided me with the name Jewiski. He also indicated that the family had hinted that several of these mystical containers were spread among the family and he even showed me an image of yet another to prove it. Certainly the image he provided shared a common motif with the Dibbuk Box. This second box included a carved Hebrew prayer, but it was not the same. Also it had a cup, but this one had two handles. It was a hand-washing cup, and I learned that one explanation of its design was that it was used to rinse off evil spirits—switching handles to the clean hand to rinse the opposite dirty hand. It also had a dried rose, a large odd coin with a swastika emblazoned on it, and a piece of granite with the Jewish word *chai* (life) carved into it. All these items were housed within a lidded wooden box made of a tree base with the roots still somewhat intact. Except for the brief image, Kevin never mentioned the second container again until we connected in spring of 2011.

So I began in earnest with the name I now had: Havela Jewiski. If the name had been correct, I should have been able to find a record of her death, but I found nothing. I learned that many Jews have both a Hebrew name and an English name, so Havela might not be the name under which she was listed. But her age at the time of her death—103 years old—would be hard to miss. The death notices for anyone near that age provided no name even close to Havela Jewiski. When I let Kevin know the name he provided to me couldn't be correct, he suggested other spellings: "Try running the name Djenzjewski for Havela. I don't know for sure if it is correct. You might also try Djenzjewsy, and Jenzjewski, and the suffix –jescu."

Of course I tried them all and a number of variations on each one too, but I couldn't find anything. I wondered what was so hard about getting the name of a family you've met face-to-face with on several occasions. But I also wondered whether Jewiski might have been Havela's maiden name or the name of her first husband. Since she had apparently remarried, had the family perhaps not given Kevin her name at the time of her death? Perhaps someone was just putting me off with a fake name. I also thought about the granddaughter Kevin said he had met at the auction and the Deborah he met at the home where Sophie lived. If Havela and Sophie were the only members of her family to survive the Holocaust and she was probably in her forties during the war, how is it that she had granddaughters? She had obviously remarried, and could have had more children. Or perhaps her new husband had children, making her a stepmother. Either way, grandchildren were indeed a possibility.

During that phone conversation, Kevin's mother said she thought I wouldn't be able to get any more information from the family and asked whether I knew that Kevin's feet had swollen the last time he visited Havela's family. I said Kevin had told me about his condition and his visit to the hospital. She then insisted, "Give me your word that you won't give the box to anyone. You didn't pay much for it. You don't want to lose control of it." Her warning grew more ominous: "I am too old to be afraid of anything. For your family—wife and kids—do not let anyone have the rights to that box. We don't know much about our world. You think a hydrogen bomb is bad? There are things much scarier—things not of this world."

She told me that she and her husband had been in the habit of going to auctions all over Portland at least once a week. They had bought many items and resold them to earn a little extra money, so her family was used to auctions. "But the auction with that box caused us to lose our style and class. This box—I am so sorry it came into our life. . . . I don't have words to describe it anymore."

"The antique shop was a fun thing for us," she said, "until the box. Frankly our lives, everything, went to hell in a handbasket. It is hard to accept that my health has been destroyed. It is a terrible thing to blame it on the box. Before the box came into our life, we were doing okay."

Since she seemed to be willing to talk about the box, I asked, "Did you recognize it as wrong? As strange?" She confided that she had never shared with her son what really happened when she touched the Dibbuk Box. Maybe he felt responsible for her pain and the health problems that followed, but Kevin never asked about it and his mother never told him.

"When I touched [the box]," she told me, "I felt an energy that I had not felt in all of my life. Not a trembling—energy! I did not feel like I was having a stroke. I didn't. I was not prepared for the energy that coursed through me. Like Mount St. Helens power. Like how that volcano near our city just came to life one day—all power. I wanted to run some place, run with fear. The next thing I knew I was in the hospital, unable to speak or feel on one side." When the stroke hit, she added, there was no pain.

Her explanation of what happened when she touched the box caught me off guard—I was expecting fear, excruciating pain, perhaps a burning inside like fire. Instead, what she described sounded like a power that might vaporize you into nothingness. "It was as if all feeling and time had stopped," she said, "like being touched by something spiritual not of this world."

She continued, "I would not hurt my son's feelings by asking him what he was doing with this—a crappy old box. I guess I should have said that right at the time. He may have trashed it right there, and then [none of this would have happened]."

She advised me to wrap the box in plastic so it wouldn't disintegrate, and bury it near a tree or some other unmovable landmark so I would know where to find it if it were ever needed. As we were speaking, I began to see luminous shapes that seemed to crawl along the floor, like warped light around my feet. The shapes moved past me—agitated little blinks of light appeared and vanished.

I tried to tell her that I would call Kevin the next day, but there was so much static on the phone line I could hear her only slightly, and she could not hear me. All I caught from her closing words was "Jason I am going to. . . been nice talking. . . . Goodbye." Then, "click."

My calls to her home the next day went unanswered. Finally I reached Kevin around ten in the evening. He was just back from the hospital. He had returned home the previous evening to find his mother unconscious on the floor. She had suffered another stroke and things were all touch and go. She got through it, but would remain in the hospital for several weeks.

During that time, I had begun to receive e-mails from Tracey, a Wiccan whose husband sold high-end guitars from their business in South Carolina. We had been corresponding for some time about this enigma, but once she started offering to assist me in banishing the thing captured with the Dibbuk Box, she noticed physical changes like oppression around her. She told me her office had grown unaccountably cold since her recent attempts to help me, and she had suffered sore arms that prevented her from typing. She took these problems in stride, telling me this is what happens when you get involved with the spiritual world. Tracey had sent me several spells in her e-mails, and in phone conversation, she indicated preparations and additional information that had become very complex and, frankly, weird by my standards. Her higher-up Wiccan priests were certain no ghost was involved, but rather a demon—a very powerful demon that had blocked all her Wiccan friends' attempts to help me. She said they were freaked out and concerned, and all of them believed the demon must be banished. They could do it themselves from afar, Tracey said, but they would expect me to take some actions too.

I did not want to believe in such a thing as an evil force or demon invading my home. Over the years I had collected a good number of ancient idols and pottery pieces. Several of these pieces were specifically created as house gods—protectors of the home and family. I hadn't thought about them as something other than artifacts before, but the words of Kevin's mom and her unexplained relapse after my phone call had unnerved me. Could any of these ancient house gods protect me and my family?

Chapter Eight

Rituals and Mysticism

IN OCTOBER 2004, I wrote in my personal journal about a series of strange events.

October 4, 2004

The Dibbuk Box has taken a new direction, it would seem—a new mode of assault. It is the reek of death and human waste. The stench invaded our home overnight. It began with the discovery of a dead mouse in the new family car. Next, I traced a foul, dead smell to the well of the grandfather clock—a dead bat. And then it got really bad. Today I picked up my kids from school, grabbed some fast-food kids' meals, and headed home. As soon as I opened the front door to the house, the stink of raw human sewage was enough to turn the kids and send them rushing back outside, refusing to enter our home. The stench was so strong and pervasive it was hard to know where to look for the cause, but I was drawn to the bathroom off the family room. I had thought the stink couldn't be any worse. I was wrong. It was impossible to breathe the air. I exited and regrouped with the kids, breathed in some fresh air, and then headed back to the bathroom to investigate.

I discovered that the toilet bowl was completely empty of any water, which meant the S pipe below it had been sucked completely dry, leaving our home open to the effluence of feces and urine from the entire town. Never had such a sickening odor filled our house. Simply flushing the toilet lever let the water flow from the upper tank and restored once more the protective water seal from the open pipeline of crap and piss. I made sure all the windows were wide open, fans running, and scented candles burning. My efforts to restore breathable air did little good until finally, many hours later, the house started to lose some of its sewer smell. It was neither pleasant nor healthy and I was concerned.

I decided to call the Schuyler County Public Water District No. 1 to ask about any pressure changes on that end, or if anything else might have caused the water in the pipes to vanish completely. Reaching the phone of Mark, who was the onsite troubleshooter, I explained the situation. I said it appeared there had been some huge suction within the sewer system, which had pulled all of the water from my toilet's S pipe and released massive levels of fecal gas into my home. Mark indicated the problem was beyond him—he had never heard of such an incident.

Next I was transferred to Dennis, in charge of machinery repairs; he was the key man in dealing with sewer-related problems within the system. Dennis told me, "I cannot imagine anything we could have done on our end that would have the power to cause such a thing." The problem had to be extremely uncommon, he said. In fact he had never encountered anything like it in all his years with the Public Water and Sewer Works.

I inquired if it could have been caused by the nearby lift station, a pump to bring up sewage from the bottom of the hill and then pump it out to the processing lagoons. Dennis said that to pull the water out of my toilet "well, that would have to be one helluva lot of suction." Besides, he continued, it wouldn't have just caused problems in my home, but would have affected every home in the entire town. So far, I was the only one who had called with this complaint, he said. He told me that these days most toilets are designed to be foolproof in preventing this very problem from ever happening.

If I were to disconnect the toilet in my home and completely spin it front-over-back in a circle and then set it down, when set back down it would still retain the water plug. That is how important it is to keep the sewer gas from coming from the pipe into the home. Dennis figured it was impossible. Based on my location near the lift station, he knew my home was close to the town cemetery.

Then Dennis suggested, jokingly, "Go next door and tell all those cemetery folks [ghosts or spirits] to stay on their own property and off of yours. It must be those cemetery folks that are causing your plumbing problem."

This is the damnedest thing. Perhaps it is the Dibbuk Box's reply to the news I'd received earlier in the morning: The *L. A. Times* writer I had helped with her article, Leslie Gornstein, let me know that she had been contacted by a major Hollywood film company who paid her for the rights to use her article, "Jinx in a Box," as the basis for a thriller-horror film, and she indicated that I too would be contacted. I wished her luck, but I told her I didn't want any part of her deal with those movie people. I had enough problems right now.

I e-mailed my paranormal expert, Steve Maass, about the fecal stink attack. He was fascinated, but not surprised. He told me that a demon would want to use the odors of feces and urine as a means of driving me crazy. But since a demon, being a nonphysical entity, can't create bad smells itself, it would look for other means. Using its energy to drain the S pipe would be both expedient and creative too. "Demons can be subtle in working within the means available to them," Steve explained. The use of my toilet to summon the foul stench might have been done in the hopes of driving me permanently from my home, and away from the Dibbuk Box too.

Steve had no doubt this was a demonic trick and he was worried for me. He hoped I wasn't headed for more problems or even some type of mental breakdown. He got the first part right. All my health problems returned with a vengeance, but I was not about to be driven from my home. My health problems seemed to be growing worse. The throat congestion had returned and now I tasted blood when I coughed. And the hives, red burning ears, and itchy eyes had tormented me all day. I decided it was time that I take serious action regarding the Dibbuk Box. I would follow Tracey's Wiccan advice—nothing else was helping me.

It was time to move the Dibbuk Box once again, this time out of my home and next door to my empty rental house. First I needed to go to town and buy fresh sage for smudging, plus basil and sea salt for a bath, materials prescribed by the Wiccans. I went straight to the farmers market where fresh herbs could be purchased cheaply. I also was reorganizing material I found useful from my journaling.

After photocopying my daily journals and picking up the herbs, I headed out to pick up my son's friend, Paul Davis, from his home. I had earlier approached his parents, Adam and Andrea, about translating the

Dibbuk Box story into German for my website. Adam, who spoke German and taught folklore in literature at Truman State University, had refused, admitting that the box frightened him too much to become involved. However, as a professor of folklore, Adam could not resist the story and had been asking me about the haunted wine cabinet since I first mentioned it to him. I eventually found a translator, Sven Sutmar, who was German and an acquaintance through the museum, to do the translation for the website.

Paul had heard his father asking me about the Dibbuk Box and when he got in the car, wasted no time in asking me what a dibbuk was. As we headed to my home I had time to explain the entire story except for one fact—that the Dibbuk Box was now in my possession. Paul assumed that someone else, not I, had bought the wine cabinet on eBay. That was probably best. Paul told me his dad often said of such mysteries, "There's not enough information to say [it really exists], but there is too much information to say something isn't there either."

Saturday, October 9, 2004—a month before the sixty-sixth anniversary of Kristallnacht, which is also the day of my son's birth.

As I write in my journal, something seems to be touching my hair, and I am sitting in a chair with nobody behind me. It is dark except for the light in the little den where I am sitting. My work painting the house is going well. I have the scaffold up on the east side. Working outside on the scaffold was great—the fall color is in the trees, the coolness, deep blue skies, crisp air, the bird and insect sounds of preparing for winter. I thought how great my life is and I don't want an old wooden box to change or destroy it. I want the Dibbuk Box contained—sealed—so whatever is attached to it and causing my problems can be neutralized. Then maybe I can move on with my life.

Sunday, October 10, 2004, early morning

I am feeling better than I have in months. I have a plan. Last night the dialogue with Tracey from South Carolina was weird for me. She was serious as could be about banishing this demon. As she says, "A ghost can barely muster up an orb in a cemetery." A demon is omnipotent and caused

Kevin's mother, me, and now Tracey to have problems all at the same time. Tracey sent me a spell or recipe for cleansing myself in a basil and sea-salt bath. She also sent a protection and banishing spell. Yesterday I had gathered the herbs I needed—basil from the farmers market and two types of sage from the museum's medicinal garden. I promised Tracey that I would do some of the spells and I would consider helping her do the banishing spell. Last night I told her the long and detailed story about Kevin's mother touching the box and her continuing problems ever since.

She had made me promise her that I would not sell the box or give it to anyone for one or even two million dollars, and that I would not give anyone rights to take the box from me. She encouraged me to bury it wrapped in plastic near a tree. Oddly, while Kevin's mother and I had talked, I could hear her telling me this, but she could not hear my responses to her. She kept repeating this information as the connection grew worse and worse, and then she gave up and hung up the phone. I learned later that his mother, after my call, had suffered another serious health episode and was taken to the hospital by her son Kevin.

After that phone call I was seeing odd flashes in my den where the very space itself seemed to bend and distort the room. I thought of Tracey saying this demon was going to get me. I thought about all my odd physical ailments—eyes, throat, hives, burning ears, and metallic taste in my mouth—they vanished and returned without reason. I decided that I would not let any spiritual energy or thoughts about such things (if it was all psychosomatic) cause me any more problems.

Sunday, October 10, 2004, 11:20 a.m.

Right now it is late morning and I am sitting on a board across the scaffold up on the east porch roof. I can see the house next door that we bought to use as a future rental income. I can see the trapdoor to the cellar where the infested little box has since been placed. As I look to the east, the sun is to my right, overhead, with a nice cool breeze. I thought yesterday was gorgeous, but today my soul feels lighter and it looks brighter than ever. I have my journal with me . . . I must write about what has just happened so I won't forget any detail (the account of the day will follow).

The odd way I lost Kevin's mom on the phone while she told me to bury the box has pushed me into action today. I didn't bury the box in the ground as she suggested—but I had a plan to put it deep and away in the darkness of a crawl space.

I went to sleep and dreamed I was at a hotel—a very nice one. And as I lay there, I realized a maid and her college-age helper were making the bed right next to mine and watching me as they worked. I was embarrassed that they had come in the room unannounced, so I vented my rage by yelling that they were doing their work all wrong, and demanding that they please leave me alone.

Next, I got out of my bed and went to the lobby where there was a large German shepherd dog being pushed around on a luggage cart. I then went into a room full of small aquariums, with all types of animals in cages much too small for their sizes. Somehow, waking from this dream, I felt as if it had to do with dark magic. It had been that unsettling to me.

First thing after waking, I went to the bathroom, and when I washed my face and eyes, my skin felt slimy and coated as soon as the water ran on it. I rinsed for some time to get this odd sticky mess off my skin. This was bizarre, and it strengthened my resolve to move the box to a more isolated location and to use the Wiccan instructions Tracey had provided me for self-protection.

I tried to open my e-mail, hoping for more details on this self-protection spell, with no luck. Something is wrong with the computer all of a sudden, it seems. I could not get on the Internet at all. Next I went over to the empty rental house to add several locks that would secure the cellar's exterior and also its inner doors—access is gained through a ground door on the west side of the rental. This ground door pulls up to open from the side, exposing cement steps that lead down to yet another door that needed to be secured. I had purchased two hinge locks because the cellar's two doors up until now had not been lockable. My plan was to use this nearby isolated location as the new holding area for the Dibbuk Box.

The task went well. Next, I tried to attach a hinge to lock what can best be described as a crawl space door, leading to a larger space that was cramped in height under the entire house. The door was about a perfect two-foot square, and as I was attaching the hinge to this small but heavy door, it fell to the floor with a loud bang. So I pulled it aside, planning instead of locking it, to just nail it shut once the Dibbuk Box was under the house. It wasn't as if I would be checking on it anytime soon.

I gathered the colored candles and herbs I would need for the ritual that Tracey had sent me. Then, I removed the Dibbuk Box from the closet in the unused room, where it had been since I moved it from my truck. Meanwhile, Lori and my kids slept, unaware of my preparations and plan. After getting the locks just right at the vacant rental house, I used a kitchen stepladder to reach the two-foot-square hole and then pulled myself into the crawl space and onto the dirt floor underneath the building. This inaccessible and hidden area was where I planned to relocate the box. Once under the house, I found that there was more space than I had imagined. I thought to myself, here is dirt that's been hidden from daylight for over a hundred years. Around me were very dry clods of earth, sharp to the touch, surrounded by deteriorating wood gnawed by generations of boring beetles.

Next, I crawled around a corner support wall to the south middle section. I set two concrete cinder blocks against the wall support and put a plywood board on top of them to create a table or low altar. I also set opened packets of De-Con mouse poison around the area. I wanted to make sure that field mice would not invade the empty house and chew off pieces of the Dibbuk Box for nesting material.

After I'd turned off my flashlight, the space felt like an empty church at night—pitch dark, a bit musty, and dead quiet. I turned the flashlight switch back on and returned to the cellar to fetch my bag of herbs, candles, and salt. I used the same kitchen stepladder to shove the Dibbuk Box, still in its shipping carton, through the trapdoor opening. It was tight and barely fit. But once it was inside the space below, I was able to push it several feet at a time, to the corner, where it would sit while I got to work. Next, I used the stepladder to squeeze myself through the trapdoor. A bent nail at the entrance had hooked onto my pants, and it held me from crawling forward to the box, but I pulled free with only a minor rip.

I crawled to the plywood "altar" where I would place the Dibbuk Box during the ceremony. It occurred to me that this quiet, church-like atmosphere was exactly right for such a ritual. I thought it would be best to lay the salt and herbs on top of the plywood. I knew nothing about occult practices like this, but I decided I could figure out the proper actions as I went. I lit the purple candle (color recommended by Tracey) and set it on the ground next to the altar. Next I made a square with the sea salt on the board. Tracey's instructions had also recommended the use of circles in the ritual, so I made one of sea salt in the middle of the square, with branch lines running out to the four points of the compass to form a diagram.

Next I put basil in each of the four sections of the circle and then added dried sage to the center. I set the lit purple candle in the middle of the circle of salt on top of the sage. Then I chose a dried branch of sage from my bag of herbs, ignited the sweet-scented sage with the candle, and trailed the smoke three times around the center circle (this is known as smudging). When this was done, I invoked the protection of Hecate against the evil spirit of the dibbuk and replaced the candle on the altar with the burning sage.

The next step was to move the Dibbuk Box, nestled in its cardboard container, to a spot beside the altar. I whispered the required incantation, "You will be contained," and gently hoisted the box onto the basil, sage ashes, and the salt diagram. Suddenly a wind picked up under the crawl space with a rumbling sound. How it got into this sealed space, I do not know. The sound grew fainter, then stopped. It shook me a bit, and I exited the crawl space.

As I looked back into the blackness, I saw a beam of white light edged in rainbow colors pouring through the space. If this was a sign, it gave me assurance that I had truly accomplished something. I was motivated to finish up the ritual and be free entirely of the Dibbuk Box. But first, according to instructions, I would have to "purify" myself before returning to the cellar to seal that area as a boundary.

Leaving my supplies in the cellar, I picked up the two-foot-square panel of wood and nailed shut the entrance to the crawl space that now held the Dibbuk Box.

I headed home with a sandwich bag containing basil and salt to be used in the ritual bath.

I knew my wife, Lori, would be up by now and she would probably freak out over any of this (it was hard enough for me, and I am pretty liberal-minded about the paranormal), so I just told her I was taking a bath.

She knew I planned to paint the house trim that day, and asked if I wouldn't rather wait until that chore was done. I said I felt too gross and needed to bathe now. While the tub was being filled, I struggled to open my e-mail. But for some reason I still couldn't get on the Internet. When I finally did get through to the Dibbuk Box forum, I found a message from Rhiamma Silvermoon, another witch who was said to be highly respected among her peers. Her e-mail informed me with the coming of fall the "veil between the worlds" was thinning, and with the anniversary date of Kevin's mother's stroke coming up, I should place the Dibbuk Box in a protective circle of salt. Oddly, that was what I'd just finished doing, and I noticed based on the time mark that Silvermoon's e-mail had arrived at the very moment I was performing the sealing ritual.

The coincidence struck me as evidence of Silvermoon's spiritual sensitivity. I had a feeling that something was guiding me subconsciously to take measures that would free me of the Dibbuk Box's influence. And I felt even more confident that I'd completed some kind of a true spiritual spell.

After shaving, brushing my teeth, and gargling with Listerine, I stepped into the hot bath of basil and sea salt. Almost immediately, I found I could breathe more easily. I felt clear-headed—almost weightless—as the stress of recent months lifted from me. I rubbed the basil onto my skin and poured the basil-scented water over my head. Once I was thoroughly soaked and refreshed, I drained the water and prepared for part two of the remaining task: to seal the area around the Dibbuk Box in the cellar next door.

Fresh and clean, I returned to the cellar. I could easily see the small trapdoor sealed with plenty of nails, denying access to the crawl space that now housed the Dibbuk Box.

In the center of the cellar, ready to continue the sealing spell, I set up a candle and tried to light it. The first and second matches both failed. I was thinking, "Something doesn't want this to happen." I said aloud that I would light it anyway, and the third match ignited. I then lit both the purple and the pink candles, set them on the concrete floor, and pulled shut the inner cellar door whose steps lead up to the yard above and the second, ground-level door. With no outside light, it was an eerie darkness, lit only by candles. Suddenly a honeybee flew at me out of the dark. I am terribly allergic to bee stings, and had nearly died of a sting when I was six years old. I knew it was odd for a solitary bee to appear— normally they'd have long since gone to their hives to hibernate. I pulled open the cellar door and the outdoor light streamed back into the cellar. I got behind the bee and swept it out into the daylight, using the paper with the spells written on it.

Again I shut the door to the cellar, and this time mosquitoes started flying at me. None of this had happened to me earlier when I had moved the Dibbuk Box to the crawl space. I killed them with my hands, and then spotted a venomous house centipede crawling toward me. Enough already, I thought, and smashed it with the paper of spells. Its legs twitched while I began my work pulling everything I would need for the spell to the very center of the cellar floor.

Then, holding the pink candle, I poured out a four-foot circle of sea salt around me, moving clockwise. I used up the whole container of sea salt—pouring a very thick line. Pleased with myself, I turned to pick up the basil and kicked over the second candle, the purple one, which fell with a clatter. The overturned glass, which had held the candle, had rolled outside the circle of salt. My instinct was to go get it. But first I picked up the purple candle, which still lay inside the circle of salt and was still burning. Before I moved to fetch the glass, a thought crossed my mind: Suppose "something" wanted me to leave the salt circle. I'd been warned that if I stepped out of it during any phase of the ritual, the spell would instantly be broken. So I left the glass where it had rolled to—I really only needed the lit candle.

Then I discovered that the dried sage, which I was to burn in the ritual, was sitting on a ledge outside the salt perimeter. Once more, I almost stepped out to retrieve it. But I found another solution. Holding onto the ceiling beams, I was able to bend down and pick up the sage without setting foot on the ground. I did not have what the Wiccans called a smudge stick, a kind of concentration of herbs that can be burned to create protective smoke like incense. But I planned to use the whole branch of dried sage I had picked from the museum's medicinal garden. The dried branch would burn easily, creating the needed spiritual smoke or smudge. I lit the sage and walked the circle three times to cleanse the space for magic. I picked up the lighted pink candle and invoked the goddess Hecate. Suddenly the flame of the purple candle flared, as it had done when I previously invoked the goddess. The extra light let me see well enough to avoid stumbling out of the magic circle. I performed the spell for protection facing the four directional points of a compass (north, south, east, and west). Then I blew out the pink candle.

Next, I wanted to do a banishing spell. But I didn't have the required black pen to write the magic words on paper—the same paper I had used to chase out the bugs. It struck me that I could burn the end of the sage branch and use the charcoal for writing. The sage gave off a sweet odor as it burned. Then, with its charcoal tip, I wrote out the occult message in black, as directed. "All blocks are now removed," I thought. The ritual had gone perfectly—even my use of the charred herb as a substitute for a writing utensil worked out well as a natural solution (important in such subtle work).

I folded the inscribed paper around the sage three times and lit it. It burned to nothing in a glass jar lid that I had cleaned with sea salt, as instructed. Inspiration had helped me complete the task, and I closed out the circle, ending the spell by moving the lit purple candle in a circular motion and blowing out the candle with my eyes closed. I could see a reddish-purple ember. It was a bright spot in the darkness, and I remained still until it faded and disappeared. I had now completed the "protection circle." It seemed to me that the two spells were completed successfully. I put the unused materials and candles to the side of the cellar. Then I left, securing the cellar door with a combination lock. Nobody would be getting near the Dibbuk Box.

Sunday October 10, 2004, 10:20 p.m.

After doing my spell to remove negativity as a seal in the crawl space, plus what was called a banishing or boomerang spell to protect the area around the Dibbuk Box, I came home feeling lighter inside my heart, energized and refreshed. The ritual must have worked. I am free of the lung congestion. My throat-choking problem cleared, vision is better, no more metal taste, and my ears are no longer red and burning. The last stage of the spell required one more purifying bath to cleanse myself in sea salt and basil. I was rinsing when I suddenly had a terrible abdominal pain that was so severe it made me nauseated. I felt like I was going to be sick, but all that came out was a mass of weird mucus-like slime. Nothing like that had ever happened to me before. I felt it may have come from being possessed by the dibbuk, or demon entity—like ectoplasm—really strange. The pain was gone. Weird, gross—but that is indeed what had happened. As I look outside into the darkness of the night I see reflections like faded faces looking back in on me. At least they are outside and not in. Maybe it isn't over after all.

Monday, October 11, 2004, 6:50 a.m.

I was up late the night before and worn out. Lori cleaned herself up and went to the laundry room, so I took my regular morning shower. While I was in the shower washing my hair, Lori called to me, "Were you in poison ivy?"

I yelled, "What did you say?" and she answered, "Were you in poison ivy with these beans?"

I yelled back, "What beans?"

What she'd said was "these jeans."

I told her no, but instantly remembered the ritual and the fresh pants I'd worn after my bath and the cleansing spell. I suspected that the spell could have been the problem. I hadn't gotten into any weeds while wearing them, and there were no bugs. I had worn the pants until midnight, but they were clean.

Lori said she had touched the pants and her hand broke out in blisters that resembled poison ivy. She said, "I am not touching them anymore."

I told her to put cortisone on the rash. When I got out of the shower I saw that Lori's hand was coated in calamine lotion. Lori told me that when she moved my blue jeans off the chair where I'd left them, her right hand instantly started to tingle, break out in watery blisters, and itch. One of the lumps had opened and started to bleed. I told her to put Ivy Wash (a prevention solution) on it, so she went to the bathroom and rinsed off the calamine lotion.

I could count seven good-sized blisters on her right hand. She rinsed it, asking if I'd seen a spider or any bugs on my pants. I assured her she would have felt a spider bite, and anyway, a spider wouldn't have bitten her seven times so quickly. Lori was angry and said she had to leave for work. I carried the jeans and all of yesterday's clothes to the washing machine. I handled the pants—took them to the washing machine stuffed them in and turned on the water—and nothing happened to me. No bugs, spiders, or poison ivy-like rash.

Lori continued to grumble about the blisters and whatever it was I'd gotten into. The Ivy Wash and cortisone took the rash and swelling down, but it was still obvious to the eye. I still wonder if, as I removed the curse, something weird had stayed on my clothing. That is why you're supposed to cleanse yourself before and after performing the spells too. Now my clothes are washed, and it hasn't bothered us anymore.

The same day, 7:15 a.m.

I asked Lori again to tell me how her hand was and what had happened. Lori said she picked up my jeans to move them to the pile of clothes near the staircase and her hand started tingling and feeling very odd. She dropped the jeans and her hand was swelling and broken out. She said it was a little better and noted how odd it was that the rash had stung and appeared so quickly from no obvious cause.

I assured her that I had not been in the woods and that those were fresh jeans from my taking a shower. She said it was strange, all the odd things that have occurred since the Dibbuk Box arrived. I jokingly said, "Yes, blame your injury on the dibbuk—but I don't know why my clothes would do that to you."

October 14, 2004

I have no plan to reopen the cellar door or pry off the crawl space door until I can decide what to do with this thing. I believe it is safe behind the locks—and that my family and I will not be harmed by it either. Perhaps this odd ritual from the Wiccan can indeed help bring better times or just get life back to normal. After my bath, I changed my usual cologne for a different scent that I hadn't used in years—Patchouli. Maybe this new scent will throw the demon—or whatever it is—off my path. Even as I write this, the taste of metal has returned to my mouth. But I don't have hives, my ears are not burning, and I can see much better.

Finally feeling free of the spiritual oppression, I decided to look into Kevin's account of the massive police raid on his antique store just moments after his mother had touched the Dibbuk Box and suffered a stroke. Kevin claimed that he had no idea what had triggered the surprise onslaught by police, but his story left me feeling skeptical. Had he left out key facts? What was he hiding? Why had all those law enforcement officers descended on such a small store, confiscated Kevin's digital records, and then returned them a year later with a weak apology and no explanation? It wasn't credible. Something was wrong. I wondered whether there was some legal problem or violation in Kevin's recent past.

Kevin had told me he named his shop Addy's Market, wanting to keep the name of the defunct mom-and-pop booze-and-cigarette store that had occupied the space for decades. My Google search for Addy's Market in the Portland Business Directory identified the shop as a retail furniture store operated by Kevin Mannis. Items sold included artwork, restored antiques, and old furniture refurbished to have a trendy or folk art look. As expected, the information was pretty routine. I then typed in the key words "Addy's Market" and "Police," and found a news story about the shop formerly located at the address. The article described what had led up to the demise of that business several years earlier, ultimately freeing up the space for Kevin's use. Here's an excerpt from Portland's *Oregonian News* story of July 8, 1998, recovered from their online archive.

POLICE STING NABS SMALL-STORE OWNERS
BY DIONNE D. PEEPLES
OF *THE OREGONIAN* STAFF

Portland police Tuesday arrested a clerk and 10 small-store owners on accusations of buying stolen small-ticket items such as aspirin, film and cigarettes that had been taken from larger stores. After a three-month investigation that included an undercover sting, a Multnomah County grand jury issued 141 indictments against 11 people on July 1 for first-degree attempted theft by receiving [stolen property] and first-degree conspiracy to commit theft by receiving, said Cmdr. Bob

Kauffman of Central Precinct. Police investigated 27 stores and found seven that allegedly accepted goods stolen from stores such as Safeway and Costco. Those seven stores were: Dr. Bill's Learning Center, 350 W. Burnside St.; 3 Brothers' Market, 638 E. Burnside St.; Old Town Grocery, 100 N.W. Third Ave.; Payless Market, 18 N.W. Third Ave; Addy's Market, 221 W. Burnside St.; Junior's Grocery, 1026 S.W. Taylor St.; and Banzai Bento, 211 S.W. Sixth Ave. The investigation began in April after police received complaints from larger stores about thefts. Police said they found stolen items on drug addicts and determined they came from the larger stores, Kauffman said. The addicts told police they stole the items, then sold them to the smaller stores, Kauffman said. About 50 Portland police officers participated in [the] undercover sting. . . . [Kauffman] said store owners and employees knew they were buying stolen merchandise. "There's no doubt that they [the small shops] knew exactly what they were doing," he said.

That article made me wonder whether the Portland police had tried to do some type of a follow-up or repeat sting on the business three and a half years later, not realizing that a different person was operating a different type of business under the name at that address. Only the officers had walked into an antique shop, not a mom-and-pop convenience store. When Kevin had described the raid to me, he may have been exaggerating the number of people involved, but if his basic story was true, it sounded like someone had made a big mistake.

Although the raid was never reported in the paper and Kevin had no formal paperwork on the incident, several family members and Kevin's mother mentioned the event in passing during conversations without any prompt by me. This leads me to believe the event truly occurred— and if my hunch is right about the raid being a bumbled bust, I can understand why there would be no report or documentation in public sources. I felt like the police mystery was solved and the Dibbuk Box was safely sealed away. I found my health starting to improve, so I decided to examine the contents of the Dibbuk Box more closely from photographs I had taken. The Hebrew writing on the back intrigued me, but I had no idea how to read it. Then an item in the university's student newspaper caught my eye. The Jewish student group was offering a free Hebrew language workshop. It was open to anyone, so I went.

Rabbi Lynn Goldstein started the workshop by explaining some basics about this ancient language. One thing I learned is that, because the name of God is considered holy by Jews, the paper it is written on is also treated as sacred, so the name of God is not written down except in sacred texts or language books. When a text is damaged or is no longer needed, it is not just thrown away, but is placed in a special collection box known as a *genizah*. When the *genizah* is full, it is buried in the cemetery. I also learned that the Hebrew alphabet consists only of consonants and markings indicating the vowel sounds were added only relatively recently.

The rabbi explained that many Jews consider the Hebrew language to be mystical and extremely powerful because it comes directly from God: "The letters that make up God's name are known, but the pronunciation is not. The Hebrew language doesn't provide the vowels . . . The high priest of the Temple in Jerusalem was the only one to know how to pronounce God's ineffable name, and only pronounced it once a year on Yom Kippur, after proper preparation, and after fasting for twenty-four hours and in the Holy of Holies in the Temple in Jerusalem. And no one else would have heard it." The four-letter name of God (*yud-hay-vav-hay*) consists of silent letters; they have a sound only when there is a vowel associated with them. With no vowels in written Hebrew, only the priests would know how to pronounce the word. Rabbi Goldstein also explained that when the Temple was destroyed and the priesthood died out, the knowledge of the correct pronunciation of God's name was lost forever. In ancient times, God's name was pronounced to bring all of God's power down on the people. Calling on a name, then, is calling on the very essence of that person, in this case, the very essence of God. That's why the name of God is so powerful and why it is *chilul HaShem* (desecration of the name) to invoke his name for selfish or manipulative purposes. For that reason, Jews traditionally refer to God as *Adonai*, meaning "my Lord, or as *HaShem*, meaning "the name." In fact, when the name of God is written in Hebrew letters with vowels, the vowels from the word *Adonai* are used to remind the reader to substitute that word. Orthodox Jews traditionally use *HaShem* to avoid the possibility of desecrating even the substitute for the name of God.

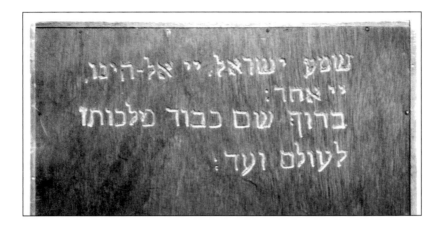

My lessons in Hebrew helped me understand why the Dibbuk Box might be endowed with power. To a mystic or a kabbalist, carving sacred Hebrew words would be enough to create power. In kabbalistic teachings, the twenty-two letters of the Hebrew alphabet are said to work with precise universal law, according to Daniel S. Krutt, a student of kabbalah whose wife was a graduate of our university's audiology program. Daniel provided me with several books, including *The Hebrew Alphabet: A Mystical Journey*, which explored the origin and significance of each letter.

I learned that *aleph*, the first letter of the Hebrew alphabet is silent—but why? One explanation is that it is silent because everything we accomplish emanates from stillness and silence. The *aleph* also begins the first name used for God in the Torah and is the primal force of creation; silence is universal unity and infinity. Daniel told me that each letter of the Hebrew alphabet has many stories. To a kabbalist, Hebrew letters, when written, invoke whatever they describe physically. I now saw the Hebrew writing on the Dibbuk Box with a new appreciation for its spiritual aspects.

In addition to her lessons on written Hebrew, Rabbi Goldstein offered spiritual insights into traditional Jewish beliefs. She told us that all events have a purpose known to God, and every action taken by each person will have an impact on all others. Those impacts can be harmful to another at times. She said it was like throwing a stone into the lake and seeing the ripples on the surface, but how that stone permanently changes the lake with the currents on the way down and the bottom by the stone lodging there. People and their actions are like the pebble in the lake. In another analogy, Rabbi Goldstein said that if a passenger has his own seat on a boat, that seat is his and no one else's, but if he drills a hole in his seat, water will rush into the boat and every one of his fellow passengers will be affected. It follows that every choice a person makes will affect the rest of humanity as all are connected in this world.

I learned that the word *shalom*, which is carved in the granite statue inside the box, means more than just "peace." It signifies an internal state of wholeness and completion—something not typically attainable, but rather a goal to be sought in life. I also learned that the Hebrew prayer carved on the back of the Dibbuk Box is the opening sentences of the Shema: *Shema Israel Adonai Eloheinu Adonai ehad* [Listen Israel, Adonai is our god, Adonai is one]. *Barukh sheim k'vod malkhuto l'olam va'ed* [Blessed be the name of his glorious kingdom for ever and ever].

In the Hebrew Bible, there are many words for the name of God, two of which are used in this prayer: *Adonai* and *Eloheinu*. Rabbi Y. Golomb, a British rabbinical scholar who had contacted me by e-mail after reading about the Dibbuk Box on the Internet, helped me to understand the significance of this prayer. "This prayer," he said, "is . . . familiar to almost every Jew who has learned something about their religion, and would be the last words that he or she would utter if they had the chance."

Carving these words on the back of the Dibbuk Box would give a degree of sacredness to this object and it would be unthinkable for its Jewish creator to not treat this item with the utmost respect and any practicing Jew who came across this item could not, in good conscience, bury the Dibbuk Box as it was reported that its creator had requested. Rabbi Golomb was extremely puzzled by the incongruence of such a request, pointing out that a knowledgeable Jewish woman would know not to request such a sacrilegious act. After examining the carved words of the Shema on the back panel he concluded that there was a kind of loophole to this incongruence within the Hebrew inscription of this prayer. The word pronounced *Adonai* is written not with the usual four letters, but as *yad-yad*, and the word *Eloheinu* has an unnecessary hyphen added between the second and third letters. Rabbi Golomb believes the carver made these alterations deliberately to allow the box to be treated as a lesser object. According to Jewish law, the words written in this manner have no sanctity. Although these precautions might seem trivial to many non-Jews, I discovered from my brief training in Hebrew that they are spiritually important to Jews. Based on the subtle alterations in spelling of key words in the prayer, Rabbi Golomb guessed this wooden box was created with the intention that it could one day be destroyed without any negative consequence.

Chapter Nine

Understanding the Dibbuk Box

NOW THAT I understood aspects of the Hebrew carving, I wanted to know more about the wooden container itself and its unusual method of opening. The Dibbuk Box doesn't have handles to open the front doors; instead, by pulling the lower drawer handle forward, the two doors above it automatically open. This design of not having pulls for opening the doors was completely new to me. I wondered whether it might be a type of opening mechanism commonly used for the *aron kodesh* (the cabinet used to hold Torah scrolls in a synagogue). While an *aron kodesh* wouldn't have a drawer whose opening mechanism would cause the doors to open, I wondered if they might use some kind of hidden opening mechanism. I looked at the websites of several companies that design and build synagogue furnishings and saw no evidence of special openers, but I did notice frequent use of grapes as a decorative motif. I later learned that cabinets like the Dibbuk Box were sold in the 1950s and '60s as liquor cabinets and found other examples of cabinets with similar opening mechanisms. Because this item was clearly not designed as a personal *aron kodesh* (which would not have had a drawer), it seemed likely that the original owner may have wanted a personal *aron*, or at least a special cabinet to hold religious items, and chose this one because of the prominent grape appliqués on the front doors. The owner then customized the cabinet by carving the Hebrew prayer on the back panel.

I also looked into the use of grapes as a decorative motif. Rabbi Barry Goodman of Or Shalom of Vancouver, British Columbia, explained that Jewish artists often use the symbol of grapes to represent personal freedom. As slaves in Egypt, the Jews were made to grow wine for others, but as a free people, Jews could grow their own grapes. According to Rabbi Goodman, grapes are a popular decorative symbol in the Jewish community. With those questions answered, I still wondered about the original owner's reason for buying the cabinet and how she planned to use it. I was to receive an interesting possibility from a young woman who was seeking her own answers about the Box.

Rebecca A. Edery of Brooklyn, New York, wrote to me through my eBay account. For this twenty-nine-year-old Jewish woman, the Dibbuk Box story had rekindled memories that had been buried for years. Her father, who had died twelve years earlier, was a kabbalist, "although he kept it a secret," she said. "But I grew up believing that 'these things' are possible, so I truly believe this whole episode of the Dibbuk Box. I come from a deeply religious Jewish family, where there is definite belief in the afterlife, reincarnation, and the tortured soul staying down on earth because [it] cannot go to either heaven or hell." Rebecca said her father had been drawn away bit by bit over the years by the mysteries of kabbalah "until he was pulled from our secular world into a world of his own creation."

I considered Rebecca's life story as a cautionary tale for me, as I seemed to be drawn more and more into my otherworldly connection with the mysterious artifact. Rebecca told me it had been quite painful for her, as a young girl, to see her father drawn into a mystical world she did not understand. Her mother had grown unhappy with her husband's emotional absence and eventually moved to Israel, leaving Rebecca to care for her increasingly withdrawn father.

> My father practiced kabbalah in private. He didn't let anyone know of his learnings and practice, and [he] was viewed by [everyone] who knew him well as a holy man. He scared me sometimes, because of how quiet and far-off he was. Nevertheless, people came to him with sick children, [and] marital and emotional problems, to which he gave very specific advice that never failed. His work with others left me with a very sensitive and questioning soul. My dad kept a book he called "The Segulah Book." It had a remedy for everything. He died when I was fifteen years old. After his death, and me being a teenager, I looked for this book but never found it. I know it is somewhere in my family's

possession, but even if I located it, I couldn't use it myself; its use would
require a kabbalah expert.

In her e-mails, Rebecca recalled that her dad's death had been difficult
because she'd been too young to understand him or the mysteries that
occupied him day and night. He was a father who connected with his
congregations, but was emotionally withdrawn from her. This left her
with many questions.

She had put all these memories away until my Dibbuk Box postings
on the Internet caught her attention and reopened the door to her past.
Now she wanted to know more about the kind of mysteries that had
occupied her father so completely. She hoped the Dibbuk Box could lead
her to both understanding and peace. Rebecca's past experiences with
her father's work caused her to look at the Dibbuk Box from a mystical
Jewish perspective. As a result, she became a great help to me—perhaps
the greatest help of anyone, to date—as I sought to understand this artifact that had come into my possession.

Among other things, Rebecca had a theory about the original purpose of the Dibbuk Box. She believed it was a small ark, an *aron kodesh*,
meant to hold a small Torah scroll. Some Jews might have such an item
in their home, a small version of the large *aron kodesh* found in any synagogue that holds the congregation's full-size Torah scrolls. However,
given that this box also has a small drawer on the bottom, which would
not be present on an *aron kodesh*, and is decorated with grapes, it seems
equally reasonable that the box was originally intended to hold wine and
other items used in the Kiddush, the blessing over candle-lighting and
over wine and bread to sanctify Shabbat and other holidays.

Since we had first spoken, Rebecca told me, she had been unable to
stop thinking about the Dibbuk Box mystery. To her and a number of
others who had visited the Dibbuk Box website, there was no question
that the wood container was a kind of *aron kodesh*, or ark, and not an
ordinary wine box. Rebecca explained that an *aron kodesh* the size of the
Dibbuk Box is used during *shiva*, the seven-day mourning period following the death of a family member. The large ark in the synagogue cannot be moved, so smaller portable arks are brought to the homes of the
bereaved for the evening service held in the home during the period of
mourning.

Rebecca wrote, "My father once told me that people can use kabbalah for their own personal gain, and it can also cause harm to others. The Hebrew term for this is called a *segulah*. My father was very into performing such *segulot* [plural form]. But again, everything was kept very confidential, and his every intent was to help heal and protect those that came to him for help. When I told my brother-in-law [a rabbi] last night how I thought your box was an *aron kodesh*, he said that giving it a proper burial is the right thing to do."

A *segulah* is an action that is thought to change a person's fortune. Some common *segulot* are the idea that carrying the baby into the room for the *brit milah* (circumcision ceremony) will bring fertility or that wearing the jewelry a bride wore for her wedding will bring luck in finding a husband. Reciting the Song of Songs every day for forty days or praying at the Western Wall every day for forty days are thought to bring a favorable response to a prayer. Many of these are like old wives' tales and many come from old traditions, in a way, no different than the traditions of knocking on wood or carrying a rabbit's foot for good luck.

In considering whether there was any significance in the materials used for the items inside the Dibbuk Box, specifically the stone statue, I also looked at the issue of using objects in Jewish magic. I learned that, as with many folk traditions, amulets and effigies were a typical part of Jewish magic and superstition, but I wondered about the use of stone in particular. In the book of Exodus there are instructions for building the tabernacle, including instructions to make an altar of acacia wood overlaid with bronze and another of acacia wood overlaid with gold. One of the reasons Jews were instructed to give gold for the construction of the tabernacle was to atone for the sin of the golden calf. Another reason, according to *midrash*, was that some things God created were, in essence, too good for man, and gold is one of those things. It is also interesting that when the Second Temple was built in Jerusalem, most of the temple complex was built of local stone, but the temple itself was built of imported white marble. Even today, objects that are meant to have special meaning, especially objects that have a religious meaning, are typically made of the best materials. The stone statue, made of especially beautiful granite in unusual colors, with an inlay of beautiful metal, makes it especially appropriate as a devotional object or item of mystical significance. Although perhaps it was not originally created as a focus for prayer, the original owner, who apparently engaged in some nontraditional practices, may have used it in that way.

In some pagan traditions, higher quality metals, rare stones, and crystals or gems, can act as spiritual cleansers, which would mean that the stone statue would have been able to cleanse the other objects in the box, which may have been considered impure—the locks of hair, the pennies, and the dried rose—and therefore unfit to be placed in a box containing sacred objects.

Of all the items in the Dibbuk Box, the one that seemed the most unusual was the stone statue. The coins, the locks of hair, and the dried rose seemed to be keepsakes, and the kiddush cup and candlesticks had clear functions, but the meaning of the stone statue was unclear. Based on the assumption that the first owner of the box had been engaged in some kind of magical or mystical practices, it seemed likely that this object had a magical or mystical significance to her. The object itself is made of four granite stones, each a different color. Each stone is beautiful by itself; together they are stunning. The statue is the largest piece found in the box, and must have been time-consuming to create. To better understand the granite statue, I decided to create a replica. I located a supplier in Michigan that had an excellent selection of granites from around the world. Comparing the stone in my statue to their selection, I discovered that the statue was made of very expensive rare granites, none of which are found in the United States. Dixie Cut Stone mostly does large orders, but I was fortunate they had the right types of granites in small remnant pieces—just enough to recreate the stone statue.

I tried to chisel Hebrew letters in the granite's surface using a stone-mason's point chisel and hammer. The granite was so hard that I shattered the stone. I tried a second time with the same results. It seemed an impossible task. Next I tried using a diamond-tipped drill bit and a power drill. It was no easy task, but the new method worked. The diamond drill bit cut into the stone and left a perfectly smooth trench with no sign of chipping. On the original stone, small scoop marks along the edges of the letters suggest that the carver used a hand chisel rather than power tools. The letters had obviously been carved with great control and accuracy; the carver must have possessed unusual skill.

Creating a copy pro-
vided wonderful insights
into the object's construction. The piece of stone
on which the word *shalom*
is carved is glued to the
base and to a small piece
of stone in front, and the
piece behind it is glued to
the front piece. Though the
piece appears top-heavy, its
stone base keeps the whole
thing from toppling over.
The statue is eternally off
balance. What's more, the

statue possesses a kinetic energy at the molecular level, because of the
quartz found within granite. Quartz has the unusual capacity to retain
energy, like a battery, so if one were to seek a potential power source
within the Dibbuk Box, this granite object would suit the purpose.

The wine cup is a silver-plated double jigger made by the Leonard Silver Company, a fairly rare item I have found in antique shops
and online auctions. The cup shows a great amount of wear and damage from use; the lip of the cup is stressed with cracks from acid in the
wine. According to the Chelsea Historical Society, Leonard Silver was
founded by Leonard Florence (a son of Russian-Jewish immigrants) in
1963 and operated in Chelsea, Massachusetts. The company specialized
in inexpensive silver-plated hollowware, and many of the early pieces are
now considered antiques. The wine cup, in a Jewish home, would have
served as a kiddush cup—used to hold wine over which the blessing is
said on Shabbat and other holidays.

Another piece of the puzzle came to me from a professor of history
with an interest in religion. She wrote to me from Colorado about her
interest in the Dibbuk Box, which reminded her of an old folk tradition
she had heard of. She told me that her mother was an immigrant—half
Greek and half Prussian—which provided her two cultural perspectives
to view this spiritual object.

Dybbuk boxes can be used in a couple of ways.... You can put together the elements of a curse and energize the spell with the trapped spirit of a demon (or a very bad spirit of some kind) ... or the spell can be done in the same way that Babylonian demon bowls worked. Two clay bowls were sealed together to form a round container, [inside of which was placed] the element for a spell or a curse. A prayer was written on the exterior and interior, which detailed the desired effect. [Some of these prayers] appeared to be gibberish, so the actual words may have been orally delivered at the time of casting the magic spell. The container was then buried in a graveyard in order to trap a [good or bad] ghost inside and fuel the spell.

The first remembrance I have of a Dybbuk Box story was in Germany in the early seventies. I heard the story orally from my grandmother's best friend when I was young. My Oma [grandmother] was Greek and married a Prussian and they lived in Berlin where I grew up. My Oma still believed some of the old ways of her ancestors, and we spoke often about Greek history, mythology and religious ethos. Her [Jewish] friend was sometimes with us and had similar interests. [We had been talking about the Greeks' practice] of cursing their enemies. [Oma's friend] added the story of [another] friend she knew, who had [created] a cursed box. The story [told] of a woman who cursed the Nazis with a spell kept in the graveyard of her village.

I also heard of a woman in Kyoto [Japan] who used such a spell to avenge her daughter, and her family house is still cursed.

The Babylonian version . . . was used at least twice [in recorded history] to win the heart and affections of a girl [whom a young man loved]. [The words of the spell] sound almost hysterical with love.

Greek history is littered with boxes such as this. One is supposed to be near my family graveyard in Mikonos. I have been looking [further into the subject] over the last few months, as I have been wanting to write a ghost story set in my husband's ancestral home.

Oddly enough, one of the items from inside the Dibbuk Box led me to a fictional account of a haunted box. The black cast-iron candlestick has four legs designed as octopus-like tentacles, an interesting design because sea creatures have been depicted throughout time as both mystical and powerful. The material and construction of the candlestick resemble the cheaply, mass-produced candlesticks of a hundred years ago. I was able to determine from antique online resources that the manufacturer was the Peking Glass Company and this candlestick was manufactured circa 1890 and shipped from China. The company went out of business after the advent of electricity made the need for candlesticks all but obsolete and a fire in the 1920s destroyed much of the company's facilities.

In researching historic uses of sea-creature motifs in occult objects, I did a Google search for the words "occult," "tentacles," "haunted," "Jewish," and "box." Interestingly, I found a short story by Tani Jantsang titled "The Statement of Richard Daniel Upton," which originally appeared in the magazine *Cthulhu Cultus* in 1995. The story involves a haunted box found by a man whose father had begged him to destroy it and then disappeared.

> "Box" really wasn't quite accurate. Chest would have been more appropriate. A great carven chest made from one of the harder woods. [Because it was] too heavy to be moved, necessity dictated that I, like my father, examine it where it stood. If only I had heeded my father's instructions and destroyed the thing on sight. Had I done that and not opened the cursed thing's lid! Oh . . . but open it, I did.
>
> The first thing I saw when I lifted the lid was an envelope bearing my name in my father's characteristic spidery scrawl. Within was a note from my father:
>
> Dear Richard:
>
> If you are reading this, then the worst is true and something terrible has happened to me. Ah son! This was supposed to be a simple journey to my father's house. Inspect the property, speak to the attorney, and return home. Now I fear it might be the death of me.
>
> When I arrived in Arkham, it occurred to me that if we were to sell the house, father's personal effects that were left in the house would have to be gone through. That was my intent in coming into the attic. Here it was that I found this cursed, haunted box, and all that it contains. Richard, for the love of God, DO NOT examine the contents of this box AT ALL! Destroy it and ALL that it contains! Since I have been in this house, horrible things have happened. I have been followed, watched, and today I was accosted on the street!

Son, I beg you, destroy this evil thing and all of the abominable
artifacts and information it contains. Good luck, my son. Godspeed.
Your father.

There are many myths and folk stories involving magical objects—
the Holy Grail, Excalibur, the armor of Achilles and Beowulf, Thor's
magic hammer, and Cupid's bow. Fewer, but perhaps more powerful, are
stories of an object associated with evil. Mythology, folklore, and literature are full of examples of people imprisoning a spirit inside a container.
In Middle Eastern folklore and mythology as told in *A Thousand and One
Arabian Nights*, the jinn can be released from its lamp or bottle only when
summoned, and several stories involve evil jinn that are imprisoned in a
bottle. In Greek mythology, the gods seal up the evils of the world in a jar
and give it to Pandora with instructions not to open the jar, but she cannot contain her curiosity and looses the evils into the world. In Jewish
and Christian mythology, Solomon's Seal was a mythical ring that could
imprison demons. A modern twist to this ancient tale is J. R. R. Tolkien's
Lord of the Rings trilogy in which magical rings imbue the owner with
unlimited life, strength, and power. Another example is the *Ghostbuster*
movies, in which paranormal scientists capture and imprison evil spirits
in New York City. Even children's literature has had it run of spiritual
beings and magical objects, most recently with J. K. Rowling's *Harry
Potter* series, which includes many creatures and objects that can be
traced to historical folklore, including the sorcerer's stone (or philoso-
pher's stone), an object mentioned in writings as early as 300 AD that
was supposed to grant its owner eternal life. The fact that these ideas are
spread throughout folklore, mythology, fables, and folk traditions suggests that people want to believe that we can contain and perhaps even
protect ourselves from evil. It seems that the Dibbuk Box is part of this
long tradition.

Chapter Ten

The Kirksville Connection

A SIGNIFICANT PIECE of information was presented to me over lunch with my mother-in-law, Joan Bauman. She lives nearby, and I often have lunch at her home. She knew I had something called the Dibbuk Box, but she had never asked about it. One day in November of 2004, she suddenly asked, "What is this Dibbuk Box? Are your children in any kind of danger because of it?" Her question caught me off guard; I assured her that the kids were perfectly safe, but that didn't seem to satisfy her and she asked me to tell her more about this strange item. With just thirty minutes left in my lunch hour, I didn't have time to go into much detail, and if I told her the full story, it would not have put her at ease. So I provided her with some general facts: it was a Jewish cabinet of sorts, going back to the time of the Holocaust. It had ended up here after several previous owners claimed it had paranormal qualities. I was researching the artifact and trying to locate the Jewish family that created it. No danger, the kids were perfectly safe to be near it. I hoped this would be enough to satisfy her curiosity and reduce her concern, and that the discussion would end there, but it didn't.

Joan stared out past me, as if she were trying to collect a memory. After a few moments, she focused back on me and said, "Oh, yes, I remember that. I was a young girl then, but I remember that." I was confused, "Remember what?" I asked. "I remember that there were all those children, and the Jewish people on that boat trying to get here," she said. "It was in the papers every day for weeks. In the end, they were all sent back to certain death in Europe."

I thought Joan had misunderstood what I was talking about; I had said nothing about a boat headed to America. Joan told me there was a large vessel, a luxury liner, that was bringing Jewish families here to escape Hitler. "There were almost a thousand on board," she said. "But no matter how hard they tried, they were not allowed to land here because of that man. He wanted the Jews to be sent back, and they were. That's all I remember, except that they were all imprisoned or killed when they returned."

I was thinking that this man must have been pretty powerful to have that kind of authority over fleeing refugees. Joan continued, "He'd been involved with all those Jewish children who weren't allowed to flee to America, they say almost 20,000 in all. It was definitely the same man who stopped them." I replied, "Oh, I see," but I was confused. I didn't see at all what this man, whoever he was, had to do with the Dibbuk Box. I smiled, told her I appreciated her help and I'd best be going back to work.

Then it happened. There was a thunderous crash and the sound of shattering glass and dishes. My heart racing, I jumped to the side and stared at the dining table next to me, which had been set so nicely for dinner that evening. The glass chandelier had crashed down onto the table, breaking glassware and plates and throwing silverware across the table and onto the floor. I looked up to where the chandelier had hung just seconds before. Somehow it had come free—I still don't know how—and fallen about five feet straight down. All of the delicate glass pieces of the chandelier were intact, but nearly everything on the table was now broken.

We picked through the clutter and threw out the remains of the dinner set. My father-in-law easily reattached the unharmed chandelier, commenting that if it had to fall, he was glad it had fallen now rather than that evening, when our family would be joining them for dinner. It seemed irrational, but I wondered whether the chandelier falling had anything to do with this man who prevented Jews from escaping to America. Was this some kind of a sign? I was growing use to strangeness in everything that had to do with this Jewish cabinet, so why not?

A little research on the Internet gave me some more information. In 1939, the German ocean liner MS *St. Louis* had sailed from Hamburg carrying 937 Jewish German refugees. After being denied entry to Cuba, the captain tried to land in Florida, but was turned away. I learned that the United States had enacted immigration quotas in 1924 that were designed to restrict immigration of southern and eastern Europeans, East Asians, and Asian Indians. I also learned that the law's strongest supporters were heavily influenced by theories of eugenics and racial hygiene. In looking at information on the eugenics movement in the United States, I ran across a familiar name: Harry Laughlin.

From my museum work, I knew the Laughlin name was long associated with the osteopathic profession, though I knew of no family members named Harry or Harold. George Laughlin was an early osteopathic physician who had married the daughter of the founder of osteopathic medicine and had taught at the osteopathic school. Later George Laughlin was president of the medical school. Two of his brothers (William and Earl) had also become osteopathic physicians. There are several buildings in Kirksville named for the Laughlin family. I had never heard, however, of a Harry Laughlin. I wondered if there was a connection, and I found one.

I learned that Harry Hamilton Laughlin was another brother of George Laughlin. He had been director of the Eugenics Record Office of the Department of Genetics of the Carnegie Institute of Washington, DC, from 1921 until 1940. He had served as the eugenics expert for the Committee on Immigration and Naturalization of the US House of Representatives from 1921 to 1931, and at the time the Immigration Act of 1924 had been passed—the law that resulted in the boatload of Jewish refugees being turned away from the shores of the United States in 1938. Digging a little deeper on the MS *St. Louis* and Harry Laughlin, I learned that when the passengers requested permission to leave Cuba, their temporary port, and land in Florida, Harry Laughlin sent a report to Congress reminding them that accepting these refugees would go against the immigration laws recently passed. In another incident, Harry Laughlin halted negotiations to accept Jewish children as refugees.

It was just moments after my mother-in-law had mentioned this man that her chandelier had come crashing down. Was her recollection of this incident related to the Dibbuk Box? I wondered why I had never heard of Harry Laughlin and his connection with the eugenics movement and World War II. I wanted to learn more. I learned that Truman State University holds Harry Laughlin's papers and their library's website includes a brief biography. Through this and other sources I learned some details about the life of Harry Laughlin and of his connection to the Holocaust.

Harry Hamilton Laughlin was born in Oskaloosa, Iowa, on March 11, 1880, the eighth child of George Laughlin, who later became a minister for a Kirksville church and language teacher at the First District Normal School (teacher's college) in Kirksville, Missouri, which is now Truman State University. Harry grew up in Kirksville and three of his brothers studied at the school of osteopathic medicine in Kirksville and became physicians. Harry graduated from the Normal School and worked as a public school teacher, principal, and superintendent before joining the faculty of the Normal School, where he taught agriculture from 1907 to 1910.

Harry's older brother George Jr., an osteopathic physician, had put his knowledge of biology into a sideline business of breeding livestock. George bred Jersey cows so well that much of the herd around the world today is descended from his herd. Individual cows sold for up to $3,000 at auction, about the cost of a two-story brick home at the time. George Jr. was equally talented in breeding hogs. Harry focused primarily on breeding chickens and racehorses. Because many people kept fowl and small gardens to feed their families, Harry was able to build up a lucrative business breeding chickens for meat and eggs. As part of his breeding business, Harry kept extensive and detailed charts showing the results of his selected breeding, and as a faculty member at the local college, Harry would often present public lectures to farmers and local people interested in improving their own flocks or in purchasing hen stock directly from Harry. I learned from materials in the Laughlin papers that in speeches delivered around the state of Missouri, Harry was vehement about the need to cull (kill off) the inferior offspring from his breeding birds. He argued that keeping all the hens alive and with the flock might seem like a money-saving idea in the short-term, but in the long run it would dilute the quality of birds until only the mediocre remained, without the desired qualities of meat, eggs, or physical attractiveness. He advised farmers to breed only the best birds in order to maintain consistently first-rate flocks. The same was true for all farm animals, Laughlin believed. Farmers aiming for top results should expect to cull about 10 percent of their stocks regularly.

Sometime around 1908, Harry started reflecting more on the human breed. Perhaps reflecting on his experiences in teaching school children who showed a range of ability, Harry concluded that human beings, like farm animals, also needed species culling to prevent genetically inferior and "feeble-minded" persons from having offspring. He didn't believe that killing citizens already afflicted with inferior traits would be necessary, but argued that they should be sterilized, even if they had to be sterilized involuntarily. One article I ran across included information on Laughlin's proposal of using a small chamber that could be pumped full of carbon monoxide to rid society of newborn children of the inferior population in a "humane" manner.

As early as 1907, Laughlin's interest in livestock breeding led him to open a correspondence with Charles Davenport, director for the Station for Experimental Evolution at Cold Spring Harbor, New York, and in the next years, Laughlin's work began to focus on humans rather than livestock. The Laughlin papers contain charts published in Germany in the 1930s that mirrored Laughlin's charts for the genetic breeding of chickens for quality traits, but were used to show that individuals from certain countries were more inclined to be what eugenicists called "genetically inferior" or "socially inadequate." When Davenport established the Eugenics Record Office, he invited Laughlin to be its superintendent, a position he filled from October 1910 to 1921. In 1921, Laughlin became director of the Eugenics Record Office and remained in that position until 1940. Laughlin also served as the eugenics expert for the U.S. House of Representatives Committee on Immigration and Naturalization from 1921 to 1931. In that position, he was instrumental in development of the Immigration Act of 1924, which established quotas designed to restrict immigration from areas considered undesirable.

In 1922, Harry Laughlin published *Eugenical Sterilization in the United States*, a book that detailed sterilization laws in thirty states and provided model sterilization laws that, he explained, would allow "seizing certain individuals proven by pedigree-study to be potential parents of degenerate or defective offspring, and by surgical operation or medical treatment, destroying their reproductive powers." In his 1922 model eugenical sterilization law, Laughlin defined the "defective strains" as the "(1) feeble-minded; (2) insane (including the psychopathic); (3) criminalistics (including the delinquent and wayward); (4) epileptic; (5) inebriate (including drug-habitués); (6) diseased (including the tuberculous, the syphilitic, the leprous, and others with chronic, infectious and legally segregable diseases); (7) blind (including those with seriously impaired vision); (8) deaf (including those with seriously impaired hearing) (9) deformed (including the crippled); and dependent (including orphans, ne'er-do-wells, the homeless, tramps and paupers)." In a 1929 article for a German scientific journal, Laughlin updated information on legislative developments in the United States, claiming that "It has been proven that sterilization is necessary to the well being of the state," and stressing the need for "prohibition of procreation for certain members of degenerate tribes" (i.e., people of certain nationalities or religions) in order to allow the state "to get rid of the burden of its degenerate members." In the Harry Laughlin Papers, I also found several of Harry's personal letters from 1935 to regular American citizens who had made inquiries on whether they should choose to be sterilized. Harry freely recommended sterilization as a precaution for people with cleft palates and for white men who learned there was "black blood" running through their veins from some distant relation.

By 1925, when Germany rejoined the international eugenics movement, German and American eugenicists were working closely, led by Harry Laughlin and Charles Davenport at the Eugenics Record Office, and by 1930 the United States and Germany were the leading forces in the international eugenics movement. When the International Union for the Scientific Investigation of Population Problems organized its 1935 conference in Berlin, Americans Harry Laughlin and Clarence Campbell served as vice presidents of the conference. Laughlin was unable to travel to Berlin, but he contributed a paper and sent an exhibit. Historian Stefan Kühl, in *The Nazi Connection*, writes that "American eugenicists were conscious and proud of their impact on legislation in Nazi Germany." The eugenicists knew that the German law was "designed after the Model Eugenic Sterilization Law developed by Harry Laughlin in 1922. The German law followed Laughlin's proposal in terms of basic guidelines, but it was slightly more moderate." The so-called Nuremburg Laws of 1935 ruled that only those of German heritage and blood could be German citizens. In 1936, Hitler enacted laws to kill the disabled to prevent weakening of the German race, and in 1937 he passed laws to sterilize black children. Soon all Jews in Germany and German-held countries had to register their locations. Laughlin proudly wrote in the *Eugenics News*, of which he was the coeditor, that the new German laws had a "familiar ring to them."

Kühl also explains that the American eugenicists were "especially impressed by Nazi propaganda that promoted the ideals of race improvement," noting that "Harry Laughlin coordinated efforts to introduce Nazi sterilization propaganda to the American people." Laughlin used his position in the Eugenics Record Office to distribute propaganda, including *Erbkrank* (*Heredity Defective*), a 1935 Nazi propaganda film that he had edited and translated and that he hoped to have shown at churches, high schools, clubs, and colleges. The film singled out the Jew as Germany's "degenerate" and the key source of social and health problems. Some of Laughlin's actions were embarrassing to his colleagues, especially the Carnegie Foundation, a chief source of his funding, which reprimanded him for his apparent anti-Semitism. At the same time, scientists and Congress were discovering that much of Laughlin's research was either botched or outright bogus; he had failed to use proper representative populations in collecting most of his data. In 1939, the Carnegie Foundation drastically cut his funding, and Laughlin took the hint. He retired from the Eugenics Record Office and returned to Kirksville, followed by a railroad boxcar full of his papers, magazines, letters, honorary German degree, and discredited research. Shortly after returning to Kirksville, Harry Laughlin developed epilepsy, one of the conditions that should have led to his involuntary sterilization under the laws he had helped Congress to develop and pass. Laughlin was quickly abandoned by his eugenics colleagues, and he died in 1943 from a massive heart attack. Harry Laughlin's grave is marked only by the initials "HHL" on a small stone block. Had he not been laid to rest in the family plot of his father, Harry Laughlin's burial place might have been forgotten altogether.

I was shocked to learn the story of Harry Laughlin, and I wondered why it was not more widely known. Kirksville is the birthplace of osteopathic medicine, where Andrew Taylor Still perfected his new science and opened the first school of osteopathic medicine, and the home of the Museum of Osteopathic Medicine. Various members of the Laughlin family were closely associated with the school, and the family name lives on through those connections. But the name of Harry Laughlin, who used his scientific researches not for the benefit of mankind as a whole, but to promote a false ideal of racial purity, seems to be largely forgotten. Although historians have studied the history of the eugenics movement both in America and throughout the world, the details of that sordid episode in our history seem largely unknown to most people. This story, and the link it provides between Kirksville and the Holocaust, is echoed in the link between Kirksville and the Dibbuk Box. My research into that mysterious box had led me to Harry Laughlin's grave and my discovery of his anti-Semitic deeds. The more I thought about it, the more I felt that the Dibbuk Box had come to rural Missouri for a purpose—to provide an opportunity to share the story of Harry Laughlin and his legacy as an inspiration for the racial purity laws of Nazi Germany. The golem in Jewish folklore was summoned to protect the Jews from their enemies, and the women who may have summoned a spirit in the late 1930s were inspired by those stories. Perhaps the purpose of the Dibbuk Box today is to play a role in spreading the history of the American eugenics movement.

Believing that, as one rabbi told me, there are no accidents in this world and each of us is connected on life's journey, I sensed that the Dibbuk Box had somehow been sent on its most recent journey for that precise mission. After talking to a rabbi and friends in the scientific community, I decided to take their advice and try to put the box to rest, but not necessarily eliminate its energy altogether, by encasing it in a container of acacia wood and gold. Scientist Bobby Parker of the Virginia Scientific Research Association (VSRA), whose association was founded in 1992 to disprove the existence of ghosts by scientific means, indicated that gold-leafing the holding container of the Dibbuk Box was probably the smartest thing I could do since gold is a strong conductive metal and I might be dealing with an electromagnetic field event. He said, "The gold will cause a grounding effect and nullification of the embedded resonance patterns in the wood [of the Dibbuk Box]."

According to the book of Exodus, acacia wood and gold were used to create the Ark of the Covenant, which held the tablets containing the Ten Commandments. I decided to build my "ark" of this same wood and to line it with 24-karat gold. It would be expensive, but I felt it was worth the trouble and expense if I could return the Dibbuk Box to a state of calm inactivity. The biggest problem would be acquiring the materials. Acacia wood is harder than many metals because it grows slowly and tightly in harsh desert regions of the world, such as the Middle East and Australia. It is almost impervious to drought, rain, bugs, and heat. The cost of shipping enough wood from halfway around the world would be prohibitive. Then I stumbled across a closer source. One of the

many hurricanes to batter Florida in 2004 had toppled an acacia that had been planted from seed shortly after World War II. The tree had grown to be beautiful and fragrant, the pride of its owner, but after the hurricane, the fallen tree was hauled off by the owner of a sawmill, who hoped to get a good price for the wood. As it turned out, the wood of this tree had an unusual characteristic, perhaps a result of growing in a wet semitropical region. The tree contained several elongated air pockets, making the sawed lumber unsuitable for highly crafted pieces of woodwork, but irrelevant to me. In the end, the seller sold it all to me for considerably less than I had expected to pay.

Now I needed enough gold to coat about three square feet of surface, the size of the interior of the ark. Gold prices had been dropping for several years, and I learned that the government of Thailand was taking advantage of the country's cheap labor to sell gold leaf at a discounted rate. I was able to purchase enough gold leaf to coat the entire interior of the ark with two or three coats of pure gold. The first challenges were resolved.

Next I had to find someone to design and build the box. The container had to be of a shape similar to the Dibbuk Box, but enough larger that the box could nest inside it. To do the work, I chose Amish craftsmen who lived nearby. When I arrived at their home to discuss the job, the sky in all directions wore a strange cloud cover. Lightening rippled and played across the cloud in veins and branches, at times lashing suddenly to the ground with thunderous explosions. I drove up to find the head of the family, "Yukey" (an Amish nickname), and several of his neighbors surveying this strange act of nature. As I joined them to share their silent awe, a bolt struck about a hundred yards away. Shaking his head, Yukey said nature was "not right" for such activity. "Best to be indoors," he said. Everyone went indoors and I followed with a scrap of paper in my hand.

I showed him a drawing of what I wanted and asked whether he could do the job. Yukey said he could do it, but told me the wood I had brought was not the standard oak, walnut, or pine he typically used. I explained that this wood was very unusual, that it was the same wood the Jews had used to build parts of the tabernacle, as described in the Bible.

Yukey looked puzzled, but gave no reply. He asked me to leave the wood slabs and the replica box so he could start work on the project. A few days later I received a call. Yukey said he had never worked with such a difficult wood. He had set his planer to shave it down into even boards of the proper width, but he couldn't make even a dent in it. He suggested I talk to Mr. Miller, a local Mennonite craftsman who might have better luck getting the wood ready for his carpentry work.

After Mr. Miller had worked on the wood for a week, he phoned me with the results. He had indeed managed to shave the pieces down into boards of equal thickness, but the task had been a tough one and had almost destroyed his electric planer. He asked me not to bring him that type of wood for any future projects.

I took the three prepared boards back to Yukey, who started the job using the Dibbuk Box as his model for the interior design. He had seemed unsure about all the lettering on the back, but seemed to relax a little when I explained it was just a prayer to God in Hebrew.

A few weeks later, one of Yukey's boys had come by buggy to my home and left a message in the door telling me the project was finished and asking me to come get the replica box and the acacia-wood container. When I arrived, I noticed that the daughter, Esther, had a thick wadding of gauze wrapped around her hand. I asked what happened. She said she'd been hauling a bucket of boiling water into the house—a chore she does daily—when the water seemed to explode from the bucket onto her hand, burning her severely. I asked when the incident had happened. She told me it was just after I'd dropped off the wood and small cabinet for my project. Odd.

I said I had come to pick up the items and asked if her father was around, and she told me her father was home but not available for visits just yet. I asked if he was all right and she said he is getting better, just still a little dizzy. She said that after finishing the box, he had headed to the barn to do a few chores in the loft. Climbing down a ladder, he was convinced he had reached the ground and so stepped off. In fact, he was nowhere near ground level. He had fallen backward, striking the back of his head on a wheelbarrow, which caused a bad gash. When they found him, he kept saying that he just knew he was on the last rung of the ladder and stepped off, only to discover he was almost three feet up in the air. He couldn't explain how he had misjudged so badly. Esther continued: "My mother thought it best you come right away to get your stuff. You can pay my father later when he's better." I had the distinct impression that the family didn't want those strange Jewish boxes around the house anymore. My possessions and I were being shooed away.

I felt bad about their misfortunes and despite Yukey's initial refusal, I insisted on paying him double the agreed-upon price, which was worth it to me to finally have the outside sealing container in hand.

From there on, I would do the final tasks alone. First I gave the wooden ark a tung oil finish. Then I set about laying the gold leaf. I knew the gold layer had to be as thick as possible, but I didn't want to risk wasting any of the materials. I learned that the glue used to attach the gold leaf is called gum arabic, which turns out to be pure sap of the acacia tree—an interesting coincidence. It took me several hours each night for several weeks to complete the gold-leafing process, working slowly and steadily with tweezers. The work was painstaking, but the results were wondrous. A bright, inviting, warm glow seemed to emanate from the ark.

It was time to move the original Dibbuk Box from its sealed storage area of the crawl space of our rental house next door. As I worked my way through the series of locked doors, I was shocked to see that during the months since I had last been there, an odd coating of white, powdery mold had coated the ceiling of the cellar. Many spiders seemed to have died in their webs from this mysterious white powder. I pulled off the trapdoor to the crawl space and saw hundreds of house centipedes. They seemed to be drawn toward the Dibbuk Box, but did not actually go onto it. I had been told that kabbalah says insects are drawn to energy and power. These seemed to bask in its presence, but my sudden appearance sent them scurrying in all directions.

Crawling across the dry soil, I thought about the fact that rain had not touched this ground since the house went up over a hundred years ago, so I was unprepared for what happened when I scooped up the cardboard container that held the Dibbuk Box wrapped in bubble wrap. The cardboard was absolutely dripping water. Had the Dibbuk Box not been wrapped in plastic, a good bit of water damage would have occurred. But it made no sense to find this dripping wet box in an otherwise dehydrated and bone-dry crawl space. I hauled the Dibbuk Box free of its wet container and took it to the house. To this day I do not understand how the Dibbuk Box container could have become so saturated that water literally ran out of it.

Finally ready to seal the Dibbuk Box in its finished container, I called my family over to take a final look. I slipped the Dibbuk Box into the Amish-made ark; it fit beautifully and the gold tones reflecting off the reddish wood of the Dibbuk Box seemed to glow and bring it to life. I was caught up in the beauty of it all, then my son interrupted the magic of the moment by asking if I had caught the foul odor of piss.

Sniffing the air, I realized he was right! It seemed to come out of nowhere. We could all smell it. I shut the doors of the ark, sealing the Dibbuk Box within, and carted the whole thing to the attic. When I returned and saw their worried expressions, I made light of it all. "Well maybe the box isn't too pleased at being sealed within its new home," I said, but I didn't really care if the box wasn't pleased. It was done and to this day, the mysterious wine cabinet has stayed in its gold-lined acacia ark.

For whatever reason, the Dibbuk Box's energy seemed to have calmed. Shadows and trailing flashes of light were gone and my health was soon restored. On the few occasions I've opened the container to inspect the Dibbuk Box, I've noticed it has taken on a completely new odor—a woody, heady scent that is strangely addicting. The smell is like no other I know or can compare it to. Just thinking of this smell makes me want to breathe in that fragrant scent again. This will sound crazy,

but I think the fragrance is a sort of tactic to lure me and others into unsealing the Dibbuk Box for yet another whiff of that beguiling scent. Oh yes, the few that have had a chance to experience this scent agree that it is unique and addictive.

In order to provide an additional layer of protection—for the box itself and for the people it might harm—I have fitted the ark with the box inside into an almost unbreakable plastic, foam-lined shipping case. This watertight, pressure-sensitive outer case would withstand virtually any kind of blow it might sustain if I needed to ship it anywhere. For now I have no such plans, but who knows?

Chapter Eleven

Incompatible Stories

I HAD SEALED the Dibbuk Box and felt safe from its influence, but I was still trying to gather more information about the artifact's history. It seemed like I had hit a dead end with Kevin concerning his tales of Havela and her family. He had refused to give me a phone number or address, and I wasn't even sure he had given me the correct surname so I could confirm aspects of the story through genealogical sources. He claimed the family would speak only to him and that he had promised to protect their privacy. It was frustrating, but it also made me suspicious. Did Kevin know something about the Dibbuk Box and Havela's family that he wasn't telling me?

About that time, November 2006, rumors of a Dibbuk Box movie started showing up on various paranormal websites. I checked the Internet Movie Database website (imdb.com), and found that all the spooky tales, testimonials, and queries about the Dibbuk Box had caught the attention of someone in Hollywood. Just what I needed—more people interested in my troublesome artifact.

I was curious about any reaction to the news, so I checked out the website's message board and found topics like "I can verify the potential truth of this story" and "Info on the Box." Then I saw a message titled "This Is Where The Story Comes From." I hoped it didn't give my name. No, instead it said:

> Sorry kids. I happen to know the guy who INVENTED the story. He created the box and made up the story so he could sell it on eBay. It's a hoax. [I] can't explain all the crazy stuff that has happened after it was sold, though.

Interesting. Well, I thought, this *is* the Internet, where anybody can claim to be anyone or know anything, and someone will believe them. I was surprised, though, because in the years I had been researching the box, this is the first time I had seen a bold statement that it was all a hoax. I needed to do some further digging.

Searching the poster's alias, Cory791, I found an ad posted by someone using the same alias for auditions for a horror film, describing it as "an independent project, done guerrilla style, so expect to get very dirty." The ad listed the location as Portland, Oregon, the same city where Kevin Mannis lived and where he said he had first bought the box at an estate sale.

I sent a message to Cory791 through the IMDb website asking him for more information. He didn't respond to my first message, so I contacted him again. In the meantime, I also learned that Cory791 was a member of a scriptwriters' and young directors' group called the Imaginarium Foundation. Interestingly, Kevin Mannis was also a member of that organization. I still hadn't gotten a reply from Cory, so I tried again: "As the current caretaker and researcher, I am curious to learn what you know, if you don't mind." Finally I got a response: "Are you involved in the [Dibbuk Box] book, movie or documentary? What does my movie have to do with anything?"

I quickly wrote back:

> Thanks for the quick reply. Don't worry—your horror movie is independent of all this. But your posting provided enough correlations to interest me in writing to you. I hope you don't mind, but this Dibbuk Box has been a puzzle of mine for the past three years, and you say you have some additional details. Your details do not seem to match what I have uncovered to date.

I explained that I had built a replica of the box and based on the effort involved and the cost of materials, I didn't see why someone would have created the box to make money, since my costs were higher than the price the box had originally sold for on eBay. And I told him that I was somewhat involved in the movie project, since I had talked to people at the studio about their offer to buy the rights to my story, although I was determined to retain the rights to publish a book.

Cory wrote back: "I'm conflicted here. I wrote what I did on IMDb to see what the kids would say in response. I didn't expect [to be contacted by the current owner] and I'm not sure if I should tell you anything." He also asked about my costs for duplicating the box. "You can't think of any way it could be made for less? Much less?"

After a couple more emails back and forth, Cory wrote, "The box isn't real. I learned of the story from the guy who made it, like I said. Hell, I know the guy who donated the hair. That's two guys who back up that it's a fake. Common knowledge to some."

Okay, so he had my interest. But there were other people who claimed to have information that contradicted Cory's claim. I e-mailed back:

. . . The point is that the box was indeed created at some point and the items installed—some items older than others, some personally crafted. And there has to be a Jewish connection, too—someone who knows and writes Hebrew well. That's one thing that intrigues me about this item.

My goal as a researcher has always been to unravel the mystery of the box's origin and purpose, so it's important that I learn more of what you know. I believe the truth is no less important to others, who are or will be involved—moviemakers, writers, scholars and so on. Those who want to profit will profit.

Understand, as I've said, that several people claim they're involved or know who made this box (so you're not the first). What evidence can you offer to prove that the person who said he created the box is legit? The guy who donated the hair and other tokens—I would like to know why he chose those items. I guess I'd like to connect with him to confirm what you say in your e-mails, and also to find answers to other questions. I would appreciate your help.

And in another message:

So the hair comes from one of the guys you know—did he say where the granite SHALOM stone came from? Did the guy you know actually make it and then sell the box and its contents on eBay to a college kid in Missouri?

I am wondering if we are writing about the same person (Kevin). You say two people were involved in making it, but I was aware of only

one first owner. Understand I am just trying to make sense of what you
are saying and compare discrepancies in stories. I appreciate your help.

At this point, Cory wrote: "Look Jason. I didn't expect this and I don't
think I should say anything more." Explaining that it wasn't really his
business, he said "I shouldn't have stuck my nose in it. . . . You have
enough to find out the rest yourself. I've told you what I know."

Cory wanted to drop the subject, but I was persistent. Kevin had
told me that the box came from a family he knew and had given me
Sophie's story of its creation. Cory claimed that the whole thing was a
fake. My own experiences after my contact with the box, as well as those
of Brian, Kevin, and Kevin's mother, and even experiences of people
who did not have personal contact with the box, convinced me there was
something more to the story, but I wanted to be sure. I asked Cory how
he knew Kevin and asked for the name of the person who Cory claimed
had donated the hair in the box. Cory e-mailed back: "The Club Underground in Beaverton, [Oregon]—Shaggy. Ask around."

I learned that Club Underground was a restaurant and bar that also
had pool tables, karaoke, and various games, as well as special activities
and contests each week. Cory told me that the staff knew the true origins of the Dibbuk Box. I wondered whether a contest might be a way
to find someone who knew the truth about the box. I talked to the owners, Randy and John, and they were agreeable. I put together a flyer that
explained the rules and said that the owners would pick the winner on
the basis of creativity, detail, and accuracy (using information I had
already pieced together). It seemed a perfect ploy for getting a knowledgeable source to talk, and I would have both a name and phone number for a follow-up interview.

Many weeks later, on February 1, 2007, I called to ask if there'd been
any success with the Dibbuk Box contest. The flyers had been set out for
several weeks, Randy said, but so far there were no takers. Well, there *had*
been one flakey dude, he added, but Randy had ended the game without
picking a winner.

I thanked him for trying, then took a new approach. This might
sound strange, I admitted, but did the club have a bartender known by
the name Shaggy? Or one who perhaps *looked* shaggy or maybe wore

his hair in a shag cut? Randy said, "Yeah, I have a guy we call Shaggy." Shaggy wasn't working that night, but another bartender who knew him well was on duty. Randy put me in touch with Shane Fox, who was working that evening. Moments after we started talking, Shane surprised me by declaring that he knew the truth about the Dibbuk Box. I told him that I had been told the lock of hair inside the box had come from Shaggy, who was Shane's supervisor and that the box's creator was a man named Kevin Mannis. Shane commented that Shaggy had gotten the nickname because of his resemblance to the Scooby Doo character.

I then asked, "Okay, Shane, so how are you involved in all this?" He laughed. Shane had learned of the Dibbuk Box from the contest flyers I had sent to the club. Figuring he could use the prize money, Shane entered the competition, following my instructions carefully. His first step was to go online, where he found my website and read it all. He also began visiting other paranormal sites. Soon he discovered that the box tale was being adapted for a Hollywood film. With the basic background facts in hand, he next decided to ask around the bar. Shane won the contest and as part of the contest rules, sent me an e-mail on March 10, 2007, that gave the details of his research and his results.

One night when I was at work [closing up], my bosses and a few regulars were still in the bar and the TV was on. I happened by the TV when a trailer for *Messengers* came on. I commented that it looked like a good movie and said aloud, "I can't wait till [that same producer] does the Dibbuk Box movie."

Instantly my bosses and the others stopped their conversation and all eyes were upon me. I was asked to repeat myself, which I did, and the demeanors of everyone changed briefly, followed by a burst of laughter. So I asked what was so funny. Shaggy (my immediate boss) asked me [how I knew] about the box, to which I replied, "Some guy named Jason sent a flyer [to the bar] the other day about a contest involving questions about this Dibbuk Box thing."

That's when Curt (my other boss) shakes his head and laughs again. So being an overly curious soul, I inquire as to what's so funny. Shaggy then turns to me and proceeds to tell me a story about the box. [I now wonder if it's really true], given the recent events of bad luck in my life since learning of the box.

Shaggy then tells me that one of our regulars, Kevin, made this whole thing up, that it is a hoax. The story goes as follows: Kevin, being in financial straits, either broke into or found in his mother's storage unit this wooden wine box and some other odd objects, too. Remembering some story about his grandmother being into Jewish magic, [Kevin] fabricated a believable story about mysticism and rituals surrounding talking to spirits.

Shaggy then goes on to tell me that the lock of [dark] hair in the box is his own, and the blond hair is from a doll. . . . my guess is a Barbie. (If tested, I'm sure the hair would [turn out to be] dyed plastic strands or some kind of animal hair.) So eventually Kevin makes this story up and puts the box on eBay, hoping to make a quick buck. Since this initial revealing of the truth, I've been spending a lot of time trying to gather more info from people [at the bar], to no avail. Seems that [everyone] who knows anything about this box is all creeped out about it and [doesn't] want to talk.

My attempts to contact Kevin [whom Shaggy told me about] have been in vain. Now, to contradict my original [opinions] on the Dibbuk Box, I'm starting to become a believer that there is some kind of strange and powerful energy surrounding this box. [I am not sure what Kevin learned from his grandma—if anything at all], but this thing isn't good. In the last month since [you and I] have talked, my entire life and all aspects of it have been turned upside-down. Granted, I've always been a magnet for random negative BS, but never to this degree or frequency. The only common denominator is the [Dibbuk] Box. As far as I know, this whole thing is a hoax propagated by a broke drunkard, [but I wonder if situations like these can tell us] the real truth. I have many ideas and theories involving the phenomena around this box, which, [if you like] I shall share at a later date. As for now, this is all the info I have. Good luck.

— Shane Fox, undetermined believer.

On April 5 in the early evening, I called Club Underground and reached Shaggy the bartender (his real name is Matt). At first he seemed taken aback by my call, but we chatted for a bit. It was obvious from the background noise that he was extremely busy, and occasionally he had to interrupt our talk to serve a customer. I told him that when I had first confronted Kevin about Cory's story and what I learned from Shane,

Kevin had told me that no one who worked there could be trusted to tell the truth.

Annoyed, Shaggy spilled everything he knew about the Dibbuk Box. When the whole thing began, he said, Kevin was working security at the club and also cooking a bit. One night, another employee called Mike was complaining that he wasn't getting enough tips, so Shaggy shaved his head and put the dark strands into Mike's tip jar. Shaggy told me that Kevin, who happened to be working that night, pulled the hair out of the jar. It was the same lock of this hair, Shaggy said, that Kevin later placed inside the Dibbuk Box. As far as Shaggy was concerned, the whole Dibbuk Box business was just a joke and nobody expected it to amount to anything. Since Kevin had come up with the tale, Shaggy didn't begrudge him making money off it, but he had no idea how much Kevin had made with the project.

I told him I had heard different stories from several of the bar's patrons and had even confronted Kevin with what I'd heard. Kevin had claimed he didn't understand what the other sources were saying about him and he had no idea what was going on. Toward the end of our phone conversation, I asked Shaggy if he'd send me perhaps five strands of the hair for comparison with the hair in the box. Shaggy said he'd think about it, but made no promises.

Shortly after that call to Shaggy, I phoned Kevin to confront him with Shaggy's account of the hair's origins. Once more, Kevin told me that the staff at Club Underground were not a reputable group. He acknowledged that he had worked at the club during the time he'd owned the Dibbuk Box, but insisted that the stories of his former coworkers were simply false. They knew nothing about the box and had never had any involvement with it.

After that confrontational phone call, he did not return any calls or e-mails for over two years. I tried to follow up on Shaggy's story. Finally, on Thursday, May 17, I connected. Shaggy insisted that he had no more to say on the topic, and pointed out that he knew little about the actual box. He had never seen it. He understood that Kevin had gotten it from his family somehow ... his grandma? His mother? Then again, Kevin may have bought it at an antique sale or somewhere. He didn't know where the box originally came from, but Kevin did take his hair to put in the box. Shaggy didn't want to send me any of his hair for comparison; the last time he gave someone some of his hair, it was used in such a strange way that he thought handing out any more hair was not a good idea.

Shaggy pointed out that he had no motivation to lie about the box and no real interest in the thing. His only connection with Kevin was through his job when Kevin had worked for him briefly as a cook, but they were not friends or anything. Shaggy added one more detail: Kevin had come by the club the other day, looking for him. Shaggy was off duty at the time, but he learned about Kevin's visit from another bartender. Kevin had asked this bartender whether Shaggy had talked to a Jason who now had possession of the Dibbuk Box. The bartender said yes, he was sure Shaggy had spoken by phone for quite some time with a man named Jason. Shaggy asked his coworker whether Kevin had seemed upset by the news. "No, not really," the bartender said. "He seemed indifferent about it."

So I now had four more primary sources about the Dibbuk Box—Shaggy, Shane, Randy, and Cory—and their stories contradicted Kevin's in most of the details. All four of my sources seemed convinced that Kevin had somehow used his Jewish family's supernatural gifts to charm the box so that it became more than the sum of its components. All four believed the box had come from Kevin's family, possibly from his grandmother, and all four shared a common attitude toward the mysterious wine cabinet: they wanted nothing more to do with it.

So I was left with conflicting stories. Kevin said that he had bought the box at an estate sale with the objects inside; certain acquaintances of his said he had put the items together himself and made up the story of the estate sale. I had some confirmation of Kevin's story, but couldn't personally corroborate it because the family from whom Kevin bought the box did not want me to contact them. His mother endorsed Kevin's version of the story, but his siblings were unable to confirm any of the details. The people at Club Underground told a different story, but who was to say their version was true? Kevin had been only an acquaintance and brief coworker, so they didn't necessarily know the whole story, and after several years had passed, they might be misremembering specific details. But even they believed that the box had some kind of power. There was no way to know who was telling the truth, and besides, I had other things going on in my life. I had sealed the Dibbuk Box and felt that any spirit it held had been contained. I had studied the artifact and pondered its strange history and the stories that surrounded it, but despite having some nagging questions about the whole thing, I was ready to move on.

I would never leave the subject behind altogether, however. The story was too interesting—and too puzzling. I continued to keep in touch with some of the people I had met during my researches, although Kevin and I had not been in touch for quite a while and he seemed to want to keep it that way. I continued to follow progress on the movie and was slowly working on putting together a book recording my experiences, in part because the movie would be a fictional story inspired by the Dibbuk Box. I had tried to interest Kevin in working with me on a book, but that didn't work out.

Then, in June 2010, I was scheduled to visit Eugene, Oregon, to present a museum exhibit and would be flying into the Portland airport and renting a car to drive to Eugene. It had been six years since I had been to Oregon and met Kevin Mannis for the first time. I still wondered about some of the details of his story, but Kevin and I had been out of touch since 2007, so I decided to try another family member I had been in contact with. Before this trip, I contacted Kevin's brother and he agreed to meet with me after I completed my work in Eugene. I told him I had a few questions, including whether he could tell me more than what was listed in the eBay sale. One of my questions concerned the dream of the "hag" when he and his wife and sister had shared the same nightmare while staying at Kevin's house. He laughed and said that neither he, his wife, nor his sister ever had this common nightmare or had associated any such dream with the cabinet. He said that if I wanted to know the truth, he would give me the details of his first encounter with the object now known as the Dibbuk Box.

One day, he said, he had gone to his brother's antique refinishing shop, something he rarely did. Among Kevin's recent purchases, he spotted the strange little wine cabinet with the grape appliqués on the doors. It seemed to have been tossed to the side, uncared for, as if it were junk. Kevin's brother said he looked it over and told his brother he would really like to have it—it was unlike anything he had ever seen—but Kevin refused to give it away, explaining that he had plans for using the box.

Kevin then moved the box out of sight. That was the last time Kevin's brother ever saw the Dibbuk Box, and he was still angered by his brother's rebuff. Kevin's brother agreed to meet with me and suggested that I call as soon as I had finished packing up my museum exhibit. I wrote about our visit in my daily journal.

Thursday, June 3, 2010

It was my plan to catch up with Kevin's younger brother in Portland, but I received a call that he was at his sister's beach house in Lincoln, about an hour and a half away. He invited me to have dinner and spend the night there, rather than meet in Portland. It sounded fine to me, as I had wanted to see the ocean sometime during my visit to Oregon.

I arrived later in the afternoon, and the first thing I did was give him a near-replica of the Dibbuk Box that I'd purchased. These liquor cabinets created in the late 1950s and early '60s were still available on the market. Both the replica and the original shared an odd feature. When a drawer was pulled out, a mechanical device simultaneously opened the box's door. The two cabinets weren't quite twins, however. Instead of the carved grapes on the Dibbuk Box, the other cabinet had golden brass adornments of a floral or multiple-leaf design.

Obviously pleased with his gift, he worked the drawer mechanism several times. He told me he'd always admired the simplicity and craftsmanship of his brother's wine cabinet—qualities repeated in the box I'd brought.

Next, I was shown to my room and I put away my suitcase. Then the two of us walked down to the beach for a long chat. The pristine beach and clean water had a timeless and healing quality to it. I mentioned how different this scene was from that of the BP oil disaster unfolding in the Gulf of Mexico waters. We discussed the long-term damage that tragedy would lead to for the people of the area, the environment, and the wildlife—all due to oil-money greed. But on this spotless beach, the disaster so far away seemed almost impossible. We walked in silence for some distance, each lost in his own thoughts.

The topic then turned to the reason for my visit—to explore what he knew about the Dibbuk Box sold by his brother on eBay. He told me that everything about that box had been bad for his family. As he spoke, a change came over his previously energetic personality. Suddenly he sounded sad and tired. He told me that he hoped one day some good might come from the thing—but so far it had brought only harm and sadness to anyone connected with it.

The energy and hopeful spirit seemed to return to his eyes, and he asked if I would do two good deeds for him. I responded, "Sure, I'll try," unsure of what might come next.

He asked that I make a donation to a food pantry he volunteered for, which fed the poor of Portland. He had worked with the organization for several years, he said, and it had helped so many needy people, especially children. He shared with me that he'd had a fire in his apartment a few months earlier and had lost absolutely everything he owned. Destitute and frustrated, he was forced to rely on friends and strangers for all his day-to-day needs. In the end, however, the fire and loss had the effect of freeing him from his reliance on those material possessions—it opened him up to greater possibilities in a life of giving. He knew what it was to need help to get back on his feet, and the food pantry really helped people. I was touched by his story.

He also asked that I speak with Kevin about what he had done in creating the box, and try to persuade him to turn the act to some sort of good. How could I refuse such a sincere request? I got some cash from a nearby ATM machine and told him to split the money up in a way that would do the most good. Tears filled his eyes.

Next, I called the phone number he'd given me for Kevin. I left my number and a message asking Kevin to give me a call—we needed to talk. This was the first time in over three years that I actually had a working phone number for Kevin.

Kevin's brother then asserted the following: There was an evil energy to the Dibbuk Box that made it harmful if one wasn't careful. The misuse of the Hebrew prayer and the writing on the box had created something very dark. From the time it was created, the thing was malevolent. It was evil at the moment he first showed interest in it.

Initially, his brother had kept the box away from him, he said. But then Kevin had tied the whole family to this accursed object. He expressed the hope that the replica box I had given him would prove the antithesis of the one created by Kevin. He told me he would fill the new box with items of life and hope.

He wanted me to know about his grandmother Ethel, his "Nana." He wasn't certain, but perhaps, or perhaps not, she had been Kevin's inspiration for building the Dibbuk Box—the reason he had included her in his eBay description. In the 1960s, Ethel had earned money investing in Rainbow Warehouse, a sundries store, one of the first department stores in the Las Vegas area when that area was not much more than desert. Many years later when the store sold, she profited in the millions and was able to live in the penthouse of the Sands Hotel in Las Vegas. Ethel played the slot machines regularly, adding to her fortune with the winnings. She lived to be 103 years old and used her own form of Jewish magic to beat the odds and win. He said she might have wanted others to think she had a special gift. However, he suspects that as a well-known resident of the hotel, she may have picked up tips or clues on which machines were ready to pay out. From his perspective, there was no magic involved.

There was no doubt she was Kevin's "Havela," he went on to say. Kevin lived with the old lady for years and she may well have mentored him some in her arts. Kevin certainly was brilliant, gifted, and a genius in some ways. He could tackle subjects like kabbalah and quantum physics and more. He had the potential to do much good, and yet for years that hasn't happened. Kevin was a hard one to understand, even for his brother.

So the story seemed to end there, not quite as the eBay listing had described events, but there seemed to be some truth to the story. That night, I lay on the soft bed, thinking of all the years I had spent learning about Kevin, the Dibbuk Box, and all the people drawn to this promising artifact. I soon fell into a deep and restful sleep . . . no shadowy figures or beatings by demonic hags disturbed my rest.

I was up early the next morning, packed and ready to head home. Maybe it was the good conversation and calm environment, but I felt lighter inside and ready for new challenges. Kevin's brother was up early too, in the kitchen making some breakfast for us. My bags by the door, we hugged without the need for words. There seemed to be an understanding between us: forgive, appreciate what you have, and try to help where you can. I waved goodbye and said we should stay in touch.

As I pulled out the driveway, I still had many unanswered questions. If his story was true, then I knew where the Dibbuk Box was first sighted. Did something transpire to make Kevin create it into the Dibbuk Box? That was still a mystery to me. I decided to enjoy the moment and drive down to the beach for one more view of the ocean. Gulls, disturbed by my sudden presence in their territory, squawked in my direction. Waves crashed. A hazy mist floated over the cliffs to the north, and I breathed in the salty air. The Oregon beach and the ocean beyond were so vast and timeless. This was as memorable a place as any to end my journey of discovery for the truth about the Dibbuk Box. The tranquil moment ended too quickly. I needed to get on the road to catch my flight back home. I would write of my meeting with Kevin's younger brother and put it in a file—maybe the last entry.

Unless . . . I really wanted to reopen the door to dialogue that had been slammed shut by Kevin three years earlier, when inconsistencies in my investigation challenged Kevin's story and his truthfulness. Hurt and angry, he had not replied to my e-mails or phone calls.

I had also fallen out of touch with Cory. After he had told me about Club Underground, our conversations turned to movie-making, and we e-mailed back and forth about Cory's film project and Hollywood horror films in general. Cory and I became e-mail friends in the end. After a while, we fell out of touch, but I heard from him again in February 2011, and wrote about our conversation in my journal.

February 22, 2011 at about 1:15 pm

I received a phone call from Cory, a cameraman, screenwriter, and independent film producer. It has been almost four years since he and I visited by phone or e-mail. It was good to reconnect and I asked him if he would mind helping me to clarify some information on the Dibbuk Box artifact and its creation from earlier when he had been somewhat reluctant. He was being conscientious not to share information that at the time he felt might have hurt the progress of the film being created. With that no longer a concern, he freely shared the following information.

He had met Kevin at the Club Underground when its popularity was waning, and as an eighteen-year-old he was happy to get into a bar that let him drink while underage. Even at that time he knew he wanted to work in the film industry. He got to know Kevin Mannis, who had already produced a film. They talked about film ideas and even worked on a few projects together. But Kevin had told him that he was never able to complete what is known as a full-blown screenplay, a point-by-point explanation for a film that includes dialogue, scene development, and filming suggestions. Cory remembered Kevin as better at producing pieces of a story line or embellishing what already existed in someone else's work.

It was about six years ago that he had met Kevin and already the Dibbuk Box story had been on a radio show podcast and was being considered for a film by a big movie company. Cory said that Kevin freely told him about the events of the film and the worldwide popularity of the Dibbuk Box on the Internet. Kevin told him he had created it all, one struggling film guy to another. Up to this point Cory had not ever heard of the Dibbuk Box.

Cory told me that Kevin had made it clear that he had crafted this item to become a "magic object" now known as the Dibbuk Box, and then had crafted a story to go with it. He said that Kevin was very open about the fact that he'd created the box itself. The bottom line: Kevin was responsible for it all.

I mentioned that a bartender named Shaggy said he had a small part in the creation. Shaggy said that within the box was a lock of his brown hair and that the other hair had been cut off a toy doll's head. Cory then said, "If Shaggy said it then it was the truth." He had never known Shaggy to tell lies. The two testimonials seemed right. Except for one detail—the hair in the Dibbuk Box is a very dark, deep black. It shines almost blue due to its rich darkness. It is NOT brown.

Kevin's friendship with Cory had eventually dwindled and the two had not communicated in years, but Cory hoped he was doing well. Cory said Kevin was a good guy and a friend.

—//—

In April 2011, I sent an e-mail to Cory: "One last question. As best you remember, what color would you say Shaggy's hair is? Light brown, brown, dark brown, black, coal black? Humor me on this one. I will tell you after you answer." Cory e-mailed back: "Shaggy has brown hair, average like mine. Not light."

I quickly e-mailed back:

> You might find this odd or not. Shaggy's hair was never put into the Dibbuk Box. Since sold by Kevin almost eight years ago, the hair is coal black—so black it glints with blue highlights. . . . Kevin and I have been chatting a good bit the past few days and he explained why Shaggy thought his hair was put in the box. He said Shaggy was going through a rough time spiritually with his faith and started messing with the dark arts in a big way. So Kevin decided to test his loss of faith by telling him he had indeed added Shaggy's hair to the Dibbuk Box. But in actuality it never was added in! He was playing him.
>
> Also Cory, know although our conversation mostly focused on the Dibbuk Box, in talking about the locks of hair in the box I mentioned both Shaggy and you were convinced it was indeed Shaggy's hair. It just isn't. That said, Kevin understands why you were convinced of it— that was his intent at the time—he is kind of sorry now. It was not a good thing to do regardless of the reason.
>
> Funny, but had Shaggy sent me a few strands when I asked him for it, he (and I) would have known the truth years ago.

Looking back, that is an interesting choice of words. If I had had one additional piece of information, I would have known the truth? Really? Do we ever have that one final piece of information that makes us sure we know the truth?

Chapter Twelve

Tying Up Loose Ends

In April 2011, I was finishing work on this manuscript. I had been researching the Dibbuk Box for seven years and had been working on the manuscript on and off for three years. I thought I had gathered all the information I could, but I was still not happy with the loose ends. I had hoped Kevin and I would work on the book together, but we had fallen out of touch and it seemed that Kevin did not want to communicate with me. But I still felt like I needed some kind of final comments from him. I talked about it at length with a friend and writing coach, who urged me to try one more time to get in touch with Kevin. So late on the evening of April 18, I sent an e-mail.

> Hi Kevin,
>
> I spent the whole day reviewing my book manuscript and I am turning it in very soon. This is a last chance to work together. If not, I will work with the film company to use their life story option that you gave them.
>
> If that is what you prefer, that is fine. I really wish you had wanted to work on the book with me.
>
> If you have a change of mind, call me on my cell phone.
>
> Best regards,
>
> Jason

Kevin not only replied to my last-ditch effort, but he wrote two pages, in essence putting his final words to this story and to my years of research. After mentioning his mother's ongoing health problems, he wrote:

> Since the advent of your first interest in the Dibbuk Box story, I have been so very honored and humbled by your interest and commitment to understanding it. Even when your zeal and enthusiasm have skewed

your path or convoluted your interpretation of my original concept and story along with what are inarguably some of the most complex concepts of human spirituality, I have been impressed and honored by your perseverance and your inexhaustible ability to share, and promote, and frankly, even delve into a matter that can be an abyss for the observant, let alone a gentile.

Up until now, with the movie having gone into production, I have not been compelled to give you any direction. . . . [In exchange for the use of his story, the movie company listed Kevin's name among the writers and production staff.]

He then commented that he understood my initial reasoning in contacting family members in my attempts to get in touch with him, but wrote,

What doesn't make much sense is trying to get some sort of background story or basis as it relates to the story of the Dibbuk Box. The estranged family members and former employees who you have interviewed about the story have absolutely no knowledge of the story nor its origins. . . . The information that you have been fed about me is erroneous at best and certainly has little bearing on the roots and workings of the Dibbuk Box.

He was also upset about what he called my attempts "to implicate [his] dear departed grandmother with aspects of [his] original story," writing, "Regardless of what you think you have discovered, my grandmother was anything but mystical or magical. She was not knowledgeable about, nor did she concern herself with kabbalah or spiritual matters in general." It seemed to me that, despite his assurance that he was not upset with me, he was not happy about some of the stories and information I had collected in my research, although he was willing to let it pass. And frankly, having talked with several members of his family, it was clear to me that the family was not of one mind in this entire matter. The family members, as well as various acquaintances, disagreed about certain events and interpretations to the extent that it would be impossible for an outsider to ever know for sure what was the real truth.

Now you know as much as anyone concerning this enigma called the Dibbuk Box that remains in my care. The box is apparently at peace—nestled

within its gold-lined wooden ark and entombed in a heavy plastic shipping case. The few times that, when the atmosphere was calm, I have taken the box from its sealed state and opened its doors, I have smelled the most amazing heady scent. Only a few people have had this opportunity and they tell me it is the smell of life. Very addictive, very familiar, and yet like nothing else.

And so I have come to the end of my story. At least for now. In my search for the truth about the Dibbuk Box, I found many possible truths. It could be a hoax, but too many strange things have happened to believe it is nothing more than that. Perhaps the box I now guard really is the latest incarnation of a vessel that held an evil spirit unintentionally summoned by a group of women who, in 1938, tried to summon a spirit to protect the Jewish people from the rising anti-Semitism in eastern Europe. If so, perhaps it was somehow connected to the evil that followed. Or perhaps evil was already loose in Germany and the women only thought the spirit they had summoned played a role in the events that followed. Or perhaps instead, the box was the result of a later person's dabbling in the supernatural and the older stories became associated with it out of confusion, or out of some desire to shift the blame.

Either way, the Dibbuk Box clearly reflects our desire to see evil as something that exists separately from humankind, something we can capture and perhaps even control. If the box is simply a more recent artifact that became associated with paranormal experiences and stories, then perhaps it reflects that belief in another way. If evil, or the paranormal, is something that can be somehow captured or controlled, then perhaps it becomes less frightening. If the Dibbuk Box was created as part of an elaborate hoax, it seems that the box became a magnet for something paranormal. Perhaps the act of creating such a story attracted the darkness that so many people have experienced when they came in contact with the box. Perhaps evil does not like to be mocked. If the paranormal is something we awaken when we mess with things we don't understand, then perhaps it becomes attached to an object belonging to a person who messes with the unknown. And perhaps once evil has been confined or associated with a specific object, it becomes possible to avoid the evil by getting rid of the object.

I do not want to be the one to set the original Dibbuk Box off on another journey. I believe it has served its purpose and shouldn't be disturbed. So what will I do with it? I am not really sure, and there is no rush. It no longer scares or worries me. Perhaps years from now, I will ask to have it buried with me when I leave this life. My son, now grown and in his third year of college, tells me he won't bury it with me. He says the Dibbuk Box is much too important—too valuable! I have learned that requesting that something be done upon one's death and actually getting it done are two different things, but it might be best to avoid any yard sale or estate sale of my belongings.

A unique human trait is that we try to find meaning in the things that happen to us. Some people are comfortable with the idea that events are random, but most of us look for connections and purpose in our lives. As I said in the beginning of this book, I believe both that the box is a truly supernatural artifact and that the box is a hoax. If I believe that there is a meaning to the box coming to me, then I also believe that the box was meant to come to me. Was I destined to win the eBay auction in which I bought the box? What if Brian had never come to work at the museum and therefore I had never heard the story of his roommate buying this haunted artifact? What if I had heard that story, but someone else had won the auction? Would someone else have found a different meaning in the box? If you had bought the box, what would you have thought it was?

Rabbi Lynn Goldstein, with whom I became acquainted during my research, believes that the meaning of the Dibbuk Box lies in the lesson it offers:

> At some point in our lives, each of us faces challenges, traumas, and tragedies that put us in a very dark place with no way out. We wonder why forces in the world seem to be conspiring against us, why we have been so hurt, why this horrible thing is happening to us. We wonder why there seems to be no light, no joy, no goodness. We feel numb and hopeless. The experience of the Dibbuk Box reminds us to open our eyes and see what is already there: a community of people who love us, friends who support us, strangers who are willing to offer assistance, all ready and willing to tackle God's unfinished work. All we need to do is choose to reach out for help and to accept support. The story of the Dibbuk Box is a story of people from all walks of life all around the

world who chose to join hands and together search for a way out, and ultimately, as a community willing to support and help each other, they succeeded.

Ultimately, the meaning of the Dibbuk Box to me is that through researching this object, I learned about the American eugenics movement and about the connection between the Holocaust and my hometown of Kirksville through Harry Laughlin, who went to school and lived here before becoming head of the Eugenics Record Office and "expert eugenics agent" for the U.S. House of Representatives, and returned here at the end of his career. I believe that the box came to me so that I could learn about these events and share that knowledge with others. But do I believe that the box was created—and caused problems for so many people—just so I could find out about these things? It seems a little arrogant to suppose that all of these things happened just so I could learn something. And so many other people participated in my research and experienced the influence of the Dibbuk Box for themselves. They, no doubt, have found their own meanings in their experiences, so my journey to discover the meaning behind the Dibbuk Box was really not my journey alone. Perhaps the lesson of the Dibbuk Box is more general— that by delving into the unknown, we learn not only about connections between events in our history, but also about connections between people who seem distant from one another. Perhaps by exploring what lies beyond ourselves and beyond our understanding, we ultimately learn what lies within each of us as individuals, and what possibilities for good or evil lie within the human psyche.

The Dibbuk
in Jewish Folklore

Howard Schwartz

The first, and ongoing, challenge for readers of *The Dibbuk Box* is to determine whether the various characters' claims that the mysterious box emanates evil are true or not. Even now, I remain uncertain. The tale this book tells is firmly rooted in the real world, down to the details of sending e-mail and buying and selling on eBay. The author, Jason Haxton, portrays himself as a detective trying to get to the bottom of a disturbing mystery. He conveys his every thought and action, including extensive quotations from his journal, as well as extracts from accounts by the other key figures. There is a great deal of documentation—everyone seems to have recorded his or her encounters with the Dibbuk Box. The suffering that follows the box wherever it goes is described in great detail, including foul smells (and an occasional scent of jasmine). This realistic grounding makes the supernatural events in the story seem plausible enough to consider accepting them as true, especially for those who are inclined to believe in the paranormal.

At the same time, there are plenty of reasons to identify *The Dibbuk Box* with certain works of fiction. It closely follows the pattern of many supernatural tales, Robert Louis Stevenson's "The Bottle Imp," in particular. That story is about a bottle with an imp inside that fulfills the

Howard Schwartz is professor of English at University of Missouri–St. Louis, specializing in the study of Jewish folklore and mythology. He is the author of numerous books, including *Lilith's Cave: Jewish Tales of the Supernatural* (1991), *Gabriel's Palace: Jewish Mystical Tales* (1994), *The Four Who Entered Paradise* (2000), and *Tree of Souls: The Mythology of Judaism* (2004).

wishes of its owners, but unless they sell it at a loss, for less than they originally paid, it will return to them, and if the owner dies without having sold it as required, his soul will burn in Hell for eternity. So it is with the unfortunate owners of the Dibbuk Box—they buy it out of curiosity or to explore its mystery, and end up desperate to get rid of it by selling it to someone else.

The extensive documentation, journal entries, and photographs strongly indicate that the author is not trying to pass off a work of fiction as a true account. There seems little doubt that a so-called Dibbuk Box existed (and still exists), and that those who came into contact with it attributed all illness and misfortune that followed to the evil spirit in the box. This does not mean, of course, that any such spirit inhabited the box, or that the box was responsible for any of the large and small miseries that took place. Thus if the accounts of paranormal experiences recounted in this book are not true, those fictions were created in the minds of the author and others who became convinced that the Dibbuk Box housed some kind of evil spirit. In that sense, this book is a study in superstition and belief in the supernatural. If anything, the author goes too far in documenting his encounters with the box and his investigations of its checkered history. He pursues any and every account of anybody with the slightest connection to the box. Haxton himself wavers from believing it is a real object of the paranormal to fearing that the whole thing is a hoax. Kevin, the original seller, sometimes appears to be a friend and confidant, and at other times seems to be the instigator of a hoax that ultimately encompasses thousands of people.

To a considerable extent, *The Dibbuk Box* is a study in obsession. In this it resembles Jorge Luis Borges's famous story "The Zahir," in which a coin, once received, cannot be forgotten and soon overshadows every other thought. Over the years spanned by his story, Haxton says less and less about the museum he directs and his family life. Instead he demonstrates his obsession with the box, an obsession that takes over his life. Over and over he expresses his belief that the box is real, but considering its dangers, he behaves in a reckless way to probe these mysteries, at the risk of his health—which is damaged from the first time he touches the box—and at great risk to his family, friends, and colleagues at the museum.

Our narrator prides himself on his rationality, and always explains his thoughts and actions in great detail, often justifying them. But it takes a long time before the widening circle of damage from the box leads him to the conclusion that he must protect himself and those around him from it. *In short, he focuses more on his obsession than on his safety.* An interesting literary echo is that found in the case of Charles Kinbote, the narrator to Vladimir Nabokov's *Pale Fire,* who first appears to be a literary critic writing a critical analysis of a poem by John Shade, but later turns out to be a madman who has been jailed for murdering the poet. While the narrator in *The Dibbuk Box* relates to the reader as a confidant and friend, the reader would be well advised to view him with a little skepticism as he is drawn ever deeper into his obsession.

Of course, there is the possibility that the box is authentic, in spite of the facts that it dates only to the 1950s, and that some witnesses claim it was intended as a hoax from the first. Kevin states that his source told him the current box was built as a substitute for a similar box lost in the Holocaust, but no explanation is given about why the replacement was created or how the deadly demon was transferred to it. It is true that the disturbances—large and small—that are linked to the box seem too extreme to be accidental. But according to Kevin, "Sophie" widened the circle of its damage to include the Holocaust and several wars, implying that its creation was a cosmic catastrophe. At that point, this reader at least felt that powers of the evil spirit in the box were exaggerated to the point of disbelief.

Since the Dibbuk Box is presented as Jewish in origin and the dybbuk itself as a figure emerging from Jewish folklore, it is very important to clarify the Jewish elements in this story. The central myth that underlies the book is the author's understanding of the term "dibbuk" (or, more commonly, "dybbuk"). Accepting the definition given by Joseph, the author sees a dybbuk as an evil spirit of nearly limitless powers that can be (and was) invoked by kabbalistic magic, but once invoked was nearly impossible to control or eliminate. Unfortunately, this does not accurately portray the traditional role of the dybbuk. Therefore let us first clarify the recognized meaning of the term, and then discuss how the author's understanding of it differs.

The dybbuk plays a very specific role in Jewish tradition. It is understood to be the spirit of a person (usually a man) who committed one of several major sins (such as murder) in his lifetime and died without repenting, and who, after death, found his spirit pursued by avenging angels with fiery whips who sought to punish him. In order to escape this torture, the dybbuk seeks out places of refuge—a flower, a rock, an animal (usually a goat, cow, or sheep), or, if it can find a vulnerable human (inevitably a woman), the dybbuk takes possession of her and refuses to depart. The woman, who is then under the complete control of the dybbuk, speaks with a male's voice, and the dybbuk refuses to depart from her, out of fear of the avenging angels waiting to punish it. In order to save the victim, a formal exorcism ceremony, involving ten rabbis, must be performed; even then the dybbuk holds out until the last second before it finally abandons its victim. S. Ansky's folk drama, *The Dybbuk*, concludes with an authentic portrayal of the rabbinic exorcism ceremony.

Consider "The Widow of Safed," a sixteenth-century folktale about a woman who becomes possessed by a dybbuk because she does not truly believe that the waters of the Red Sea parted as described in Exodus. A rabbi is sent to help the widow; he interviews the dybbuk, extracting his name, where he lived, and the nature of his sin. Here is the story:

> A widow living in Safed, whom everyone considered pious, suddenly began to speak with the voice of a man, until it became apparent that a wandering spirit, a dybbuk, had taken possession of her body. The woman was greatly tormented by this spirit, and she sought help among the disciples of Rabbi Isaac Luria, known as the Ari. Rabbi Joseph Arsin was the first to visit her, and when the voice addressed him by name, he was amazed.
>
> Then the dybbuk revealed that he had once been a pupil of Rabbi Arsin's when they had both lived in Egypt, and he gave his name. Rabbi Arsin recalled that he had once had such a pupil and realized that the former pupil's soul was now addressing him.
>
> Rabbi Arsin demanded to know why the soul of this man had taken possession of the pious widow. The dybbuk readily confessed that he had committed a grievous sin. He had caused a woman to break her marriage vow and had fathered a child with her. And because of this sin, he had been enslaved after his death by three angels, who

had dragged him by a heavy chain and had punished him endlessly. He had taken possession of the widow's body in order to escape this terrible punishment.

Then Rabbi Arsin asked the dybbuk to describe the circumstances of his death, and the spirit said: "I lost my life when the ship on which I was sailing sank. Nor was I able to confess my sins before dying, because it happened so quickly. When the news of the wreck reached the closest town, my body was recovered along with the others who had drowned, and I was buried in a Jewish cemetery. But as soon as the mourners left, an evil angel opened the grave with a fiery rod and led me to the gates of Gehenna [Jewish hell]. But the angel guarding Gehenna refused to allow me to enter, so great was my sin, and instead I was condemned to wander, pursued by three avenging angels. Twice before I tried to escape from this endless punishment. Once I took possession of a rabbi, but he invoked a flock of impure spirits, and in order to escape them I had to abandon his body. Later I became so desperate that I took possession of the body of a dog, which became so crazed that it ran until it dropped dead. Then I fled to Safed and entered the body of this woman."

Rabbi Arsin then commanded the dybbuk to depart from the widow's body but the dybbuk refused. So Rabbi Arsin went to the Ari and asked him to perform the exorcism.

The Ari called upon his disciple, Rabbi Hayim Vital, to do this in his name and gave him a formula, consisting of holy names, that would force the dybbuk to depart.

Now when Rabbi Hayim Vital entered the house of the poor widow, the dybbuk forced her to turn her back to him. And when Hayim Vital asked the dybbuk to explain this, the spirit said that he could not bear the holy countenance of his face. Then Hayim Vital asked the dybbuk to tell him how long it had been cursed to wander. The spirit replied that its wandering would last until the child he had fathered had died. Finally, Hayim Vital asked to know how the dybbuk was able to enter the body of the widow. The dybbuk explained that the woman had made it possible because she had little faith, since she did not believe that the waters of the Red Sea had truly parted.

Hayim Vital asked the woman if this was true, and she insisted that she did believe in the miracle. He made her repeat her belief three times, and on the third time Hayim Vital uttered the formula that the

Ari had taught him. After that he commanded the dybbuk to depart from the woman by the little toe of her left foot. At that moment the dybbuk did depart with a terrible cry, and the woman was freed from the agony of that possession.

The next day, when the Ari ordered that the mezuzah on her door be checked, it was found to be empty, and that is why it did not protect against that evil spirit.

(*Ele Toledot Yitzhak* in *Sefer Toledot ha-Ari*, pp. 253–56)

The legends concerning dybbuks, spirits of the dead who take possession of the living, multiply in the later medieval and Hasidic literature. There are scores of such accounts of possession in Jewish lore. "The Widow of Safed" reveals the basic pattern to which all such possessions are subjected. The dybbuk has been able to enter her house because the mezuzah *is* defective and has been able to take possession of the woman because of her lack of faith in the miracle of the crossing of the Red Sea. The latter was the standard test of true faith among Jews in the middle ages. Today the test question is whether a person believes that God dictated the Torah to Moses on Mount Sinai.

It is interesting to note that the majority of these accounts of possession include details of name and place that far exceed the usual anonymity of folklore. Gedalyiah Nigal has compiled a Hebrew anthology of dybbuk tales, *Sippurei ha-Dybbuk* (Jerusalem, 1983), and virtually every account includes the place and year where the possession and exorcism occurred and the names of the witnesses. The tales almost always follow the same pattern: 1. someone becomes possessed by a dybbuk; 2. a rabbi confronts the spirit and demands that it reveal its name and history; 3. the dybbuk tells its tale; and 4. the dybbuk is then exorcised, and the one who was possessed recovers. This suggests that the pattern established in the earliest of these tales, such as this one, was repeated in succeeding generations and became, in effect, a socially recognized form of madness, especially for women. More recently, such possession has been identified primarily as a psychological aberration. In *Legends of the Hasidim*, the editor, Jerome Mintz, reports a twentieth-century case of such possession in which the Satmar Rebbe supposedly advised someone said to be possessed by a dybbuk to see a good psychiatrist (pp. 411–12).

It should be apparent that the description of the dybbuk found in *The Dibbuk Box* differs considerably from the traditional role. The author accepts the definitions provided by Joseph of a dibbuk as "a misplaced spirit that can neither rise to Heaven nor descend into Hell, essentially stuck in Limbo or purgatory," "a demon that enters the body of a living person and controls that body's behavior," or "the spirit or soul of a dead person that inhabits the body of a living one, with sometimes evil, sometimes positive results."

Although these definitions include the correct one (a spirit that takes possession of a living person), this is not the meaning the author and others portray in their accounts. For them, a dybbuk is a powerful evil spirit that can be invoked by kabbalistic magic. *But in none of the traditional accounts does anyone ever invoke a dybbuk.* That would be the last thing anyone would want to do. The dybbuk arrives on its own, taking possession of vulnerable people, especially women. Dybbuks aren't held prisoner in boxes, bottles, or anything else. They are free to depart from any container they find refuge in, including a person's body, but they are highly reluctant to do so, since as long as they remain in the body, they are protected from the avenging angels who pursue them. Therefore the evil spirit in the Dibbuk Box cannot be identified as a dybbuk. It is simply a misnomer to do so. What, then, is the evil spirit in this story? It appears to be some kind of demon. A demon and a dybbuk are not the same thing. A dybbuk is the spirit of a person who has died. A demon is an evil spirit who was never alive. A demon can be invoked by a spell, can be imprisoned in some kind of container, and often has the kind of destructive power described in the book. All demons have names (such as Ashmodai, the king of demons, or Lilith, the incarnation of lust), are invoked by magic spells that include these names, and different demons have different roles and powers. Note that the spirit in the story of the Dibbuk Box never reveals its name, without which it is impossible to defeat it.

Like Jorge Luis Borges in many of his stories, such as "The Aleph" and "The Zahir," Haxton incorporates his sources into the narrative, mentioning the jinn in Middle Eastern folklore, Pandora's box, and Solomon's Seal. These are relevant sources, and the Greek myth of Pandora's box (originally a jar) is far closer to the role of the evil spirit in the Dibbuk

Box than the traditional role of the dybbuk. Indeed, the Dibbuk Box is very much a Pandora's box, and Haxton, who intends to discover the secret of its powers, inadvertently sets free a force of evil much like that released by Pandora, who sets free the winged Evils, the misfortunes that plague mankind: Old Age, Labor, Sickness, Insanity, Vice, and Passion (see Robert Graves, *Greek Myths*, 39j).

It is also important to emphasize that the box itself is not part of any traditional Jewish ritual. It does appear to have been intended as a wine cabinet, and blessings over wine are traditional for the Sabbath. While wine cabinets are not a required part of the Sabbath ritual, many different kinds exist. We know this cabinet (or the one it was modeled after) was Jewish because of the Shema prayer inscribed on it. We know it was a wine cabinet because of the grapes on its doors and the bottle holders on the inside. The cup inside of it is called the kiddush cup, and is used in making the Sabbath blessings. So, yes, the original box was intended for a Jewish purpose related to the Sabbath. But the idea that young Jewish women using kabbalistic spells from the books listed could somehow invoke an evil spirit that would take vengeance on everyone who came near the box is absurd. Of the books mentioned in Kevin's account of Sophie's story, *Sefer Yetsirah* is an oblique eighth-century text that contains no spells, and the story of Rabbi Judah Loew's creation of the Golem actually derives from the nineteenth century. Both books have no relevance to the kabbalistic spells that were said to invoke the evil spirit of the box. Nor is the folk account of the creation of the Golem relevant to the story of the Dibbuk Box, as is suggested in Kevin's account of Sophie's story.

The book of stories about the Golem, a man said to have been made out of clay and brought to life by Rabbi Judah Loew by writing the word *Emet* (Truth) on its forehead and reciting kabbalistic spells, is *not* a manual of kabbalistic meditation. It is a book of stories, actually composed in the nineteenth century by Rabbi Yudel Rosenberg. Thus it is not an authentic sixteenth-century text, as it claims, nor does it contain a single spell. Nor is the Golem related to the spirit in the Dibbuk Box. The Golem, according to Jewish folklore was brought to life to protect the Jews of Prague from the blood libel, the false claim that the Jews used the blood of Christians to make matzoh, the unleavened bread used for

Passover. The spirit of the Dibbuk Box, which has a destructive and not protective function, was supposedly invoked by pronouncing kabbalistic spells. The problem is that there are no spells in the book, nor is any spirit brought to life. The story of the Golem is simply irrelevant to that of the Dibbuk Box.

In his search for ways to protect himself from the evil spirit, Haxton turns to Wicca, the practice of witchcraft, and receives instructions and spells that he directs to Hecate—a figure out of Greek mythology. If the danger of the spirit of the box had emerged from Jewish folk tradition, it would make sense to try to stop it using Jewish magic. But instead the author draws on a potpourri of magical and mythical traditions. Thus, although the Dibbuk Box did originally serve a Jewish purpose (as a wine cabinet), neither the invocation of the evil spirit, which is never fully explained, nor Haxton's efforts to protect against it, derive from Jewish tradition.

The reader of *The Dibbuk Box* follows, with the author, any clue that might shed light on the ultimate mystery, but most of them do not. There are hints that the spirit of the box is actually the spirit of an angry old woman who beats her victims in their dreams, leaving marks that remain when they awake, but we never learn the identity of this woman or why her spirit is so furious, and this primary path of the mystery is not pursued. We are left with an explanation that during the Holocaust, some women, furious at the Nazis, somehow blindly invoked an evil spirit, locked it in a box (various people beg the author not to open the box), and discovered that it offered them no protection, only grave danger. No redeeming features of the evil spirit of the box are ever suggested. For those who believe in the paranormal, it would seem reckless to intentionally invoke powers of evil, but that is the theme of *The Dibbuk Box*. For the author and many of those he encounters, the secret of its powers is more important than the risks it exposes them to. In this it is a modern retelling of the story of Pandora, with similar results. But this story also reveals something of the psychology of the fascination and dangers of superstition and obsession. The story follows a classic pattern of supernatural fiction, but in this account of the author's experiences, the reader is left to decide for himself what is true and what is not.